Bete was crying.

He was all alone now. Sitting there beneath the light of the moon, he howled at the heavens.

IS It WRONG to TRY to PICK UP GIRLS iN A DUNGEON? ON THE SIDE

*Sword Oratoria*

# CONTENTS

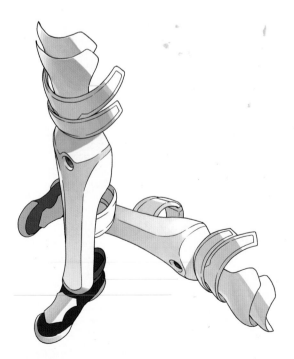

© Kiyotaka Haimura

# VOLUME 8

## FUJINO OMORI

### ILLUSTRATION BY
### KIYOTAKA HAIMURA

#### CHARACTER DESIGN BY
#### SUZUHITO YASUDA

NEW YORK

IS IT WRONG TO TRY TO PICK UP GIRLS IN A DUNGEON?
ON THE SIDE: SWORD ORATORIA, Volume 8
FUJINO OMORI

Translation by Liv Sommerlot
Cover art by Kiyotaka Haimura

This book is a work of fiction. Names, characters, places, and incidents are the product of the author's imagination or are used fictitiously. Any resemblance to actual events, locales, or persons, living or dead, is coincidental.

DUNGEON NI DEAI WO MOTOMERU NO WA MACHIGATTEIRUDAROUKA GAIDEN
SWORD ORATORIA vol. 8
Copyright © 2017 Fujino Omori
Illustration copyright © Kiyotaka Haimura
Original Character Design © Suzuhito Yasuda
All rights reserved.
Original Japanese edition published in 2017 by SB Creative Corp.
This English edition is published by arrangement with SB Creative Corp., Tokyo, in care of Tuttle-Mori Agency, Inc., Tokyo.

English translation © 2019 by Yen Press, LLC

Yen On
1290 Avenue of the Americas
New York, NY 10104

Visit us at yenpress.com
facebook.com/yenpress
twitter.com/yenpress
yenpress.tumblr.com
instagram.com/yenpress

First Yen On Edition: February 2019

Yen On is an imprint of Yen Press, LLC.
The Yen On name and logo are trademarks of Yen Press, LLC.

The publisher is not responsible for websites (or their content) that are not owned by the publisher.

Library of Congress Cataloging-in-Publication Data
Names: Ōmori, Fujino, author. | Haimura, Kiyotaka, 1973– illustrator. | Yasuda, Suzuhito, designer.
Title: Is it wrong to try to pick up girls in a dungeon? on the side: sword oratoria / story by Fujino Omori; illustration by Kiyotaka Haimura; original design by Suzuhito Yasuda.
Other titles: Danjon ni deai wo motomeru no wa machigatteirudarouka gaiden sword oratoria. English.
Description: New York, NY: Yen On, 2016– | Series: Is it wrong to try to pick up girls in a dungeon? on the side: sword oratoria
Identifiers: LCCN 2016023729 | ISBN 9780316315333 (v. 1 : pbk.) | ISBN 9780316318167 (v. 2 : pbk.) | ISBN 9780316318181 (v. 3 : pbk.) | ISBN 9780316318228 (v. 4 : pbk.) | ISBN 9780316442503 (v. 5 : pbk.) | ISBN 9780316442527 (v. 6 : pbk.) | ISBN 9781975302863 (v. 7 : pbk.) | ISBN 9781975327798 (v. 8 : pbk.)
Subjects: CYAC: Fantasy.
Classification: LCC PZ7.1.O54 Isg 2016 | DDC [Fic]—dc23
LC record available at https://lccn.loc.gov/2016023729

ISBNs: 978-1-9753-2779-8 (paperback)
978-1-9753-2780-4 (ebook)

1 3 5 7 9 10 8 6 4 2

LSC-C

Printed in the United States of America

## VOLUME 8

## FUJINO OMORI

ILLUSTRATION BY **KIYOTAKA HAIMURA**
CHARACTER DESIGN BY **SUZUHITO YASUDA**

PROLOGUE

# SCORN OF THE STRONG

Гэта казка іншага сям°і.

Насмешка моцнага чалавека

Myriad stone blocks formed the walls of the underground chamber, far beyond the reach of the sun above. A scream cut through the dank chill.

"I need a healer, now! Gimme something—an item, anything! Just do it quick!"

Over *Loki Familia*'s panicked shouts came the cries of the catgirl Anakity, body wounded and voice ragged after ceaselessly shrieking orders.

They were in the man-made labyrinth Knossos.

After being drawn into a trap, they quickly fell into chaos and confusion as they struggled to find a way out of the maze. Though the adventurers of *Loki Familia*'s main party had nearly been annihilated, once Riveria's group infiltrated Knossos, they had rallied around a solid core consisting of Aiz, Bete, and several others, regrouping before heading back into the labyrinth to rescue the companions they had been forced to leave behind earlier.

Until the sound of that piercing scream, when the world in front of them turned red with blood.

"Ahhh…Ahhhhhhhhhh?!"

"This…this can't be true! T-tell me it's not true…!"

"Oh, shit, Lloyd! Shit, shit!"

The companions they'd broken bread with, their friends, were splayed out on the ground before them, drenched in blood.

It was a massacre.

The gore covered the walls and floor so completely that calling it a red room would have been appropriate—a nauseating indicator of the slaughter that had transpired. Some of the bodies had been cut while others had been stabbed, but a blade had inflicted every wound. This was no monster attack.

On the wall was a message scrawled in blood: THIS IS YOUR DOING, BRAVER!

Beneath it, the Trickster emblem had fallen to the floor, blood spatters forming red tears flowing from its eyes.

"Over here! Someone's still alive!"

The shout alerted the newly arrived healer, who darted over in a flash. Soon, the telltale glow of healing magic flickered, but—

"It's...It's not working!"

"Aaggghhhhhhh...!!"

The gaping wound simply wouldn't close. Potions were equally ineffective. No matter what they tried, blood kept flowing from within the armor. They could do nothing but watch, despair welling up inside them, as yet another one of their companions breathed their last.

"It must have been a cursed weapon...Just like what they used to attack the captain...!" Raul clenched his fist, tiny red rivulets squeezing out between his fingers.

An Unhealable Curse. Those cut by the blade of a weapon imbued with this curse couldn't be treated. Anyone who fell victim to it was as good as dead. Realizing that all their fallen companions' wounds had been affected by it was enough to dash what little hope the adventurers had left.

"We don't have anything that can lift it?"

"C-can't someone go get something?!"

But even as Anakity and Raul shouted their desperate pleas, they knew it was too late. Aiz was dashing around in search of survivors, but she understood as well.

Aiz, Raul, Aki—they'd been part of *Loki Familia* long enough to have experienced this countless times before. What they hated the most was the smell of death it left on their skin, impossible to wipe off. This stone room deep within the labyrinth's halls had become nothing more than the tomb of adventurers.

"..."

Amid the chaos of the group, only Bete stood in silence, his gaze glued to the scene in front of him.

His amber eyes were ice-cold, almost like he didn't even care as he completely suppressed his emotions.

"—! Leene!!"

"...M-Miss...Aiz..."

Aiz flew toward the far corner of the room to where a girl lay sprawled on the ground. It was none other than Leene Arshe, the young healer, her body bearing the same bloody scores as the rest of her group. Aiz gripped the girl's shoulders in her fingers in an attempt to lift her, but strength had already drained from Leene's body.

Jutting from her ribs was the same cursed dagger that had spilled her companions' blood. It had been left there in what seemed to be a final insult to *Loki Familia*, like a gravestone marking the resting place of their comrades.

Rage seethed across Aiz's face, and she wrenched free the blade still disgracing the body of her friend and threw it away.

—*It's no good. We're too late.*

The Sword Princess had seen enough of her friends die to know that this girl was past saving. When Leene saw Aiz's face twisting in agony, she merely gave a tiny, mirthless smile at how unusual it was for her to make such an expression.

Finally.

"Mister...Bete..."

The werewolf's shadow was looming over them.

His amber eyes were lowered toward them—toward Aiz, who was glancing up over her shoulder, and toward Leene, whose feeble gaze was rising to meet his.

And then the young werewolf laughed.

"Damn, look at yourself. Just like I've always said: Weaklings only get in the way."

The completely inappropriate comment, coupled with an icy laugh, stunned Aiz.

But Bete didn't stop there.

His lips pulled back in a derisive grin, leaving his fangs bare.

"And what a pointless death for you and everyone else! Curse how stupid and weak you are until you never forget it. Taste the shame. Make sure you remember this long after you die so pathetically."

All their fellow familia members, who were weeping or groaning as they clung tightly to the motionless corpses of their friends, now had their eyes on Bete.

Under the tear-stricken gazes of the weak, the strong one continued his speech.

"So long, then. I never wanna see your sorry ass again. Don't ever come out of this damn hole."

His mocking laugh echoed off the walls of the stone room.

Both Raul and Anakity glared at him, like he was the very enemy responsible for this atrocity. Many of their companions whose cheeks were still stained with tears scowled in rising anger as well.

Aiz furrowed her own brows as she made to stand—then she froze. She looked at those amber eyes, distorted with contempt, heard the final words he muttered beneath his breath, and let her hand drop, no longer able to strike his cheek.

"...Ngh."

And then Leene opened her eyes.

The faintest traces of a smile formed on her face before her hand went limp.

A single tear beaded in the corner of her softly closed eye, marbling with blood as it traced a red line down her cheek. Her final expression was peaceful, almost like a young maiden whose love had finally been requited.

The far-off howls of monsters echoed throughout the maze's chambers.

And from within their stone room, the blood painting the walls seemed disdainful of both the living and dead alike.

Raul, Aki, and the other adventurers trembled as they angrily watched the wolf sneer at those weaker than him. Only Aiz saw something else, the contemptuous smile fall from the young man's face as he stared at the girl on the ground.

That was four days prior.

# CHAPTER 1

# Lonely Wolf

Гэта казка іншага сям'і.

самотны воўк

"This is the first time since Lefiya and the others joined that we've had…casualties."

Riveria's heavy sigh echoed in the large room. The three of them were in the captain's office—Riveria, Gareth, and the owner of the room himself, Finn. Though it was still early, the dizzying events of the last few days necessitated a prompt meeting. The list of things they needed to do loomed like a mountain, with the burial of their fallen companions merely being one of many duties.

In response to the comment Riveria made from her spot at the far wall, both Finn and Gareth offered grave looks of their own.

"The fault is ours. We weren't able to protect Leene and the others, divided as we were…I'm sorry."

"A disgrace, we were. Too caught up in our own pride."

"I'm not blaming either of you, so stop that now. It's simply…difficult. This is the one thing I've never been able to get used to. Losing those whose names and faces I've long etched into my heart…"

Finn and Gareth were lamenting how they let their subordinates die while infiltrating the enemy's hideout, but Riveria shook her head, her jade-colored eyes dropping to the floor in pain.

The only sound in the quiet room was the continuous ticking of the tall grandfather clock.

Almost as though standing in silent prayer, they allowed a few moments to pass with their eyes closed before Finn finally spoke.

"We've no choice but to accept our loss. The one question now is, how do we reclaim our honor?" he posed, resting his elbows on the desk. There was an unusual strength to his words. At the moment, more than self-vindication and guilt, his narrowed green eyes burned with the thought of a rematch—almost like an unspoken pledge to those who'd lost their lives.

The time to mourn the dead was over.

They hadn't a single moment to waste. The three familia leaders began reviewing what they knew.

"Not that it does us much good now, but…We really underestimated those Evils blokes. That much we can say for sure."

"Indeed. If we can believe Valletta, the official name for that labyrinth is 'Knossos'…"

"A second dungeon right beneath our feet…I know the floor I reached doesn't compare to the depths you two descended to, but I can already say now—we should leave this place alone."

Gareth, Finn, then Riveria spoke in turn, shifting the topic to the maze that served as their enemy's hideout.

The man-made labyrinth Knossos.

Residing deep beneath the winding roads of Daedalus Street, the Evils had made it their lair, an underground maze that boasted a size and depth that was far beyond anything they knew. Finn believed it was as large as the entire city of Orario, while its depth was reached near the middle levels of the Dungeon, at least. Even for the goddess Loki, this was a discovery that defied common sense.

"And that convoluted snarl of a dungeon wasn't the only thing we had on our plates, either. Orichalcum doors, cursed weapons, creatures, demi-spirits…And to top it all off, that demon witch Valletta was still alive," Gareth muttered.

"I will say that I could hardly believe she was dead when I heard her corpse had been found after the Twenty-Seventh-Floor Nightmare six years ago…"

The face of Gareth and Riveria's longtime enemy wasn't one they'd soon forget. Both of them had fought tooth and nail against the agents of the evil gods and their attempt to upset the order of Orario fifteen years ago during a period in the city's history known as the Dark Ages. Their expressions clouded before Gareth continued.

"The lot of 'em already packed a punch, but more important was the overwhelming advantage they had in that maze. No way they'd pick a fight outside it. Actually, there's no point in the first place."

"Right. According to Aiz, there are already seven crystal orb fetuses…demi-spirits…on their way to the surface. At this point, they're just waiting. Why plan their own strike when they can simply wait?" Riveria nodded, relaying what Aiz had reported earlier.

After the group split up, Aiz had found tanks in Knossos's abandoned lab.

Though they'd been empty, she was sure the dregs still coating the broken glass had come from the spirits. Which meant the crystal orb fetuses were somewhere in that labyrinth, already evolving into the frighteningly powerful demi-spirits, just like the power bull femanoid Gareth, Tiona, and Tione had struggled against.

"*I will destroy Orario.*"

That was the ultimate goal of the creature forces belowground and the remnants of the Evils.

And they would accomplish it, too, if all those demi-spirits fully matured—it would spell both the end of *Loki Familia* and the rest of Orario.

"At any rate, we need to come up with a plan right away. We have to get back inside Knossos."

"That we do. Just talkin' ain't gonna get us anywhere."

The two first-tier adventurers had had their fill of grief; the melancholy had left their voices. They immediately began consolidating their ideas, Finn taking the lead.

Once the prum captain had issued his orders to the dwarf and high elf respectively, he brought up a new topic.

"Now that *Ishtar Familia* has been completely annihilated by *Freya Familia*...what's the situation like?"

"What's there to say? Not even sure I'd know where to start. At least we know that its members have scattered to the wind..."

"They don't have much choice given how the person we suspected of being connected to the Evils, Ishtar herself, was sent back to Heaven. There was a high chance she had info that would've benefited us greatly, but..."

It had been only three days ago that *Freya Familia* had attacked and destroyed *Ishtar Familia*. Sorting through the convoluted morass of info they'd received about this major event was merely another reason the three of them had met so early for the day's meeting.

"We still haven't figured out the reason *Freya Familia* chose this particular moment to attack Ishtar and her people. At least from our perspective, it seems a bit more than simple bad luck."

"I've gotten a whiff of a rumor Ishtar had her hands on Freya's man," Gareth piped up, having been in charge of gathering info the last few days.

"To think it would come down to something so inane..." Riveria brought a hand to her head as though sensing the approach of a headache.

Finn, meanwhile, seemed lost in his own thoughts. "Hmm..."

All of a sudden, Riveria came back to her senses with a start.

"There's one more thing, Finn. Though it has nothing to do with Knossos..."

"And yet it must be important if your face is anything to go by. What is it?"

Riveria's fine brows were drawn together, creating a frown on a face beautiful enough to make the goddesses jealous, as Finn prompted her to explain.

"It's about Aiz and the others...No. It's about Bete, to be specific."

At the mention of the werewolf's name, identical knowing looks crossed Finn's and Gareth's faces.

"Right now, among members of the familia, there's—"

At that very moment, the raucous sounds of a fight reached the office.

It was coming from another of the mansion's towers.

"...Seems we mighta been a bit too late on this one," Gareth murmured before heading toward the door.

"Really, what a handful..." Finn sighed with a pained smile of his own as he followed the dwarf out.

The last one to leave, Riveria brought a hand back to her forehead. Apparently, the headache from before was flaring up again as she quickly headed toward the hallway.

"Mister Bete is unbelievable!" Raul's shout echoed off the rafters of the large dining hall. It was breakfast time in *Loki Familia*'s home, Twilight Manor. But rather than eating, the members of the familia who were currently gathered were in the midst of an uproar.

Their anger with a certain member of the familia had finally peaked.

"How could he say something like that? That…that Leene's and the others' deaths were pointless?! To even think of saying something like that about your own companions…What makes him think he has the right?!" Raul sputtered. The normally indecisive, confrontation-hating peacemaker of the group was unable to hold in his rage any longer.

"Yeah, it's not like he's ever been the most approachable of guys, but…this is just too much," Anakity, herself a candidate for the familia's upper echelons, weighed in from beside Raul. Her own anger was evident on her face. Leene had been a close friend. Anakity was attempting to keep her emotions in check, digging her nails into her arms.

The event currently on everyone's minds was, of course, what had transpired in Knossos. The source of their outrage was a certain werewolf who'd laughed at their companions' deaths.

Bete might have been a well-known powerhouse in *Loki Familia*, but that didn't stop his fellow familia members from fearing and reviling the way he constantly looked down on and abused those in the lower ranks. Now that he'd even gone so far as to mock their companions' deaths, their enmity toward the young wolf had reached a breaking point.

Watching the tumultuous storm of condemnation swirling about the dining hall now, Lefiya stood stock-still near the door.

"What's wrong?" The voice belonged to Aiz, who had come running to investigate the commotion.

"Hmm? Oh, Miss Aiz! It's…Well…" Lefiya started, hurriedly attempting to explain the situation, but all it took was a few words for Aiz to understand what was going on. The swordswoman's eyes quickly scanned the room.

The red-faced, teary-eyed Raul wasn't the only one condemning Bete. Every one of the adventurers who'd been there in that stone room shared resentment for the werewolf. The elf Alicia, the chienthrope Cruz, the human Narfi—all of them second-tier familia members just like Raul. They were not at the point of joining in openly lambasting Bete, but their mouths were certainly tense. Even Tiona and Tione were acting particularly chilly at their spot by the wall. Neither of them had been at the scene of the crime themselves, but they had obviously caught wind of what had happened.

Aiz had never seen her fellow familia members like this before, and for a moment it left her dazed, unsure what to do.

Not a single person present was standing up for Bete.

Not that they would be, considering what he'd done.

He'd simply gone too far this time.

"...What do you think...Lefiya?"

"M-me? I, uh, well...Of course I'm mad at Mister Bete, but, I mean...I can't be too mad...After all, he did save you and the others..."

She was referring to what had happened in the pantry on the twenty-fourth floor when she, Filvis, and Bete had formed a three-man party to rescue Aiz and the others.

"After what happened down there, I always just kinda thought Mister Bete was scared, but...but after hearing what Mister Raul and the others are saying, I...I guess I don't really know what to think..." Her directionless response quickly fizzled out.

Aiz could empathize with her indecisiveness. It was understandable why she was leaning toward Tiona and Tione's view.

Lefiya's voice was unmistakably discouraged, and she even seemed to be losing hope entirely. "...What about you, Miss Aiz?" she posed, her eyes still trained toward the ground.

"Me? I..."

She didn't have an answer.

All Aiz could think about was the look on Bete's face. The way he'd been unable to put into words the feelings building inside him that led to irritation, then anger, before he'd finally snapped.

*"We can never repay them for what they've done!!"*

As Aiz was still trying to find her words, Raul's voice cut through the food hall.

And it was at just that moment that a certain gray-furred wolf decided to make his entrance.

"Pretty early for y'all to be so goddamn annoying, don't you think?"

It was Bete.

A sudden hush settled over the dining hall, all eyes on him.

"M-Mister Bete..."

He walked straight past Aiz and Lefiya, both still standing by the door in stunned silence, and into the center of the hall. His usual aura of antipathy was plain on his face, and one of his lupine ears lay flat in indignation.

His appearance, however, solicited a variety of responses from the crowd of adventurers. Some cowered in fear, others furrowed their brows in anger, while still others couldn't hide the animosity building up inside them. But one thing they all had in common—their castigation of Bete.

Bete, however, was the same as always despite having opponents on every side.

"Moan, moan, whine, whine. If you've got somethin' to say, say it to my face! You little shits can't do anything on your own!"

Every brow in the room rose. Raul even seemed ready to lunge forward. But Bete paid their reactions no mind and simply made his way lazily toward a nearby chair.

Or he would have if a certain copper-colored leg hadn't blocked his path.

"M-Misses Tiona and Tione..." Lefiya whispered, her eyes trembling as she watched the twin Amazonian sisters step in front of Bete.

Tione's eyes were narrowed in icy wrath, and even Tiona's smile had disappeared as she glared at the werewolf.

"You got a beef with me, Amazons?"

"..."

Tione didn't respond. Her sister, however, did.

"Don't you feel anything, Bete?"

"..."

"Leene and the others—they're dead. Don't you understand that? You'll never be able to see them again!" Tiona's voice was quiet amid the protective gazes of her peers.

She continued:

"Leene liked you, you know?...You really don't feel *anything*?"

The question, coupled with Tione's silent glower, was the last straw.

The room fell utterly still.

Bete said nothing for a moment. Then—he laughed.

"Sorry to burst her bubble, but I hate weak girls most of all."

His words were the trigger.

All of a sudden, the bodies of the two sisters became a blur.

Their faces blank, they came at the wolf and his unchanging, characteristic derisive smile.

From the left came a punch and, from the right, a front kick aimed at his head.

Some of the women in the room yelped. But before the two iron hammers could fall—they were stopped by a massive fist and a long spear, respectively.

"That'll do, you two."

"Gareth...!"

"Any further and this will have gotten entirely out of hand."

"Captain...!"

Gareth's fist had grabbed Tiona's wrist, and the handle of Finn's spear had blocked Tione's kick. The two of them had raced into the dining hall just in time.

Joining them was Aiz, standing firmly in front of Bete. Despite being empty-handed, she'd reached out to restrain the werewolf's arm, already extended in the process of delivering a counterstrike.

Lefiya and the others had barely been able to respond, all of them frozen where they stood. They gulped at what had just transpired in front of them.

"Outta my way, Captain! This piece of shit thinks—!"

"As a high-level member of this familia, you have a standard to uphold, Tione. Or is that not what I've always told you?"

Tione bit down on her lip, Finn's unwavering gaze cooling the fire that had been about ready to rage out of control inside her. She scowled at Bete.

Bete also stood down, cursing beneath his breath.

"Ain't it a little early to be gettin' all riled up, guys? You're a real hot-blooded bunch, you know that?"

"L-Loki..."

The familia's patron goddess herself strolled into the dining hall past Lefiya at the door. Her vermilion eyes took in the explosive situation currently gripping the hall before widening ever so slightly.

"That's enough, Bete. Get outta here and go cool off."

"...Hmph." The wolf cursed beneath his breath but did as he was told. Turning his back on Aiz, he made his way out the door.

Riveria took the opportunity to approach him, moving from where she'd been watching over the proceedings to stand in front of Bete.

"Whaddaya want, ya old hag? You wanna have a go, too—?"

"I'd choose my words more carefully if I were you, Bete," the high elf queen warned, half interrupting the wolf's tirade. "I don't care how you choose to feel, but that's no reason not to mourn the loss of your companions."

Bete snorted. "Oh yeah? And what's mourning gonna do for 'em? I'd cry myself to sleep every night if it'd do a damn thing. But it won't, will it?"

"..."

"They died 'cause they're weak. Or am I wrong? Tell me I'm wrong, huh? I'm not gonna deny what's true." He looked back over at the group behind him. "You bastards, too. You slow us down and that's what happens!" he spat before pushing past Riveria and leaving through the door.

Tiona clenched her fists as Tione kicked over a nearby chair with an enraged yell. "Piece of shit!" This earned her a swift smack on the back of her head from Finn's spear before Loki, Finn, Gareth, and Riveria all heaved a simultaneous sigh.

"This has really gotten out of hand. At this rate, it may end up forming a rift in the familia," Finn lamented, turning away from Tione, who was squatting on the ground with her hands to the back of her head.

"Maybe a bit late in sayin' this, but…that boy may have been more trouble than he's worth," Gareth mused.

"We knew this would happen…sooner or later…" Riveria agreed as she made her way over to rejoin the two. One eye closed, she scanned the dining hall while the lower-level familia members around her trembled in fear. Raul and some others continued to stare daggers at the door Bete had gone through.

"C'mon, people! Enough of this, yeah? I'm starvin'! Fix me up a heapin' big plate of the good stuff, won't ya, Lefiya?" The sound of Loki's relaxed voice sliced through the tension. "Food, food, I need food!"

"Huh? I, erm, o-okay…" Lefiya sputtered at the goddess's carefree request before she and the others quickly moved to obey.

"…"

Only Aiz stood alone, the clatter of plates on the table ringing in her ears as she gazed toward the corridor where she had last seen the young werewolf.

There was still much information to be gathered—not only to further their knowledge of the events in Knossos but also to investigate *Freya Familia*'s attack on *Ishtar Familia*. That night, the members of *Loki Familia* were issued their respective orders.

It was around that time that Bete was making his way down the hall, one eye on the sun setting over the city through the nearby window.

"…Hmph."

Everywhere he went, his fellow familia members fled. They didn't even look him in the eye, never mind utter a greeting. In the hallway, in the parlor room, everyone he passed kept that same silent distance.

Not even Raul or Cruz, the two he'd spent the most time with, acknowledged his existence. The second they noticed him coming down the hall, the emotion left their faces as they passed by in silence.

"Ah...M-Mister Bete."

Then there was Lefiya.

The young elf glanced up at him when they unexpectedly encountered each other, looking as though she was about to say something—

"This way, Lefiya!"

"M-Miss Tiona! Miss Tione..."

But before she could finish, Tiona and Tione arrived to grab her arm, pulling her away from the werewolf. Normally, the Amazons would start fighting with him the moment they made eye contact, but this time, they didn't so much as glance at him.

People had a tendency to change gears once their anger had risen too much. They began to ignore the source of their anger, behaving as though it didn't even exist.

That was exactly what was happening to Bete.

It made him feel like he was walking on a bed of nails. While he wasn't so emotionally delicate that their treatment bothered him, he also wasn't so uncaring as to simply do nothing and take it.

Bete was well aware that his refusal to behave any differently from normal painted him as the ultimate evil to the rest of his familia.

"—Bete. I don't know how much we can do for you."

An hour earlier, he had been summoned by Finn after his duties for the day had come to an end.

"It doesn't matter what Riveria, Gareth, or I say—none of it's likely to get through to Raul and the others. While I've no wish for dissension in this familia, I'm also aware that no amount of persuasion is going to help. Quite the opposite, really."

The two of them had been in Finn's office, the prum sitting at his desk with shoulders sagging.

"If we covered for you, we'd simply bring the hostility of the familia onto ourselves. And, unfortunately, I'm not really in a position to let myself become a target at the moment."

They didn't want any outrage directed at them. It was such a refreshingly honest answer, Bete couldn't even be mad. It wasn't an issue of Finn's personal preference, either, only an objective decision. After all, the familia's morale would take a big hit if its members disagreed with their leaders. And with the underground organization of creatures and the Evils' Remnants practically at their doorstep, they had to be at the top of their game. This wasn't the time for discord among their ranks.

Bete knew this, which was why he hadn't interrupted Finn's speech.

"Thus, I'm placing you on leave. Once all this dies down, you can return to the manor. Until then, I ask that you stay at an inn. I'll provide you with the funds—though I doubt you'll accept them," Finn finished, placing a bag of coins atop the desk separating them.

Unsurprisingly, Bete pushed it back with an "I don't need this shit."

Bete didn't care about money. All he cared about was the Dungeon. And he wasn't about to let someone else become involved with his personal problems—which was exactly what Finn had been afraid of. Bete couldn't shake the look of sympathy Finn had directed toward him as he'd left the room.

There was no place for him right now in Twilight Manor.

"...Hmph."

Grumbling beneath his breath, he made his way toward the main entrance. There was no one there to see him off. The only witness to his exit was the scarlet sky smoldering overhead.

His destination was the Flaming Wasp, a pub in Orario's fifth ward.

It was just one of many pubs in the sprawling Shopping District located at the city's southern quarter. Nestled into one of the many alleyways some distance from the main road, the pub was distinguishable from the surrounding buildings by the bright-red wasp signpost hanging from its wall.

This establishment was well-known for its wasp liquor—colored a red so deep, it might as well have been liquefied ruby, and boasting a fiery heat that burned the throats and stomachs of its patrons. The combination of its unique flavor and the pain drew regulars back time and time again. That night, as the sun neared the horizon, the Flaming Wasp was indeed a hive of activity as per usual.

Normally, Bete would be here with Raul and the others. This time, however, he had no company for obvious reasons. Nevertheless, he was fully prepared to drink in solitude…or at least, he had been.

"…What the hell you doin' here, Aiz?"

"…Because I felt like it?"

Bete's lips curled into a scowl at the golden-haired, golden-eyed swordswoman cocking her head from the other side of the table for two.

Had she followed him from the manor? Either way, she was sitting across from him. Even among the raucous cacophony of drunken patrons surrounding them at their center table, a strange aura seemed to settle over the two of them.

"You follow me?"

"…I did."

"And why the hell would you do somethin' like that?"

"You looked…lonely?"

"Like hell I did!"

Bete brought his mug down hard on the table, interrupting the halting conversation he was having with the girl of few words. Aiz, however, just tilted her head curiously.

Around them, the carefree jubilance of the other patrons continued, oblivious to Bete's inner turmoil. There was a whole host of customers today, everything from dwarven adventurers to humans, animal people, and even a few Amazons. The prum girl tending to them was in constant motion bringing out orders of liquor and food.

But some of them also seemed to be foregoing drink, and some were throwing glances at Bete and Aiz. More than a few, in fact. They were *Loki Familia*'s Vanargand and Sword Princess, after all. No matter where they went in the city, they were likely to draw attention—that was simply what it meant to be a first-tier adventurer.

Aiz's looks, in particular, drew more than a few lewd gazes. Bete was quick to glower back at the demi-human culprits, who responded by keeping their eyes well enough to themselves afterward.

Bete had no problem with Aiz sitting there. What he did have a problem with was her silence.

She ordered nothing and simply sat there, staring at him prettily from across the table as Bete's features twisted into an expression of discomfort far greater than anything he'd displayed back at the manor.

Then his drink arrived, mistakenly placed in front of Aiz.

He grabbed and downed it before Aiz even had a chance to react.

"...So? You're here...why? Finn ask you to come babysit me?"

"Finn...? No, this has nothing to do with...Finn..."

"Then why the hell come here?"

"I guess I was...worried about you..."

"—GBWWOOOFFF?!"

Bete choked on his drink, drawing a startled look from Aiz.

Though flustered for a moment, he quickly recovered. "Goddamn airhead doesn't even realize what she's saying..." he mumbled begrudgingly, leaving Aiz more than a little bewildered.

*I suppose I...haven't spoken with Bete very often...*

She thought to herself, reflecting on how this was the first time she and the werewolf had done anything alone together outside of battle (and consequently missing the fact that Bete was downing drinks at an increasing pace).

Similar to Tiona and her sister, Bete had also converted to *Loki Familia* from a different familia. It had been almost six years since then, which was before the two Amazonian sisters had joined. He'd looked down on her back then, but after seeing her combat prowess in the Dungeon, he'd changed his mind, eventually growing to even respect her.

His previous familia was *Víðarr Familia*.

Aiz had heard from Finn that he'd left them on bad terms. In fact, *Víðarr Familia* itself didn't even reside in Orario anymore. Even though she'd known Bete longer than Tiona and Tione, she still felt like she didn't understand anything about him.

*...When I think of Bete...*

The emotion she usually held was doubt—specifically, wondering whether he had taken something too far.

His strength was unquestionable. In fact, she couldn't help but think the werewolf's views on strength were quite similar to her own. In that regard, he was considerably different from those like Tiona, who simply enjoyed fighting for fighting's sake.

These thoughts running through her head, Aiz finally spoke up again.

"Why is it you...look down on others so much?"

"Huh?"

Bete's face had already taken on a decidedly reddish hue from his continued alcohol consumption. He shot Aiz a curious look before curling his lips into a smile.

"Weaksticks are weaksticks. What's wrong with lookin' down on those weaker 'n you? They're pathetic."

Aiz closed her mouth at the werewolf's response.

No. She couldn't. If she did, she'd get the same exact results Riveria and Tiona always did.

Instead, she tried to rethink her question.

"Okay, then...What is it that drives you...to become stronger?"

"..."

It was a question she felt would provide her an answer similar to her own.

If Bete really did share the same reasoning as her, the same unyielding tenacity to grow stronger, then maybe, just maybe she might be able to uncover what it was that made him tick.

Bete was silent for a few moments, then smirked.

"Isn't this a rare treat. You actually showin' interest in someone 'sides yourself."

"..."

"Pretty rich coming from the girl who never said anything about herself and didn't care about anything 'cept crushin' monster skulls."

"Ngh!"

Aiz's eyes narrowed, her mouth opening for an instinctive retort, but Bete continued before she could find her words.

"How 'bout this, then? I show you mine; you show me yours? I'll answer if you answer, too."

"!"

Aiz didn't have a response. All she could do was avert her eyes.

Bete knew she wouldn't answer, and he didn't blame her for it, either. Instead, he simply continued, words hissing out between his teeth.

"Don't get so upset, Aiz. S'not like there's a point in carin' about other people's problems. Let 'em care about themselves." Finishing up a glass of wasp liquor, he tossed it down on the table. "You're strong. That's all that matters."

"..."

"So long as we keep stayin' strong, we'll be fine."

He was looking straight into her eyes now, almost as if he was trying to advise her through his intoxicated haze.

"When you're strong, you can do anything. You'll never have anything taken away from you."

But then, his grave expression shifted into a glib smile.

"For instance, I could serve up the chicken livers of all these cowards to go with my drinks!" His voice was booming now, loud enough to swallow up the cacophonous frivolity of the entire bar. Ignoring Aiz's shock, he put his arm on the back of his chair and let his eyes travel the room. "You hear that, you yellow-bellied shits? Keep on yukkin' it up! I'm sick of you and your pig-ass faces! Every day, killin' nothin' but small fries! Is that how you wanna live? Spendin' your measly-ass coins for watered-down piss like this? What the hell kinda life is that?!"

The entire bar went silent as Bete's words echoed against the rafters. It didn't take long for things to go south from there, as murderous gazes turned toward Bete from every corner of the room.

"Bete!"

"Stay outta this, Aiz! You know I'm not wrong! All they've got going for them is numbers. There ain't a single one of 'em with the guts to fight back on their own!"

And it was true. Despite the multitude of scowls, the adventurers in the pub were quick to back off at the wolf's antagonistic peal of laughter. Averting their eyes, lowering their eyes, even, their actions seemed to confirm the slander being thrown at them.

"What a bunch of sorry losers…If you can't even defend yourself now, how the hell are you supposed to defend yourself in a real battle? Cowards! Every last one of you!"

But even as their faces reddened and their fists trembled in anger, the armor-clad adventurers could do nothing. There wasn't a single person in the pub who stood up to Bete's mockery. They were far too afraid of the true "monsters" of the Dungeon—the first-tier adventurers.

Even Aiz with her general lack of emotion found herself brimming with anger, and she moved to put a stop to Bete's tirade, but then…

"—How charming."

Someone moved forward to step in front of Bete before she could.

It was an Amazonian prostitute, stepping away from the rest of her group in a corner of the pub, her long, silky black hair swaying behind her.

"Aisha Belka…"

"Antianeira."

The murmurs from the crowd identified her, and Bete and Aiz immediately recognized her and her crew as part of the Berbera and former members of *Ishtar Familia*. They were a strong group of women, most of them second-tier adventurers at Level 3. And from the looks of it, they'd been continuing to meet for drinks even though they had all converted to different familias after Ishtar's return to the upper world—a ritual that Bete had just interrupted with his earlier spiel.

"Don't group us with the rest of these fools. My sisters and I aren't so spineless as to take your insults sitting down…First-tier or not, don't get full of yourself." Her final words were so low that they sounded practically murderous.

The rage burning inside her after listening to Bete's rant was tangible, and it seemed her fellow Amazons lined up behind her weren't too pleased, either. Her eyes flashing, her clothes revealing much of her copper-colored skin, she had the aura of someone all too familiar with the brawl scene.

"Ha! So the fishies wanna play?" Bete's lips pulled back in a ferocious grin as he watched the group of Amazons rise to their feet. He almost seemed elated. "You learn to use that mouth of yours in bed, you whore? You want my foot to bash your skull in?!" he shouted, once more rising to his feet and sending his chair flying.

"Bete, stop—!" Aiz started, leaping up in an attempt to stop the fight, but her cry was quickly swallowed up by the crowing of the Amazons.

"Bring it on, you uncivilized mutt! I'll enjoy beating the shit out of you!"

And with jeers from the surrounding patrons egging the combatants on, the fight began. Plates, chairs, tables, blood—everything went flying. Screams and shouts shook the walls, even while the dwarven pub owner stood calmly wiping plates by the counter as though this happened every night.

Abandoned and alone, Aiz stood off to the side in shock as a grand brawl erupted around her.

As a soft sliver of the moon peeked through the clouds, the quiet curtain of night fell once again as the furor cooled.

One after another, the pale-faced patrons of the bar watched the bodies pile up on the floor.

"Heh. All bark and no bite, I see."

"Gnngh…!"

Bete had his hand wrapped around Aisha's neck. She was the only one left out of more than ten Berbera he'd already taken down. They hadn't even been able to scratch him.

Aisha, however, refused to give up, fighting against him even as he curled his fingers tighter around her throat.

"Vanargand…!"

The outcome may have been decided, but the glint in her eyes had yet to dissipate.

Her continued ferocity despite the pain made Bete grin all the more.

He would end her right here, right now.

"Let her go."

The edge of a blade met his throat—Aiz's sword, Desperate.

Bete's smile was gone in an instant, and he turned to see the Sword Princess shooting him an icy glare.

The fight was over. The Amazons had fallen, the spark inside them soundly snuffed. This wasn't simply self-defense anymore. That's what Aiz was saying.

Bete did as he was told, letting out the last of his malice with a huff before releasing his grip on Aisha's throat. Aisha herself fell to the ground, choking and sputtering.

"Why do you…always have to hurt people like this?" Aiz asked, attempting to find her words.

With his fist. With his words.

Bete didn't have an answer.

Aiz's gaze never left him, even as the other wounded Amazons gathered around Aisha.

"That's what I…hate about you."

"…Heh. That so?" Bete snorted. "I'm done here," he said, walking away. He tossed a bag of coins toward the dwarf behind the counter before turning toward the door, not even bothering to throw a look of contempt at the group of Amazons glaring up at him from the floor.

The same scowls of resentment that had accompanied him in *Loki Familia*'s dining hall followed him all the way out of the building.

Bete threw them a glance before letting the wooden door clatter behind him on his way out.

"…"

Aiz herself remained silent, still standing in the center of the room with her brows lowered in heartache. Not even she made to follow him this time.

The Shopping District was a bevy of activity.

The twinkling lights, the flashing windows of casinos and theaters—Bete pushed past it all without so much as raising his head, almost as though attempting to escape the gaudy effulgence. He preferred the dim blue glow of the moon overhead to man-made lamps.

On and on he walked until, upon reaching a deserted bend in the road, he lowered himself to a crouch.

Or perhaps it should be said he dropped into a froggish squat.

"I've really done it now…"

The antagonizing smirk from earlier was nowhere to be found; instead, he hung his head dejectedly as the self-deprecating words tumbled to the stone below.

*This happens every time you drink too much…Damn loose tongue, then starting a fight…*

Already, the alcohol had left his system, leaving him in cold sobriety. Aiz's words had made sure of that. Her straight-faced "That's what I hate about you" had taken care of the buzz like a direct hit from her Airiel.

He didn't regret what he'd done. What he'd said. No, it was far too late for that. He didn't even care about the cold stares he'd received as he'd left the bar. What bothered him now were Aiz's words. He didn't even know why they were affecting him so much. Not too long ago, Bete had caused a ruckus at The Benevolent Mistress when he made fun of that kid who resembled a rabbit, comparing him to a tomato and whatnot, but this commotion might have been the last straw.

It was as though a whirlpool of self-loathing had opened up beneath him. That he was one of those very same cowardly adventurers he'd been vilifying only minutes earlier. Bete was finally reaping what he'd sown, and this thought sent his tail drooping to the ground below.

If there had been anyone around to see him, they surely would have been unable to believe their eyes. "Goddammit…" he muttered, letting out a sigh that shook his entire body.

Just as he was thinking he would like to just pass out on the cobblestones right then and there—

"There you are, Bete Loga!"

—an annoyingly cheerful voice called out from behind him.

"…Whaa—?"

Glancing back, he saw an Amazonian woman. Though perhaps "young girl" would have been a more accurate description. She was clearly far from maturity; her copper-colored arms and legs were slender and lean, and her chest, while larger than Tiona's (not that this was a difficult accomplishment), couldn't be called more than a slight bulge. A short vest covered her torso, and hanging from her hips was what could barely be considered a loincloth—it covered slightly more area than what the other Amazons might wear, but it was still considerably revealing, her belly button bared to the world. The only part of her appearance that wasn't childish was her long black hair, currently done up in a ponytail.

At the moment, she had her finger pointed in Bete's direction, cheeks flushed with excitement, golden earrings jangling, and looking very much like a small dog about to pounce on him.

"I can't believe I finally get to see you after all this time!"

"Who the hell are you…?" Bete started, rising to his feet and taking a few steps backward as the girl landed in front of him with a mighty *thud*.

Bete was fully prepared to land a kick with his Frosvirt if she took so much as one more step toward him. The girl, however, seemed oblivious to that as shock appeared in her euphoric smile.

"Hey! You didn't forget me, did you? I remember you, after all! I could never forget *you*, Bete Loga!"

"Like hell I'd be associated with a dopey Amazon like you! And stop tossin' my name around like that, you little shit!" Bete spat back, clearly irritated at the young girl and her refusal to listen.

"How rude! And after everything you already did to me, too!"

She was annoying. *So* annoying. A different kind of annoying from Tiona. This wasn't one of those "hyperactive wackos" Loki was always talking about, was it?

Or was she simply *that excited*?

About what? Meeting him?

One of Bete's eyebrows arched skyward.

He didn't have any memory of this little girl, but there was something about her shrill squawking that seemed to trigger something in his brain.

"Wait a minute…You're one of those whores from *Ishtar Familia* we fought in Meren…!"

"Bingo! That's me! Do you remember me now? Huh? Huh?" She was nodding fervently now, eyes sparkling.

It had been back when he and the rest of the familia's men had gone to aid Aiz and the others in Port Meren outside the city—when *Kali Familia* had made Tiona and Tione perform that sadistic rite and *Ishtar Familia* had faced off against them on the docks. Yes, this girl had been there. She'd aimed a scimitar right at his back after he'd gone into beast mode and subdued that ugly frog of a woman, Phryne. He hadn't been able to see her face thanks to the clothes she'd been wearing, but he did remember landing a heavy punch right on that stomach.

What was it one of the other Amazons had called her…?

"I'm Lena! Lena Tully! So you better not forget it this time, Bete Loga!" She finished his thought cheerily, face beaming. "Oh, right! I heard you just had a big, huge fight with Aisha and the others, huh? Man, talk about bad timing on my part! I went and missed the whole thing! What a missed opportunity!"

It seemed this girl, Lena, had been en route to meet Aisha and the other Amazons at the Flaming Wasp for drinks. Then what—had she shown up to see her friends on the ground, heard what happened, then come running after him…? Looking at her all restless and fidgety and clutching her cheeks now, Bete figured that was probably what happened.

*But why…? What's this brat's deal?!*

Bete's brows furrowed even lower as he watched the girl continue to giggle and squirm like a puppy. Bete wasn't exactly a popular guy. He was well aware of this. Used to it, even. Answering others' malice and hostility with snubs of his own was pretty much an everyday occurrence for him.

But this girl was different. In fact, she actually seemed to *like* him.

Him. The lone wolf even the members of his own familia feared, wouldn't come close to.

"Hey, hey, hey! Wanna grab a drink or somethin'? We don't have to go back to where Aisha and the others are if you don't want. We can go somewhere else! Just the two of us!"

…Not only that, she was close. Ridiculously close.

*This woman.*

"Get the hell away from me, would ya? Just who the hell you think you are?"

"It's Lena! Like I said earlieeer, Bete Loga!"

"That's not what I meant and you know it! And didn't I already tell you to stop tossin' my name around like that?!"

He simply couldn't understand this chick. Why was she being so clingy? Somehow he could already hear his own emphatic goddess's words ringing in his head: *"Oh-ho! Look at you, Mister Popular!"*

"You look right here, you Amazonian brat. I don't even know you, so stop actin' like we're best friends or somethin', yeah?" Bete shouted as he attempted to bat the girl away.

"But I can't heeeelp it! I've fallen for you!"

At this, Bete came to a stop.

He stared at her, his lupine ears twitching.

Looked back down into that wistful expression.

He saw eyes that resembled two bright-orange pearls, not much different from Bete's own, directing a sultry, seductive gaze at him.

More specifically, it was the expression of an Amazon who was sizing up her prey—

*—Now hold on just a goddamn second here!*

The face in front of him now was one he knew all too well.

It was the face of an Amazon in search of her mate. And the same face Tione gave Finn as she chased him halfway around the world.

A shiver snaked its way up Bete's spine.

"I haven't been the same since I saw you that day in Meren, Bete Loga. I'm a changed woman! Just thinking about you turning those handsome dark eyes my way gives me tingles all over!"

For you see, Amazons were attracted to strong men.

Amazons gave their hearts away to any strong male who could best them.

This oh-so-troubling tribal tradition dawning on him, Bete pulled his lips back in a terrified grimace, tattoo and all. Certainly, he had "bested her" that night in Meren. It had been a one-hit kill, the extraordinary power of his beast form turning his fist into a veritable hammer of iron.

—And now she was in heat!

Suddenly, everything made sense.

As he stood there, glued to the ground, Lena continued to gaze longingly at him, fingertips grazing her slender chin as she let out a libidinous sigh.

"It was fate, you know? The moment your fist plunged its way into my stomach...I just knew we were meant to be!"

Thinking back, he *had* felt a sort of ominous chill as he'd blown her away.

But to think it would mean this. That beating the shit out of her would actually *attract* her to him. *Amazons are too strange!*

"...My confession may be a little out of order, but know that my feelings are true! I love you, Bete Loga!" she finished, head popping upward and both arms outstretched as she leaped toward him. "My heart beats for you, Bete Loga! *Have my children!*"

Just in time, Bete noticed her coming for him, and he curled his hand into a fist.

"Guwauugh?!"

His response to this once-in-a-lifetime confession was none other than a full-throttle wolf punch to the gut.

Lena curled in on herself before crumpling to the stone below, and the sound of the collision brought Bete back to his senses.

"H-hey...you alive?"

Damn. He'd really put everything into that one. Anyone would be down for the count after a direct hit like that from a first-tier adventurer. The moment he showed concern, however—

"Heh...heh-heh-heh-heh...! You did it again...Right in the baby-maker...Now I'll...definitely get pregnant...!

*What the hell?!*

Bete instantly took a step backward.

The girl was a terrifying writhing mass moaning on top of the stone, both hands to her exposed belly. The drool leaking from her ghastly smile only added to the effect.

Suddenly, the very same Bete who had never turned his back on a battle before wanted so badly to get the hell out of there.

"...There ain't a single one of you Amazons who's worth a damn."

*Cough-cough.* "That's not...true...At least we're...always true to... ourselves..." Lena muttered, rising to her feet with a lurch like a zombie. Despite the teary smile on the girl's face, there was something almost sobering about the image, and Bete narrowed his eyes.

"You *do* know I just beat the shit out of your friends, right?"

"I sure do! And I think it's amazing! To think you're even stronger than Aisha and the others—it gives me chills! It makes me love you even more!!"

There was no getting rid of this girl.

It didn't matter what he tried; he'd never win. Realizing this, he simply turned around and started walking away.

"W-wait! Where are you going?!"

"Gonna get some actual sleep! At an inn! Don't follow me!"

But, of course, the girl was hot on his heels.

Black ponytail bobbing up and down, she cocked her head to the side curiously. "An inn...? Why not your home?"

Bete could have punched himself. Him and his damn mouth.

"Don't tell me...You got into a fight with your familia? And now you don't have anywhere to go? Is that it? Huh? Is that it?!"

Shut the hell *up*.

He spun around, only to see Lena bouncing about in her most disgusting display of excitement yet. He wanted to hit her so badly.

"Come back with me, then! I've got a nice bed! It should fit two people just fine!"

"Like hell! I'll choose where I spend the night myself, thank you very *much*!"

"Do you have money, though, Bete Loga? Huh? The hotels around here are veeeeery expensive!"

Bete stopped cold at this, his second error in judgment dawning on him.

—*Shit. I don't have any money.*

The bag of money he'd tossed so haughtily at the owner of the Flaming Wasp to pay for the damages had been everything he had.

Sure, he could head to the Dungeon now and make as much as he wanted, but…to be honest, that was more work than he was willing to do right now. What's more, he didn't have a single person he'd call a friend outside of the familia, which meant he truly had no place to go. Bete was surely and truly the most despised adventurer in all of Orario.

As though attuned to the subtleties of Bete's mind, Lena sidled next to him. "Stop right there, my good sir! Have I got the inn for you! Won't cost you a thing, and it comes with some mighty fine company, to boot! Our girls will keep you satisfied *all* night long!"

*"Mighty fine company"…Just how cocky is this chick?!*

Bete shot her a menacing look.

Looked straight into those hopeful orange eyes—and made up his mind. He wouldn't go with her if she was the last girl on earth!…But then a new idea seemed to cross her mind, her eyes flashing.

"If you won't come with me, then I'll go to *Loki Familia*'s manor! I'll yell 'Heeey, this guy assaulted me!'"

"The hell?! Gimme a break! This's got nothin' to do with my familia. You go there and I'll straight-up grind you to a pulp, you little shit!"

"I wouldn't mind! It would be a dream come true to be killed by the man I love!"

Now Bete was really starting to sweat.

Any other day of the week, he'd have been fine teaching this girl a lesson, but his current situation put him between a rock and a hard place. No doubt, everyone would think he'd gotten drunk and assaulted some kid, which would make it considerably more difficult (if not impossible) to restore his dignity in the familia. Tiona, Raul, and the others would truly lose all respect for him. No, laying a finger on Lena would only bring him more trouble than it was worth.

What's more, this chick was actually considering attacking *Loki Familia*, the greatest familia in the city, without even thinking about what this would spell for her own familia. Was this complete disregard for the means she took to sate her own lust just another one of the "bonuses" that came with being a running-on-instinct Amazon?

Anguished, Bete felt an overwhelming rush of anger rise up in him.

Face flushed and teeth grinding against one another, he finally grumbled: "…This is never happening again, you hear? If I stay tonight, you better run like hell if you ever pull a stunt like this again!"

"Hooray! No worries! I'll never extort you ever again! At least not like this!"

"You p-piece of crap!" Bete sputtered as Lena hopped about with a complete lack of concern. Cheeks now a brilliant pink, she grabbed Bete's arm and started walking.

"Let's get going, then! This place'll be so much nicer than an inn—I promise!"

"Stop pullin' me, you damn whore! Let go of meeeeeeeee!"

And so, the two of them continued like that, Bete still struggling to shake the girl off him, for some ten, twenty minutes. The place Lena was leading him to was in the city's fourth district to the southeast.

"Hey! Isn't this the Pleasure Quarter…?"

"I-it's nothing like that! This isn't some shady brothel where you're gonna get ripped off, I promise!"

The bewitching flush of the magic-stone lamps and telltale bawdy musk of the Night District surrounding them, Bete glared down at Lena as though she were a goblin or some other impish creature. Lena, however, hastily attempted to explain herself.

*He has a fight with his familia and then runs off with some harlot in the Pleasure Quarter!* Bete could already hear the gossip. It was enough to spur him toward the back alleyways and away from prying eyes, though it seemed Lena was actually headed toward the other side of the southeastern main street, where the third district met the northern tip of the Pleasure Quarter.

"I joined a new familia after Ishtar was sent home, but bringing a man back with me so soon after converting might not be the best idea."

"I'm pretty sure bringing someone from another familia would *never* be a good idea…"

"That's why we're going somewhere else! A *secret* place!" she insisted before strolling right into a very obvious no-entry zone. Pulling Bete along, she guided him deftly past the guards the Guild had assigned to keep everyone out.

"Is this…*Ishtar Familia* territory?"

"Used to be."

The once prosperous city of iniquity had been reduced to nothing more than rubble and ash after the loss of its goddess. Its many brothels were in a horrid state of disrepair, their walls collapsed, roofs in pieces, and shutters littering the streets. There were even large halls still bearing the crosscuts of cinder and flame. The entire estate was devoid of light, most of its magic-stone lanterns snuffed and leaving it illuminated only by the moon. It was empty, not a soul in sight.

It might as well have been a castle city ransacked by an enemy nation, still in ruins after its fall. And there in the middle of it all soared Belit Babili, *Ishtar Familia*'s former home, bearing its own fair share of wounds. The resistance against *Freya Familia*, against the Goddess of Beauty's blitzkrieg, had turned the district of ill repute into rubble in the course of a single night, and it was currently scheduled for redevelopment.

"*Freya Familia* pretty much went to town, but the building itself's still surprisingly intact. All right! We're here!"

It turned out the "secret place" Lena had so professed was a building situated right next to one of the city walls to the southeastern corner of Orario's already southeastern-most third district. It was a four-story abode that drew heavily from the culture and architecture of the Kaios Desert of the middle continent. Its stone had been lacquered white, which, when coupled with the elaborately designed windows, made for an impressive sight. No doubt, it had been a high-class establishment back when it was still in business. From its position hidden away on one of the neighborhood's side streets, it was easy to see how famous top-tier adventurers and ambassadors from other countries might have slipped in and out unnoticed.

Bete observed everything with apathy as Lena dragged him inside.

"Only Aisha and a few others even know about this place. It's like my castle! I used it as a place to sleep until a room freed up in my new familia."

The vacant brothel was, indeed, luxurious. The hallway connecting to the main entrance was well-furnished, from the velvet sofa covered in a thin layer of dust, to the gorgeously vibrant rug, to the bevy of expensive-looking vases. Just when Bete was thinking this place would be easy pickings for thieves: "It's gonna be redeveloped, yeah? So the guards here keep everyone out, even those bums who come down from Daedalus Street," Lena explained. "That means we've gotta be careful, too, yeah? Don't wanna get caught, so ix-nay on the ights-lay!" she continued, bringing her hands together in a pleading gesture.

"Whatever," Bete simply tossed back in response. "Can I just take whichever room I want?"

"Ah! Wait, wait, wait, wait! H-higher is better! The top floor! That's where the best room is! And you can definitely, definitely still use it!" Lena quickly blurted as Bete prepared to start investigating the place on his own.

Bete narrowed his eyes in suspicion…only to see the girl reaching a hand toward her glossy hair. With a *swish*, she pulled out the blue clasp that had been keeping her hair up, letting the long black strands cascade down her back and create a much more sensual image. In that instant, she transformed from an innocent child into a woman well versed in the ways of love, her eyes narrowing like a small cat's as she shot him her most sensational smile yet.

Bete, however, couldn't have cared less.

Hands still shoved in his pockets and brows lowered in disinterest, he simply trudged up the stairs.

"Huh…? *H-hey!*"

But he ignored the impassioned cries coming from below, not stopping until he made it to the top floor and kicking open a nearby door that wasn't entirely closed.

The carpet here was much fancier compared to the one in the hallway, and rather than magic-stone lanterns, candlestick sconces had been affixed to the walls for mood lighting. As for the room itself, it was big enough that ten people could have lounged in it easily, and a grand four-poster bed stood alongside the wall, its long columns stretching toward the ceiling. It was every bit a VIP room.

There was the faint smell of *something* still coloring the air—Lena's residual scent? She had said she'd been using this room for a time. The corners of Bete's mouth curled downward.

"There's no way I'm sleepin' in a bed like that. Who the hell knows what's been done in it…"

He'd rather die than sleep in the same spot some other guy had gotten his canoe shellacked, so instead, he found himself a spot on the floor near the window and slumped down. The velvety carpet was a soft welcome to his body, and he let his eyes wander off to the side, where a view of the Pleasure Quarter greeted him from the open window.

From far above, the grand temple of the Goddess of Beauty soared

© Kiyotaka Haimura

over the rest of the Night District, making for a none-too-paltry view if he had to say so himself.

"This is the life…huh?"

Being solicited by a girl, spending the night in the prime seat for looking out across this ruined city…He let his gaze stay there awhile, taking in the situation and finding the whole thing just a bit ironic, considering he'd just been chased out by his own familia (albeit temporarily).

Finally, he turned away to get some sleep, resting his arms behind his head and closing his eyes. Sleep came quickly, too, no doubt because of the copious amounts of alcohol he'd earlier imbibed. Letting the cool night breeze caress his skin, he felt himself begin to drift off…until, *clink*.

He heard the door open ever so quietly.

"—Bete Logaaaaa." A sickly sweet purr made his lupine ears twitch.

It was Lena. And what's more, she'd changed her clothes.

Now, she donned a black negligee…which, while certainly covering more skin than her previous attire, was so see-through it might as well have been transparent, a veil covering what looked like nothing more than undergarments beneath. From the gentle curve of her body to the vivacious glow of her copper skin, every bit of her seemed to emanate an alluring, pheromonal redolence.

"Why not forget all those bad things for a while, hmm? I can take you into a wonderful, enchanting dream." Smiling softly, she made her way toward Bete on the floor, her slender toes quiet atop the carpet. When she knelt over him, he could feel her breath and its primal heat, and then the rest of her, descending toward him, looming just above his virile powerhouse of a body.

Her Amazonian instincts were controlling her every move, and there was only one thing this girl desired: a child.

Even from within her perfume, the man-killing scent of her musk was unmistakable. And as she came toward him, moonlight drenching her delicate shoulders and limbs seeking out his own—

"Get away from me."

"Guh?!"

—she was sent flying.

A single leg had risen from the floor, stubbornly kicking her away and sending her tumbling across the length of the room. Bete flashed his pointed incisors to tell her he was far from amused.

"Hey, what gives, huh? You're really just gonna go right to sleep?! Not even violate me a little?!"

"Who was it who said we had to be quiet or we'll get caught, huh, you damn brat?!"

Lena shot to her feet, only to immediately bring both hands to her mouth with a gasp. Her stunned silence didn't last long, however; with an indignant puff of her cheeks, she was crawling back toward him once more.

"Come on, hmm? Let's have a little fun! If we try really hard, I'm sure we can whip us up a little bundle of joy. Make me pregnant, hmm?"

"Shut the hell up, you whore."

"Why won't you even touch me, hmm? Is it because I'm not endowed like Aisha and the others? Is it?! Or...You're not impotent, are you?! No, wait—you like men?!"

"I'm going to murder you!"

Lena stealthily reached toward him, still whining and cooing, only to meet Bete's foot once again. He wasn't about to let her touch him, let alone sleep anywhere near him. Again and again, she went sailing through the air, until finally, when she crash-landed on the bed—"*Whuaaagh!!*"—she let herself collapse backward onto the mattress.

"This isn't how it's supposed to be! I got myself all ready so you wouldn't be able to resist! So that Bete Loga wouldn't be able to *live* without me!"

"Because that's not at all nefarious!"

Lena was crying now, her tears soaking the bedsheets.

Bete just stared at the ceiling with a spiteful sigh, glad the storm had passed.

"Wh-why don't you like me?"

"You think it's just you? I hate all you wimps! Sleeping with any of you'd just make all that weakness rub off on me."

"Hmm? But Bete Loga, is there even a woman stronger than you out there?" Lena asked, currently curled up among the sheets.

"..."

Bete went quiet. Rolling over, he closed his eyes.

"...I hate weak women most of all," he muttered in irritation.

*Goddammit. I should have known this would happen.*

From within the floating depths of his consciousness, a tangible sense of dread came to him.

He knew this feeling. He was about to dream of his past—

It had been half a werewolf's lifetime ago.

Bete Loga had been born into the world in the land to the north—to a tribe of wandering animal people with no ties to any city or country, let alone the Labyrinth City of Orario. Unlike typical nomads, they were a people focused solely on hunting, the Beastmen of the Plains, and Bete was the son of their chief.

It was just him, his powerful father, his bighearted mother, and later, his sister. And if he left the large tent his family had been allocated, he had his peers, the smiling faces of his many werewolf brothers awaiting him. The entire tribe was his family.

"It's a dog-eat-dog world out there, Bete, so keep those fangs polished."

His father, stronger than anyone else he knew, had drilled that into him time and time again.

As a tribe without a god to worship, everyone had to be strong, even the women and children. They'd fight off the monsters that roamed the surface, crush rogue caravans along with their guards, and do it all without the blessings of a Status. More than anything else, their power as a race of people who awoke under the light of the moon came from their untamed skills and knowledge—the techniques and strategies they'd long cultivated as a tribe. They were the Beastmen of the Plains, capable of taking on even low-level familias, and though many envoys from their surrounding countries and familias solicited their aid, Bete's father had always heeded the teachings of his ancestors and refused them.

They lived as nature; their bodies turned to dust and, from that dust, new life emerged.

And young Bete revered them all, from his tradition-honoring father to the staunch, brave warriors of his tribe.

*"Good morning, Bete!"*

There had been a girl, too—born on the same day, she'd been a friend of his growing up. Her long, softly golden hair was rare for a werewolf, and she was beautiful, standing out from among the others of her generation like a brilliantly glimmering jewel. Like clockwork, as Bete had grown, so had his feelings for the girl, and so had the scuffles with his male peers over her.

*"You want it? Take it!"* That had been the simple rule hammered into him by the tribe, and Bete had heeded the call, training day in and day out until he was the strongest among the tribe's children. Until, finally, he could claim her for his own. It was her warm sigh, fading into the wind, *"...Even with you, I can't be strong..."* that had left the strongest, most genuine impression on him to this day.

For you see, the uncommonly reserved girl had been weak. Frighteningly frail, almost.

Which had forced Bete to train even harder, knowing he had to protect more than just himself. Going to his father, he'd asked to be treated as one of the tribe's warriors, venturing out with the adults on their many hunting missions. It even got to the point where he could take on goblins, orcs, and other similar monsters completely on his own.

That was how he'd spent his youth: roaming those green hills surrounded by majestic mountains, the gaze of his childhood friend watching over him, joined every once in a while by his precocious sister, and simply training with everything he had.

Then, Bete's twelfth birthday had arrived.

And all of that had changed.

"Father…Mother…Luna…"
The moon had been positively golden that night.
The night everyone in his tribe had been killed.
It had been a massacre.
A strange new monster had suddenly appeared on the plains, slaughtering everyone.
Everyone except for Bete.
Though he would only come to know this later, the beast had come from one of the world's three great frontiers—the Valley of Dragons to the far, far north.
The colossal, flightless dragon boasted scales that could ward off any attack. With one mighty roar, it had punctured the very eardrums of the plains people, and it had devoured even the tribe's warriors in their awakened beast modes. His father and mother had been torn to shreds. His sister had been crushed to death. Bete had been more fortunate: After a swipe to the face from the beast's claws, he'd been sent hurtling into a nearby outcropping of rocks, the impact knocking him out cold until the battle was over.
When he'd crawled out later, dragging his battered body across the ground, nothing but rivers of blood and lumps of gnawed flesh remained; the black shadow of the creature was disappearing along the far horizon.
It was the new Master of the Plains. It had devoured the weak and robbed the once strong of their privilege, turning them into nothing more than food.
Bete had lost everything that day.
In that one merciless attack.
It was a tragedy the gods were all too used to: an everyday occurrence in that vast, sprawling world, not even warranting a glance of interest.
Survival of the fittest.
The values of the dog-eat-dog world that Bete's father had long impressed upon him finally hit home. It was just how the world was.

Divine providence. The real truth. The weak could have their happiness taken away from them in the blink of an eye. Bete's tribe had finally had the tables turned, becoming nothing more than the same prey they themselves had hunted. It was simple, really. So simple, everything in his stomach came bubbling up right then and there.

The strong could get away with anything. They could take anything.

And the weak could do nothing against them. Nothing of theirs was safe.

The weak couldn't survive.

His father had been weak. The warriors in his tribe had been weak. His mother; his sister, Luna; Bete himself; and yes, even *she*—currently scattered into hundreds of fleshy, bloody chunks across the ground—had been weak.

*"Renee...!"*

Bete had cried.

His wound still carved deep into his face, he'd cried tears of salt and blood.

He was all alone now. Sitting there beneath the light of the moon, he'd howled at the heavens.

After that, Bete, the only surviving member of his tribe, had washed his hands of his homeland. Directly disobeying the teachings of the Beastmen of the Plains, he'd sought out places with people. He had no intentions of trying to revive his tribe—they'd been weak. Even banding together, weaklings were still weak. Natural selection would weed them out. So he'd tossed them aside, together with all the feelings he still had for them.

What he craved was strength. Fangs that couldn't be broken. He vowed to cast off his weak flesh so he could fight back against the strong, to take down the Master of the Plains.

It was from a passing peddler that he learned of another of the world's three great frontiers: the Dungeon. It rested on the westernmost tip of the continent, within a city known as the Labyrinth City.

And it was in this city that the strongest of adventurers and their gods gathered. Thus, Bete's journey for power began.

As a lesson to himself and to his frailty, he had a reminder carved into his face, a symbol of his past self that he would never forget. And with that, his hunger grew—hunger to grow strong, to never have to lose anything anymore. The first time he saw it, the bolt of lightning the artist had tattooed across his face from his eye to his cheek, he'd laughed. It looked almost like the very same unbreakable fangs he so craved.

His hunger for strength and his symbol of weakness had become one—the fang of a wolf.

"...Shit."

Bete grimaced the moment he opened his eyes.

Shaking off the lingering thoughts of his past and the phantom pain running up and down the length of his tattoo, he furrowed his brow.

But then...

"——Ah."

The girl who'd creeped over next to him froze, as though she believed the grimace had been directed at her.

More importantly, though, she wasn't wearing a thing.

"...What the hell do you think you're doing?"

"Eh-he-he...he-he-he-he...Dropping by for a nightcap? Or I guess it would be a morning-cap in this case..."

Bete didn't even wait for Lena to finish, kicking her and her long, dangling hair away.

She gave a startled "*Guphwah!*" as she was sent sailing toward the far corner of the room, then shot him a series of death glares as she righted herself.

Outside the window, the light of dawn was just beginning to warm the sky. Its faint traces could be seen ever so gently wrapping themselves around the Pleasure Quarter from their position in their hideout along the city's walls. For a moment, Bete let himself watch the transition, silently cursing the dream that had seized his attention so thoroughly he hadn't even noticed Lena's approach.

*Can't go home yet, but that doesn't mean I can just sit around on my ass all day. Guess I'll head to the Dungeon, see if I can make myself a valis or two...Maybe check around for that thing Finn and the others are looking for.*

His eyes narrowed as he took in the sight of the soaring temple on the other side of the window—the former castle of the Goddess of Beauty.

Finally, he turned around and looked back toward the still-groaning girl on the other side of the room.

"Hey, brat."

"What is it nooooow?" she moaned back, tears in her eyes.

"You ever seen some sorta red key? With a weird symbol thingy carved into it?"

A cold wind whistled against the stone path underfoot.

It was in a tunnel deep underground, in a labyrinth untouched by the sun up above.

As a multitude of water spiders scuttled about, conducting a revolting symphony of pitter-patters with their legs, an angered shout cut through the air.

"That goddamn shithead of a goddess!"

The voice came from a human girl dressed in a fur-lined overcoat. It was Valletta Grede, one of the upper echelons of the Evils' Remnants, and she was currently stalking about the mural-adorned hallway of relics deep within the maze of Knossos, her maddened screams bouncing off the walls.

"After all we did for her, she goes and lets herself get trashed by *Freya Familia*!"

"This was an unexpected move by Freya. If everything had gone according to plan, none of this would have happened," the God of Death, Thanatos, responded in an attempt to placate the girl, a forced smile pulling at his lips.

Valletta's raging refused to cease, the rest of the familia's high-ranking officials watching from all sides.

"Oh, it would have, would it? A whole lot of good that does us now! And you know what's even worse? We gave her one of our keys! And now it's who-knows-where!"

Ishtar had been one of the sponsors the Evils had enlisted to help expand Knossos.

Thus, they'd provided her with a key to the labyrinth.

One of the appropriately named "Orbs of Knossos."

They were magic items that could be used to open the many orichalcum doors littering Knossos's halls.

Only now, with Ishtar's sudden defeat, they'd lost track of the one they'd entrusted to her.

"Yes, yes, this is indeed a bit troubling, but we're already searching the ruined Pleasure Quarter, are we not?"

"Yeah, and we haven't found squat! Do you even realize the shit we'd be in if Finn and his little goons got their hands on it first...?!"

The man-made labyrinth Knossos had two main advantages: It was unbreakable, and it was inescapable. But as soon as the enemy possessed one of its keys, whatever edge they had would be reduced to nothing. Chewing viciously at her nails, Valletta positively radiated enmity as the face of her sworn rival, Finn, who'd just barely slipped past her fingers, flashed through her head.

Currently, Valletta was the only major player left in the maze. Barca, and his Daedalian pedigree, was gone, as was the creature Levis. They'd taken off, leaving Valletta and the others to deal with everything in the aftermath of *Loki Familia*'s attack. The former would do what he could to fix the decimated labyrinth, and the latter likely planned to protect the remaining spirits.

*Damn ingrates!* she seethed, her anger only rising.

"Where'd that little Tammuz shit run off to, huh...?!" she growled as the face of Ishtar's manservant popped into the back of her mind.

The goddess's most trusted right-hand man, he came with her time and time again on her visits to Knossos. Only, he'd gone missing the night of *Freya Familia*'s attack.

"What's going on in that head of yours, Valletta dear?"

"...We're gonna look for that key. Turn over everything in that shitty woman's home if we have to. There's no way I'm letting *Loki Familia* get the drop on us! Get out there and search, you good-for-nothings!"

There was a resounding "Yes, ma'am!" from the rest of *Thanatos Familia* before the whole lot of them went racing toward the exit.

Valletta shot a look of contempt at Thanatos. The way the god's eyes were narrowed in what seemed to be amusement rubbed her entirely the wrong way.

# CHAPTER 2

# Did Someone Order a WOLF?

Гэта казка іншага сям'і.

Ці з'яўляецца парадак воўк?

"We need to get our hands on one of the keys."

It was morning at *Loki Familia*'s home.

They were conducting a meeting in the dining hall, and Finn was speaking to the rest of the familia.

"While most of them certainly are secure within the Evils' grasp... there is one we may still have a chance with."

"You think that *Ishtar Familia* might have had one? They were the ones hauling the violas to Meren, after all," Tione pointed out.

"Indeed. Considering the close relationship between Ishtar and the Evils, there's a strong possibility she may have been given one of the keys," Finn confirmed. "Due to the surprise attack from *Freya Familia*, Ishtar should no longer have any contact with the Evils. The key may have gotten lost in the attack. There's also a chance one of her ex-followers may know of its location. We have no choice but to take our chances...Which is why, from today forward, we'll be putting all our efforts into finding that key."

The air in the dining hall grew tense.

"I'd like everyone to start by gathering as much information as possible. Scout out the Pleasure Quarter; interrogate any former members of *Ishtar Familia* you can find. Do try to keep things on the down low, though, if you would. Does anyone have any questions?"

"I do; I do!" Tiona's hand shot up just like always. "This is about something else but...where's Riveria? I haven't seen her anywhere."

"Riveria has already left on an errand."

"I see...Well! That stupid wolf! Where's he?"

"Worried about him, are you?"

"As if! Just wondering if he was skippin' out. Totally in-ex-cusable!" Tiona hurriedly added, unable to hide her petulance. Neither she nor the rest of the familia members knew Bete had been placed on leave.

Unsure if it was for better or for worse, Finn shot the Amazon a smile all the same, deciding it would be best to cover for the wolf for the time being. "Bete is, well…Let's say he's probably out sniffing around for something on his own at the moment, hmm? Anyway, if that's all the questions for now, let's go ahead and split into teams: I want a search team and an interrogation team…If you would, then, Loki?" Finn added, his last comment whispered in the goddess's ear.

"Roger that, boss! Leave it to me!"

As everyone in the hall rose to their feet to start forming their teams, Loki wove through the hustle and bustle, surreptitiously sliding up next to Aiz.

"Got a favor to ask of ya, Aizuu."

"Loki…? What is it?"

"Keep an eye on Bete for me, would ya? No reason to go outta your way, though—just while yer out 'n' about doin' yer own stuff is fine."

Aiz's eyes widened ever so slightly.

"Poor thing may have gotten the boot 'n' all, but, well, Bete's still Bete. He'll be out there lookin' for clues on his own. Doesn't matter how he talks in front of y'all." Loki's eyes were filled with nothing but trust in her lupine follower. It was a different kind of trust than Aiz and her peers had in one another. This was the unconditional faith of a mother.

"Now, I'm pretty sure the enemy's not gonna try anything aboveground. I also don't think Bete's stupid enough to go wandering about Daedalus Street on his own. But still. Look for 'im for me, would ya?"

"…But I…"

"Huh? Somethin' wrong, Aizuu?"

"I told Bete that I…hate…him…" Aiz mumbled, her gaze pointed downward.

Hearing this from the girl of few words was enough to make Loki bring her arms to her stomach in a giant belly laugh.

"Bwa-ha-ha-ha!! Now you've done it! Poor Bete's prolly lyin' dead in the street right about now!"

"S-so, I…I just think that…maybe it's not so good if…we see each other now…" Aiz continued despondently.

Calming herself, Loki turned toward Aiz, speaking as she would to a child. "Whaddaya think, Aizuu? About Bete? And the rest of the familia?"

"…Well, I…Maybe I told him I hate him, yes…but I…" Aiz started, searching for the words inside her as though attempting to take another look at what was really in her heart. Loki watched gently all the while. "…I can't help but remember before…when Tiona and Bete would fight, and…Raul and Lefiya and the others would all panic, trying to stop them, and…everyone would laugh…"

"Right."

"…I want it to be like that again…The way it used to be…" she finished, her golden eyes turning momentarily toward Tiona and Tione. Even with Raul and the others there, it felt like there was something missing. The familia just felt off.

When Aiz glanced back up, Loki had a huge smile on her face, and she reached forward to tousle the swordswoman's golden hair as though awarding her a gold star. Aiz scrunched one of her eyes shut, not even bothering to push the goddess away despite how much it tickled.

"I feel the same, Aizuu. But considerin' how stubborn Tiona and the others are actin', there's no one else I can go to to help fix this but you. Finn's got my hands tied, after all."

"…"

"If yer still feelin' a little anxious, though, you can always go to Lefiya for help. Whaddaya say, huh? Can I count on you?"

"…Yes, I'll…do it."

The short answer brought another smile to Loki's face, and the goddess patted her on the shoulder. As the rest of her colleagues filed their way out of the room, Aiz threw her gaze toward the window and the sunlight filtering in.

"A magic item with a weird symbol thingy carved into it…?"

Back in the Pleasure Quarter and the high-class brothel Lena had been using as her secret spot beneath the shadow of the city's eastern wall…

Having moved to the courtesans' old living quarters on the first floor, Lena was currently stuffing her face with bread from her stash, gazing down at a piece of parchment in her hand. On it was a rough sketch of the item in question—Bete's handiwork, with just enough detail to be discernible.

"You're looking for this thing? By the way…you sure you don't want anything to eat?"

"You think I wanna be even more in debt, you hag? I've got enough on my plate as it is!"

"It wouldn't be like that at all, and you know it! I even made this myself!"

"All the more reason not to…" Bete grumbled to himself as though he hadn't heard.

Indeed, sandwiching Lena and the table was a whole smorgasbord of simple Amazonian dishes—cut it up, toss it on the fire, and serve. Throwing a glance at the sliced dried meats and bread, the cheeses and honey, Bete looked back up, returning to the topic at hand.

"Your damn goddess mighta had somethin' like this. Ain't it familiar at all?"

"Hmm…" Lena murmured as she took a swig of magic-stone-refrigerated milk. Staring long and hard at the $D$ symbol carved into the surface of the ball in the sketch, she raised her gaze to search Bete's face. "…Though I can't say for absolute sure…I feel like I've definitely seen *something* like this before…maybe?"

"Really?!" Bete demanded, hand on the table as he leaned toward the girl. Lena nodded boastfully. "Then hurry up and tell me, would ya?!"

"For free?!"

"Huh?"

"That was some embarrassment you put me through last night…I may need a little something to get my mouth working again," she continued, eyes closing as her lips curled upward with salacious intent.

Bete's cheek twitched. "You askin' for a beating, you damn witch?"

"Such violence! This is the negotiation table, don't you know? The whole point is *not* to offend the opposing party...Even an Amazon like me knows that!"

"Oh, quit your whining! If that mouth of yours won't listen, I'll make sure your body does!"

"Then you'll question my body? Oh my, Bete Loga! I see you're quite bold even in broad daylight!"

"Stop hearing only what you wanna hear!"

The fight from the night prior continued, but no matter how much he yelled, it had no effect on Lena, who was sitting prettily with her hands clasped against her cheeks for the moment.

She was possibly the most vexing human being Bete had ever come across. If she had been a normal adventurer, he'd have grabbed her collar right then and there and beat the daylights out of her. But considering the girl in front of him now would probably enjoy that, this made her particularly difficult to deal with. If not *nauseating* to deal with.

Never in his life had he imagined that someone being attracted to him could be worse than someone who hated or feared him.

Though perhaps it was a little late to say it, he was finally starting to empathize with Finn, given how Tione was usually glued to him. He almost wanted to apologize to the prum captain.

"If you're not gonna tell me, I'll just ask another one of you damn Amazons!"

"But maybe I'm the only one who knows about this little ball, hmm? Plus, do you really expect Aisha and the others to bare everything to the one who took them to town last night? It's just like back in Meren, hmm?"

"Guh...?!"

She had a point. The "repulsive werewolf" was more likely to get spit on than get any sort of information out of the other Amazons. Which meant the only negotiation partner he had left was Lena.

As Bete struggled to find his voice, Lena shot him a wink, drawing a miniature circle in the air with her finger. "Besides, isn't that the rule of you adventurers? To always pay for your information?"

Bete clenched his canines together as hard as he could.

He already knew the incorrigible girl in front of him wasn't going to ask for money or any other "normal" payment for the information he sought.

"…What do you want, then?"

"For you to give me a baby! —Kidding, kidding, just kiddiiiiing!" She quickly backpedaled as Bete raised his fist up in a sincerely murderous move. Sweat soaking her forehead as she racked her brain, she finally popped her head up with a smile.

"Go on a date with me, Bete Loga!"

Later that day, when the morning sun had just crested over the city's walls and the thrum of daily life had returned to its streets…

Northwest Main Street, nicknamed Adventurers Way, was as busy as always, filled to the brim with demi-humans on their way to explore the Dungeon. The nearby *Dian Cecht Familia* facility, as well—the solid-white field hospital—boasted its own fair share of visitors.

It was here, in the hospital's pharmacy, that the high elf Riveria stood.

Across from her at the counter was the silver-haired human girl Amid Teasanare.

"Were you able to discern anything from the dagger in question?"

"Indeed, we've completed our inspection. However, I really must say…There is something undeniably queer about that weapon," Amid replied, her voice hard as she dropped her eyes to the obsidian dagger lying atop the counter.

It was a cursed weapon—endowed with an Unhealable Curse.

It was also the same weapon that had been used to slay Leene and the others down in Knossos, retrieved by Aiz herself.

"It boasted quite a curse...I still remember when you brought Captain Finn in with it. None of the items currently in circulation had any effect. It was only by my magic that we were able to make any headway, and it required an extraordinary amount of Mind..." Amid's tiny hands clenched visibly as she relived the memory in her head. "I even tested it on my own body later. Not even protective accessories or magic items had any success in resisting the curse," she finished, voice grave.

"No way to defend against it and nigh un-liftable save for the magic of Dea Saint. A powerful curse, indeed..."

Existing equipment and items were entirely ineffective, both in protection and as restoratives. Though perhaps what worried Riveria even more was the thought that there were more of these weapons out there.

The sword the creature Levis had used against Aiz and Finn, the abandoned dagger before them now that had been used against Leene and the others, and even the weapons Tione's assassin opponents had used against her had all been capable of inflicting this dreadful curse with merely a single graze.

Which meant the enemy had at least one person crafting these vexing weapons for them.

"For a hexer to be able to craft cursed weapons such as these... their power must be incalculable—far beyond our wildest imagination. Either that...or they're being guided by some kind of crazed delusion..." Amid mused, the outline of some faceless yet assuredly unbalanced hexer beginning to take shape in her mind.

Riveria couldn't have agreed more.

There was a chance these Evils' Remnants had all the cursed weapons they could possibly want, which meant going in without a plan would only force them to make more sacrifices. If they were going to return to Knossos, they not only needed to get their hands on one of its keys but also do something about these weapons.

"Then the anti-curse I ordered. Do you think you'll be able to craft it?"

"...It will be difficult, to be frank," Amid confessed, the fatigue

Kiyotaka Haimura

plaguing her features evidence enough as to the countless times she'd already attempted to craft the curse-repelling medicine in question. And thanks to her near-translucently pale skin, the fatigue looked almost painful. "But…I will do my best. I can't allow such a weapon to exist," she finished, dauntless will coloring her voice. It was a rare sight to see the delicate doll of a girl express such strong emotion. After throwing a bitter glance down at the dagger on the counter, she returned her gaze to Riveria. "I will defeat this curse."

"…We're counting on you," Riveria pleaded, almost as though entreating a saint.

The blade of the scimitar bisected the monster's chin in one clean swipe.

"*Gwwwwuuuuooooogggh!*"

"Yah!"

Continuing through, it sent the head of the bull-headed minotaur flying. Her long black hair tied up in a ponytail, the girl sliced through the dim gloom of the grotto in a flash. The monster dealt with handily, she continued forward and toward the large swarm now gathered in front of her, aiming a sweeping kick.

"Bete Loga! C'mon, let's go! We're on a date! We're on a date!"

"I never imagined the dating scene would be so brutal…" Bete grumbled, a bit stupefied at the antics of the smiling, waving, *slaughtering* girl. His hands shoved in his pockets, he delivered a kick to an incoming hellhound that shattered its cranium.

They were in the Dungeon's middle levels, the "Cave Labyrinth."

More specifically, on the seventeenth floor—the stronghold of the third-tier adventurers.

It turned out what Lena really wanted was a "Dungeon date," quite possibly the least romantic idea for a date ever. Certainly, fighting and killing together as a method of increasing one's affinity with another made perfect sense when it came to the brute-force social skills of the Amazons, though Bete wasn't sure if this truly applied to all Amazons or just the one in front of him in particular.

If they weren't fighting on the streets, they were fighting between the sheets.

That was all Amazons knew. Though for Bete, this was more of a godsend than a flaw, as the idea of a normal "date" about made him want to puke.

"Look, look, look! Isn't this al-miraj the most adorable thing you've ever *seen*?!" Lena cried out as she sent the lovable rabbit monster sailing with a mighty *SPROING!*

*"Gyaaaaaaaah!"*

"You say as you beat the living shit out of it."

The brutish spectacle was so far removed from an ordinary date that had Lefiya and the others been there, they'd have fainted on the spot. As the girl annihilated everything in her path in her excited, happy flailing, her slashes cut deep despite her feminine antics.

"Just knowing that Bete Loga is here beside me is enough to shoot me to the moon!" she announced, scimitar in her right hand and gold-lined arm protector on her left. She used the thick metal to ward off her enemies' attacks as she set her blade awhirl in a dance allegro. It was an altogether unique battle style; the rapid movements made her look more like a spinning top than anything else. She held nothing back as her slender curved limbs executed her every power-packed move and her bare feet slammed into the teeth of the nearby liger fangs with such force they rendered their faces unidentifiable. Every attack sent her undersize loincloth dancing, revealing again and again the white undergarments and copper thighs beneath. Even the arm protector on her left hand became a weapon when she smashed it straight into the monsters' flesh and shattered the bones inside.

*A Level 2, huh? And about to level up again, by the looks of it...* *Seems she's got no problem against monsters up to the twenty-fourth floor or so,* Bete mused, eyes narrowed as he watched the girl throttle swarm after swarm of monsters with no need of help from him.

She was undeniably beautiful—radiant, almost, with the way the sweat was flying off her. And suddenly Bete realized her plan: After all, what man would be able to resist seeing her now? Well, sans the terrifying howls and spattering blood, perhaps.

"Outta my way," Bete growled, aiming a kick at a nearby minotaur that Lena had let escape and debilitating it with a single strike.

"*Gwuuuaaaagh?!*"

"Oh, I knew it! You really *are* strong!"

And with that, the battle was over. The Amazonian girl seemed satisfied, taking deep, heavy breaths. She then proceeded to run around from pile of ash to pile of ash, collecting the fallen magic stones and drop items in place of the completely unhelpful bump on a log, Bete.

She didn't seem the least bit concerned that her perpetual high was starting to grate on Bete's nerves. Just thinking about what they must look like to any other adventurers passing by made Bete want to melt, and he twisted his face into what must have been the thousandth grimace already since the night before.

"This is so much *fun*! On a Dungeon date with Bete Loga!"

"Yeah. 'Fun.'"

"My heart feels like it's about to burst out of my chest! But since I can't see your face that well, I wanna hide it by throwing myself into battle after frenzied battle!"

Bete truly didn't understand how the girl could be having so much fun.

Bouncing over, she shot him a grin, her tiny tongue poking out from between her lips.

This girl, Lena Tully, was an entirely different kind of "simple" than Tiona. Bete's one consolation was that she was at least *smarter* than the other Amazon, but she still couldn't "read the room," so to speak, for the life of her. Perhaps this was thanks to the fact that her naivete was more lovesick-induced than hereditary.

"...Do you Amazonian witches flaunt your gravy at any old macho thug who walks by?"

"Huh? Oh, no! Not at all! Not. At. *All!* That'd mean Aisha and the others would be all over you right now, hmm? Since you beat them and all?" Lena protested, fighting back against the common misconception about Amazons.

She did have a point.

"All of us have our types and such, you know? For me, well, mine's more like an alarm going off. *Beep-beep-beep! He's the one!* And then I just know! Like I said yesterday—it's made me believe in fate!"

"..."

"Which is why!…I just *knew* I had to have your children!"

It was an admission of love so direct, an elf might frown in disapproval.

Indeed, the Amazons made no effort to hide their procreation-inclined intentions.

With a blush warming her cheeks and a hint of shame coloring her features, Lena shot Bete another smile, almost as though plucking up her courage. "If we keep going much farther, we'll end up having to stay here overnight. You probably don't want that, hmm? Do you, Bete Loga? What should we do, then? Maybe…maybe if we could meet again, we could…go all the way down to the lower levels sometime?"

But despite all her efforts, the werewolf's heart remained as cold as ice.

His amber eyes stared indifferently at the still-smiling girl.

*Affection. Pah.*

Adventurers didn't need it. And even more certainly, the *strong* didn't need it.

It was nothing more than white noise.

And for Bete right now, a werewolf detested not only by others but by himself as well, it just made him want to gag.

"—Are you really that stupid?"

"Huh?"

And so he pushed her away.

The rotten werewolf, selfish beyond measure, violent to a fault, and capable of nothing but hurting those around him, raised his head.

He was going to make this confused girl understand whether she wanted to or not.

To turn her affection into revulsion.

"You sure talk big for someone who doesn't even know her place."

"Th…! That's…I—I know I'm not as tall as Aisha or the others and…and that maybe I'm not so strong yet. And maybe I even got pushed around by that frog lady a lot, but…From now on, all that's gonna change! One day, I…I'll even become as strong as Bete Loga!"

Bete smirked. "You're a chump. And you'll always be a chump!"

This made the girl's orange-pearl-colored eyes widen with a start.

"Doesn't matter how much you keep yappin' about 'someday, someday'—fish bait like you'll never amount to more than just that: fish bait! So quit your whining! Ain't gonna do you any good!"

"I…But I…I have to try…"

"Yeah, you and everyone else! You're all alike! Goin' on and on about your big dreams, then you don't regret it till you're halfway down a monster's throat. You're disgustingly weak. Nothin' but stupid, flimsy dreams and a whole bunch of baloney!" Bete continued, scenes from his past playing out before his eyes one after another. He wasn't even looking at the stupefied girl anymore, but through her and toward the blood-strewn field of his memories beyond.

And from the middle of that scene came the sound of his own laughter.

"You're nothing. And you always will be. Ignorantly spewing lofty goals that you'll never come close to reaching. And I hate it. More than anything else in the world, I hate it."

"I—I…"

"You don't even have the guts to tell me I'm wrong, do you? Heh… Well, you can't polish a turd," Bete finished, still sneering at the stock-still girl in front of him.

"Weak and strong just don't mix."

It was a statement forged of pride, of utter arrogance.

And with it came the contemptuous echoes of his laughter in the dark, quiet grotto where neither human nor monster dared approach.

Lena's gaze sank slowly toward the floor. Her thin frame began to tremble, almost as though holding back tiny sobs.

Bete's laughter faded, and for just a moment, he felt a sort of dried-up cynicism (along with just a tiny bit of disappointment) seep out from the corners of his tattoo. But then the feeling was gone, and the smile was back on his face, accompanied by an almost too-forced snort.

At long length, Lena looked up at him.

"Then…does that mean once I'm not a piece of fish bait anymore…I can be with you?!"

Her voice crescendoed into a full-out belly roar.

"…Wha—?!"

The orange pearls that were Lena's eyes were glittering more violently, more radiantly than ever before. Bete, on the other hand, could only stutter in bewilderment, his mouth hanging open in a stupor.

"Yippee!! All I have to do is get stronger and then I've got me a first-tier adventurer as a hubby! The wife of one of the most truly coveted males in the species!! Yes, that's it! That's all I have to do! Everything's going according to plan!"

"Wh-whaaaaaat?!"

"And that means I'll get to bear Bete Loga's children!!"

"Y-you idiot! The hell are you going on about—?!"

As Lena raised both arms in a sudden burst of exuberant triumph, Bete felt his heart cry out in agony.

*—That's not it at all, you lunatic!*

This wasn't the reaction he'd expected. No, Lena had truly punched a hole in that strategy, leaving him trembling and confused in its wake. This was, without a doubt, the strangest, most off-kilter response Bete had ever received after shooting off one of his cruel smirks.

"Stop that right now, you baby-obsessed bush leaguer! Were you even listening to me?!"

"Of course I was! And now I'm more pumped up than ever! I'm gonna get strong! The strongest you've ever seen! If I can just make it to Level Six, then…he-he-he…he-he-he-he-he-he…!!"

"What the hell…?!"

*What in the world is wrong with this girl…?!*

The nigh-unparalleled depravity behind her smile was enough to shake Bete to his very core. Lena, however, was ignoring the werewolf's terror while pushing herself so close to him that their chests were practically touching, then gazing up at him.

Her eyes consumed him, spinning like twin orange whirlpools. *S-somebody help me!*

"Once I become strong, please make me Bete Loga's—make me your wife!"

*—It's Tione! Oh god, a Tione just showed up!!*

The Finn-obsessed, two-screws-loose Berserker had appeared on the scene!!

He should never have let his guard down in front of this lovesick Amazon.

Not even scorn and ridicule were enough to divert the beating, lovelorn heart of this carnivorous girl, loyal to nothing but her own instincts. No, those would have only thrown more fuel onto the fire.

"Oh yeah! And I get it now!"

Lena continued to speak, her voice like daggers plunging into the werewolf's short-circuiting brain.

"When you call people fish bait or weaklings…those aren't insults at all!"

"_____"

It was at that moment.

That time came screeching to a halt.

"They're more like…worms on the end of a hook, you know? Like a carrot in front of a donkey!"

"…"

"Which means…you're just trying to cheer me on! Yeah, that's it!"

"…Like hell I am, you pinhead."

But those were the only words he could manage to squeeze out.

Lena blissfully ignored him, skipping on ahead, almost as though she was in such high spirits that she couldn't control her own feet.

"..."

Around them, the blue phosphorescence emanating from the walls seemed to brighten, light seeping slowly into the gloom of the normally silent cave. The derisive laughter of the strong had been replaced by the cheery chirping of a young girl, the sound echoing off the stone. The werewolf stood in stunned silence, his shadow stretching toward the wall with no one left to bare its fangs at.

Bete watched the girl leave before letting his gaze drop slowly toward his right hand.

A scene from his memories was rising up to meet him.

Of a girl who'd once told him the same thing.


"You useless roaches! Gettin' in our way again! You think we enjoy gettin' slowed down by all this excess baggage, huh?"

Bete had been hurling profanities that day, as well.

"Bete, calm yourself! There's no reason to disturb the peace!"

"Oh, cram it, you old hag! You know I'm right!"

It had been two years ago, on one of *Loki Familia*'s expeditions.

On their way down to their target floor, they'd gotten attacked by monsters, and the lower-level members had quickly found themselves battered. This stalled them for quite some time, which was what had led to Bete's tirade (and Riveria's subsequent admonishment; the high elf couldn't let his words go despite the situation).

The whole affair was enough to steal what little morale the lower-levels had left, even with Finn's and the other elites' mediation. Heads were drooping, tears were building, and teeth were biting hard on trembling lips. They were completely incapable of fighting back against the first-tier adventurer's censure.

That girl, Leene Arshe, would have been with them.

"Hey, you! Dum-dum with the glasses! Why're you here, huh? You think you're a healer? You can't even protect yourself! Worthless piece of shit!"

"Ngh..."

"All you fish bait should just crawl back into your hole. You don't belong on the battlefield...and you never will!"

It was later, when the whole group had finally been able to settle down for a longer rest, that Bete had run into the human girl, Leene, in the shadow of a nearby rock. He'd chided her then, only for the girl to gaze up at him, trembling.

She'd looked him straight in the eye through those large glasses of hers, fear and hesitation all but gone.

"This is the seventh time you've yelled at me, Mister Bete."

"Huh? You've actually been keeping track? Heh, you really are hopeless."

"This is true. I am hopeless. Already, you've saved me seven times...no, much more than that." Gathering her courage, she took his right hand—the one that had been injured protecting Leene and the other lower-levels.

Bete simply stuck out his tongue. *Stupid injury. It's what I get for involvin' myself with weaklings, is all*, he thought, cursing his own ineptitude.

But he wasn't about to say that out loud. Instead, he prepared to lay all the blame on the "weaklings" themselves, but before he could get the words out, Leene shot him a smile, almost as though seeing through the barrier of his heart.

"I think I...finally understand. What you keep calling us... weaklings...fish bait...They aren't insults."

Time had stopped for Bete then, as well.

His hardened features twisting.

The tattoo on his face—his fang—distorting.

Leene's braid shook, tears in her eyes as she turned a gallant smile toward him.

"I may be one of these weaklings, but...I can still heal you."

"..."

"So...would it be all right if I...stayed by your side?"

A warm light formed around his hand as she spoke, already working at healing the gash on his skin.

Still, she continued to smile, gazing up at him with cheeks flushed.

"..."

How had he responded to her back then?

For some reason, Bete couldn't seem to remember.

Maybe...maybe if he'd said something different...she and the rest of his fallen comrades wouldn't have lost their lives deep within that cold, dark labyrinth.

"Bete Loga!"

Lena's sharp call brought him back from the sea of his memories.

And when he looked up, he saw a face completely different from that of the girl in his mind, but smiling back at him all the same.

"I'm gonna do my best, okay? And when I finally prove that I'm not weak anymore, you've gotta make me your number one, yeah? Promise!"

"...Would you shut up already...?"

But his words didn't have the same oomph behind them as before, and Lena cocked her head curiously and started back toward him. She took his hand, giving it a gentle tug.

Bete took one look at their hands clasped together before sullenly jerking his away.

*Why, you!* Lena's face conveyed her thoughts clearly, her cheeks puffed out in anger, but it didn't last long; her lips curling back into their usual smile as she renewed her cheerful step.

How sentimental. Maybe it wouldn't have changed anything at all. But there was a question he couldn't push out of his mind.

It was something he should have forgotten long, long ago, but this Amazonian girl had dragged it back to the surface, and now it was expanding in his thoughts like rings on water. Gazing off at nothing and no one in particular, he went with Lena into the winding corridors of the seemingly endless Dungeon.

"So…you got any idea of somethin' you mighta seen that looked a bit like a key?"

"Like I've been saying this whole damn time, I don't know!"

It was later that day, and just around when the sun was beginning its descent toward the western horizon, Tiona was accosting one of her fellow Amazons in the city's Central Park.

"You're sure you don't have aaaaaaaany idea at all? C'mon, Salami! Do your fellow Amazon a solid, would ya?"

"My name is Samira! Not some food! Now you're just messing it up on purpose! And don't you try that with me. Amazon or not, you know the wants of *Loki Familia* are of no concern to me!" shouted the cocoa-skinned Amazon with the short ashen hair, her speech decidedly masculine as she stormed off.

"Well, that could have gone better…" Tiona moaned, scratching her head at the ex–*Ishtar Familia* captain's rejection.

"Any luck?…Though it looks like I don't even need to ask."

"Ah! Tione! How'd you do, huh?!"

"Horribly. But that's beside the point! Damn *Freya Familia* assholes. Dropped by their home with a letter from the captain but couldn't even get them to answer the door. A bunch of jerks—all of them!"

"Well, our two familias have never really gotten along…"

Finn had tasked the two sisters and the rest of their group with seeking out any information they could on the man-made labyrinth Knossos. While it made the most sense to question the former members of *Ishtar Familia*, they'd also hoped to make contact with *Freya Familia*, given how they were the ones who'd effectively wiped *Ishtar Familia* off the map.

Tiona and her group had come up with a grand total of nothing.

Tione, meanwhile, hadn't fared much better, completely ignored by Freya and her cronies.

"We were supposed to rendezvous back here with Aki and everyone, but…I'm guessing the results will be pretty much the same across the board."

"Pretty much, yeah…Huh? Ah, there's Lefiya!" Tiona suddenly exclaimed, bringing a hand up to wave at their stock-still companions a short distance away. It was the two elves—Lefiya and Alicia—the former of whom dashed straight over upon seeing the two sisters.

But the look on her face said immediately that something was wrong.

"M-Miss Tiona! Miss Tione!"

"Huh? What's got you all worked up?"

"It…I-it seems that Elfie and the others recently caught sight of Mister Bete…!"

"…Yeah? And what of that damn werewolf, huh?"

Just the mention of Bete's name was enough to put the two Amazons in a sour mood. Lefiya, however, couldn't keep the flustered tremble out of her voice as she continued.

"M-M-Mister Bete, he…he seems to have been…out walking with an A-A-A-Amazonian girl…Almost as though they were on some kind of d-d-d-date…!!"

""WHAT?!""

Tiona's and Tione's eyes widened with almost audible snaps.

"So he thinks he can go around chasing tail while the rest of us are bustin' our asses, does he?!"

"WHAT DOES THAT DAMN WOLF THINK HE'S DOING?!"

The two cries of rage were enough to shake the ground where they stood.

It was simply too much—not only had all their information-gathering efforts failed, but that detestable werewolf was off chumming it up with girls.

"And after all that time ignoring Leene! That son of a————!!"

…*Perhaps telling these two wasn't the best idea*…Lefiya couldn't help but think, finding the information hard to believe herself as the whole dumbstruck group watched the twins flail and rant.

For just a moment, she could have sworn she heard Leene's ghost weeping in the air next to them, but it was just her imagination.

Around the same time that Tiona and Tione were blowing their lids…

Lena's Dungeon date had come to a close. That didn't mean, however, that the "date" itself was finished.

"Hey! Bete Loga! Over here! Do you think this looks good on me?"

"It looks like shit."

"Heeeeey!"

They were in one of the small back alleys set off from the main street, Lena having posed the question while standing excitedly in front of a small accessory stand. Returning the hairpin she'd picked up to the cloak laid out across the cobblestones, she turned to Bete with a harrumph.

"Shit, shit, shit! Is everything shit to you? You're never gonna get any girls to like you like that, you know!"

"Yeah? Great. Then maybe you'll stop following me around."

"Yooooooooooou!" she moaned, bouncing around in frustration.

It had been like this since they'd returned to the surface, to the point where Bete felt he didn't have any sighs left in him to sigh. He couldn't even find the effort for his usual ascerbic remarks.

Lena's eyes trembled in anguish as she looked up at him, until her usual smile returned in an instant mood shift.

"Are you gonna tell me about that key already or what?"

"No way! As soon as I do, you're gonna leave me high and dry! You will! I'll only tell you if you stay with me aaaaaall day!" she declared before taking off down the bustling backstreet, glancing back and forth between the stalls of jewels and accessories on either side.

Bete had already gone past the point of caring. Lena may have been an Amazon, but she was also a teenage girl, so it only made sense she'd want to date like one, as well. Bete only half paid attention to her. *The hell is fun about this?* he silently grumbled as she picked up one item after another, eyes sparkling—"Look at this! Look at this!"—as she turned back to show him.

"You don't like exploring the market? I thought you would."

"Like hell I'd enjoy playing house with you, you dumb brat."

"Cold as always, I see, Bete Loga...Ah! A florist!"

Upon leaving the backstreets, the first thing to cross their path was a small flower shop. Named "Dia Floral," it was run by a young, free girl who'd stocked its shelves high with an assortment of colorful flowers. The human girl herself must have just come back from making a delivery. Her goddess-rivaling beauty drew all manner of adventurers' gazes as she made her way toward the store.

Lena, meanwhile, was perusing the flowers out front thanks to an arrangement of tiny light-blue blooms that had caught her eye.

"Hey, Bete Loga!"

"What is it *now*?"

"Wanna hear what I like the best? And I mean something that I'd be super-pumped, super-jazzed to get as a present?"

"Nope."

"Then I'll tell you! There's nothing that makes me happier than getting forget-me-nots!! They can make me fall in love with a man all over again! Wink, wink!"

Bete almost hurled.

Which was a feeling that was becoming as common as breathing for him at this point as Lena shot him an all-too-expectant glance next to him. He didn't even have to try to look fed up—his features had already formed the expression for him.

"...Lena? And is that...Vanargand?!"

As the two of them were standing in front of the florist, a voice accosted them from behind.

Turning around, they came face-to-face with a long-haired, long-legged prostitute.

"That woman from the bar...!"

"Guh! A-Aisha?!"

"Just what the hell do you think you're doing, Lena? Why are you fraternizing with his type?"

It was none other than Aisha Belka, one of Lena's sisters from her former familia and the same Amazon Bete had gone toe-to-toe with in the pub the night prior. Brows raised in surprise, she quickly grabbed Lena's arm and prepared to pull her away from the werewolf.

"W-wait, Aisha! Bete Loga and I are on a date right now! Th-this is the chance I've been waiting for!"

"A date? With this werewolf? Fool! Just how low have your standards dropped?! You'd do better to find yourself someone with at least an ounce of integrity!"

"I'm right here, you know..."

"Flowers are about the last thing you can expect from a man like *this*," Aisha continued, still testy about the fight in the pub and not even trying to hide her disdain. She must have heard their conversation, as she threw a disgusted look in the direction of the light-blue flowers Lena had been ogling (and she certainly didn't pay Bete's annoyed comment any heed, either).

Lena, however, wasn't one to give up, and she implored the woman who was as good as an older sister to her. "Pleeeeeease, Aisha! Just gimme some time! Let me pop out two kids!"

"Say that one more time."

"I see. Like a studhorse, then?"

*"Say that one more time."*

"Mm...More like a stud*wolf*!"

*"JUST TRY SAYING THAT ONE MORE TIME!"*

Bete's indignant commentary grew louder and louder as the two girls talked around him.

"So, just let it go, yeah? Pretty please? What're you doin' out here anyway, huh?"

"I seriously can't believe you...Me? I'm out on a walk is all, and keeping an eye on things while I do. I like to make sure our fellow sisters and Berbera who've been scattered to the wind aren't in any trouble."

"Really? You old softy!"

"Oh, don't patronize me. Which reminds me—you haven't been using that 'secret place' of yours in the Pleasure Quarter again, have you? I heard you didn't return to your familia last night!"

"Guh?! F-forgive me, Aishaaaaa!"

"How many times were you told to stay away from those old buildings?!"

The conversation continued as though Bete wasn't even there.

Whether the first-rate courtesan, who had a decidedly more

put-together look and sexually alluring body than Lena, had been persuaded by Lena's arguments or not, she finally let out a sigh and gave up on her lecture. This didn't stop her, however, from menacingly advancing toward Bete before taking her leave.

"Hey, Vanargand. I'll permit you to drag her along for now, but if anything, and I mean *anything*, should happen to her, you'll wish you'd never been born."

"*She's* the one doin' the dragging here—not me," Bete grumbled under his breath as the older Amazon walked away with a final glare.

"Aisha may not look it, but she's a real sweetheart underneath everything. I can't count the number of times she's helped me out, and I'm basically nobody among the Berbera. She's even looked after the old crackpots of the group who everyone else had already given up on. She just does a whole lot, you know?"

"You think I care? And, *hey!* Stop pullin' me!"

Lena had taken to clutching Bete's arm in her glee, rattling on and on about the older woman like a proud younger sister. Bete attempted to peel her off, grimacing internally.

*I shoulda known this would attract more attention than the Dungeon. I don't even wanna think about what'd happen if we bumped into someone I know...*

The fact that Aisha had discovered them so quickly only added to his already growing sense of paranoia. If any member of his own familia were to see them, it would only be worse.

Indeed, if even Aisha had noticed them—

"...Mister...Bete?"

—then anyone could.

"...A-Aiz?"

It was her, Aiz, and the moment he sensed her shock, his face froze in terror.

Sweat began leaking down his skin like a waterfall as the tail protruding from his backside tensed up like a lightning rod. Aiz, too, was staring at him with an expression of sheer disbelief, almost as though she'd just encountered the most outlandish of phenomena.

She looked back and forth between Bete, his cheek twitching, and Lena, who happened to be clinging to his arm.

A strange sort of tension wove its way between the two first-tier adventurers, neither one making the first move.

"Huh? What's going on, huh? Don't tell me…the Sword Princess is your wife?!"

Fortunately, there was someone there to break the ice for them—a certain reckless Amazon.

"Nuh-uh! No way! *I'm* gonna be Bete Loga's wife, you hear? I'm the one holding him in the middle of a crowded street, aren't I? And I've already promised him a pair of healthy bundles of j—"

*"Would you shut the hell up already?!"*

"Gwwwuaagh?!"

Bete didn't even try to restrain himself this time, aiming his elbow at the back of the girl's head. The impact practically knocked her eyes out of their sockets, and with a sharp yelp, she was out like a light, Bete lugging her body up under his arm.

Aiz had yet to get over her shock, and as Bete continued sweating buckets, he did the only thing his lupine instincts could think to do—he *ran*.

"D-don't get the wrong idea, Aiz!" he shouted back as he picked up Lena and fled.

Meanwhile, *Why am I running?!* was all he could think, unsure as to why he was sprinting like his life depended on it. But that didn't stop him from hightailing—or perhaps *wolf-tailing* would be the better word—it out of there, the passersby on the street looking on in bewilderment as he raced by at full speed.

"W-wait!"

Finally recovering her senses, Aiz took off after him.

"Oh, sure! You choose *now* of all times to chase me!"

"I'm supposed to…to watch out for you…!"

"Well, that's news to me!"

"I know you're upset, but…children, Bete? Don't you…think you're being a little too…hasty?!"

*"You've got it all wrong!"* Bete howled back.

Aiz must have taken Lena's words to heart, the airheaded swordswoman now trying desperately to warn him against the dangers of having children across familia lines. She was like an assassin, ready to do whatever it took to carry out Loki's orders, and Bete put everything he had into his legs to increase his speed to its utmost limit.

Just when it seemed he might get away, Aiz sped up, too.

"Damn it, damn it, damn it…!"

*"Awaken, Tempest!"*

*"Damn iiiiiiiiiiiiiiiiiiittttttttttttttttttttttt!!"*

Throughout the streets, they ran, the golden-haired swordswoman gaining, the limbs of the Amazonian girl bouncing wildly, and one final scream ripping its way out of the wolf's throat.

Sweat pouring off him, Bete fled.

"Haah…haah…gnnagh…Damn…woman…"

Night had descended upon the city.

Having arrived safely back at Lena's secret place in the ruined Pleasure Quarter, Bete tossed aside the girl beneath his arm and collapsed to the ground.

He was still the fastest runner in *Loki Familia*, able to outpace Aiz even when she used Airiel. As he sat there, shoulders still heaving, Lena gave a small moan—*"Ngh…"*—from where he'd thrown her as she finally came to.

"Huh? Is this my…secret place? And…Bete Loga, why are you all covered in sweat?!" she furiously inquired, though she was quickly silenced by the werewolf's bloodshot glare (*"Gngh?!"*). Taking in his worn-out state, she seemed to postulate what had happened, letting out a forced laugh. "Aha…ah-ha-ha-ha-ha! Sorry, it was…my fault, wasn't it?…Though now what're we gonna do, huh? It's night already, which means I won't be able to…"

Finish the date? Fulfill the requirements for the date?

Either way, their time was up. And from the look on Lena's face, she was greatly regretting the time lost.

Bete pressed his lips together in a tense line, picking his spent body off the floor and sluggishly rising to his feet.

"...I'm tired. It's too much trouble to go anywhere else at this point, so I'll just stay here."

"Huh?"

"But you're gonna help me search for that thing tomorrow, you hear?!" he quickly snapped as Lena looked up in surprise.

"You'll stay here again? Really?"

"...Whatever."

"You'll really stay here with me?"

"Do I gotta say it again?" Bete growled.

A smile popped onto Lena's face, and she jumped to her feet, arms flailing. "W-wait! I'll cook dinner! We can eat together! So just... You can just go upstairs and rest, okay?!" she urged excitedly before racing toward the kitchen.

Bete watched her disappear down the hall, not saying a word before trudging his way up the stairs to the bedroom on the top floor. Same as the night before, he disregarded the bed, sitting himself in front of the open window.

"...I shoulda gotten what I needed and left..." he mumbled. As the night breeze played with his gray fur, he narrowed his eyes. "...I'm not even thinkin' straight anymore..."

Was it because it'd been so long since anyone had shown him any sort of affection? Or because the girl downstairs had repeated those same words Leene had told him so long ago? Bete wasn't sure. All he knew was that little by little, his lips were starting to forget how to sneer.

Down below him, the Night District was as tranquil as the sea, the whole of the Pleasure Quarter drenched in shadow. Maybe today, too, beneath the lights peeping out from the surrounding buildings, men and women were giving themselves up to passion, whispering the sweet nothings of love. Even if that love was nothing but a fleeting night's dream.

Bete could feel his eyelids grow heavy as he gazed out across the night landscape.

He was tired. For many different reasons. So many reasons. The past haunted him, and the words of a girl no longer with him kept creeping into his thoughts, drowning him in a strange sort of sentimentality. Somehow he knew he was going to dream again—a continuation of the one last night.

Even as he heard Lena's footsteps dance lightly up the stairs, Bete could already feel himself succumbing to the darkness like waning moonlight.

When was the last time anyone had shown him any affection?

Waiting for him at the end of his long journey from his homeland were the towering walls of the Labyrinth City of Orario. And his first order of business upon arriving was to get himself a blessing from the gods. He already had a pretty good idea what these "gods" were, given how many had passed through his tribe's village on their way to Orario: insincere, pleasure-seeking hedonists, the whole lot of them. For an adventurer to get picked up by a good god, it required considerable luck—and a few hints from the rumor mill, as well. No one could afford to simply wait for a god to choose them on a whim. No, a great deal of meticulous care had to be taken.

Fortunately for Bete, he was picked up rather quickly by a god who didn't really care one way or another if he joined, and he was soon inducted into *Víðarr Familia*, a Dungeon-type familia led by the god Víðarr.

Víðarr himself was a god of few words and just about as far removed from Bete's philistine image of the gods that one could get. More of a hermit than anything else, he had two defining features: his long auburn hair and matching eyes. There was something about the god's calm, tranquil features and oracle-esque speech that pulled at Bete's heartstrings.

"Protect that jaw of yours—and that fang—at all costs, yes?"

—*Just let anyone try!*

The words of his god brought a fierce grin to his face.

His peers had been much the same, all of them purebred adventurers, relatively young, and quite a few animal people were among their numbers. It almost reminded him of his tribe on the plains, and it didn't take long for Bete to decide this was the familia for him, even if the decision itself might have been nothing more than atonement for abandoning his own tribe.

He butted heads with his colleagues even back then, but that didn't keep him from slowly making a name for himself in the familia. The experience he'd gotten fighting in the wild as a Beastman of the Plains became a powerful weapon even far beneath the earth in the Dungeon. But more than anything else, Bete wanted to continue tempering his fangs, plowing through the monsters of the deep with a sort of fierce desperation, giving himself up completely to the days of combat. His insatiable desire to feed on the strong was enough to earn him not only the trust of his fellow familia members but their commendation, as well. Before he knew it, he'd become a sort of beloved father figure to the rest of the familia, like an alpha wolf looking over his pack.

All of a sudden, the completely unknown *Víðarr Familia* was making news. Led by Bete and his superior skills, the familia saw the number of its members leveling up rise. Even when other familias attacked, they were able to pull out ahead, and soon they found themselves sitting nicely among the other midsize familias of the city. It was during this time that Bete received his first title: Fenris.

The familia itself acted about as terribly as most civilians imagined a group of battle-crazed animal people would act, Bete included. That said, none of them was the type to commit any misdeeds that Bete would've deemed "lame" or "stupid." They weren't about to become chumps who tormented the weak. There was no room for the arrogance of the strong. If anyone had so much free time they could afford to waste it harassing others, they should've been using it to sharpen their fangs. Under the leadership of their captain, Bete, *Víðarr Familia* quickly positioned itself as the strongest combat familia in all of Orario.

*It'll be different this time. Not like before with my childhood friend.*
*Make 'em stronger. Show 'em how it's done.*
*That way, even those weaker than me'll be able to bare their fangs.*
*Become warriors who can fight back against that whole survival-of-*
*the-fittest mentality.*

Even the weak could become as strong as him. That's what he believed. Protecting them as they ran along after him, seeing their smiles when they flipped the tables and protected him in return—yes, he'd been able to believe that.

To Bete, who'd lost everything, *Víðarr Familia* suited him just right.

They were a group of idiots who risked the Dungeon for drink money, pulling their god into all-night booze fests. Patronizing the pub with its newly hung red-wasp sign and causing a commotion every single day, not sparing a thought for their antics as they exchanged insults with the unsociable old dwarf who ran the place. Bete, too, had run his mouth off at him innumerable times. And sometimes, even Víðarr himself would give a speech, letting his hair down just a little too much and eliciting terror from the boys and laughter from the girls. It really seemed like Bete had recovered the one thing he'd lost so long ago—his family.

There'd been a girl in the familia, too. One of the few humans.

She was the vice captain of the familia, second in line to Bete when it came to sheer power and resentful of the fact that he constantly had to look out for her. Her long chestnut-colored hair had run down her back like silk, and she'd always had a determined grin on her face—and was always first in line to scold Bete when he was injured, tending to his wounds in reticent silence.

She'd been a good woman.

From the way she'd felt in his arms, to the way her sighs tickled his ears, to the slight trouble she had with her words sometimes—she'd been his warmth. They'd gotten into a huge fight one time. Bete had complained about her perfume (the smell was hard on his sensitive nose), but sure enough, he noticed the scent was nowhere to be found the next day or the day after that. She'd always tried to be strong for Bete's sake. For the sake of a man hungry for power.

Everything about her, from her looks to her personality, was different from his childhood friend back on the plains. But that didn't stop Bete from falling for her.

Somehow, something inside him told him that she'd be able to heal the scar of his first love.

He'd been infatuated. A love so sweet, he would've been lying if he claimed he didn't want to lose himself, to drown himself in it.

But Bete's fang wouldn't allow that.

No, the blue tattoo on his face, racing across his cheek like a bolt of lightning that represented all those irreparable wounds guiding his actions, would allow only one thing:

*Be stronger.*

*Feed on the strong.*

Indeed, Bete was already stronger than anyone and everything he knew.

The young, weak boy he'd left behind on the plains was nowhere to be found.

It was four years after he'd arrived in Orario. Sixteen years old and now a Level 3, he knew it was time. He was going to take down the Master of the Plains.

He was strong now. And past the point where he could leisurely bide his time, telling himself he just needed to be a little bit stronger, a little bit stronger. Even here in Orario, people knew of the creature stalking the plains far, far to the north. If Bete didn't kill it, surely somebody else would. And Bete wasn't about to let that happen. No, Bete was going to take that thing down with his own hands.

Receiving permission from Víðarr and the rest of his peers, he departed alone from Orario. He left his anxious companions with nothing but a few off-color words, telling them not to worry and to look after the place in his stead.

That girl, too, had tried to keep him from leaving. But Bete had simply shaken her away. He knew she liked him. Knew she loved him. But this time, Bete refused to face her. He'd chosen his fang, after all.

To this day, he couldn't get that final image of her out of his mind, that resolute smile of hers as she watched him leave.

Víðarr, too, left him with a final set of words as Bete made his way past the gate.

"Bete...someday, you'll understand the true meaning behind your fang."

The trip took him three months with all the stopovers he was forced to make.

But finally, he arrived—the plains of the north and the place of his birth. The wide-open fields stretched out before him like an ocean, followed by the deep green of the forest past the short hills, and even farther than that, the steely mountain range whose tips were covered in white snow. There was even the large lake he remembered swimming in together with his sister and friends. They'd wandered across it time and time again, their backyard rich with nature's bounties. But now it had become nothing more than a parched land of bones, its surface ravaged by the new master who'd laid claim to it. Bete clenched his teeth together as he looked out across the plains he'd once called home, anger coloring the old memories.

He ended up finding the beast, strangely enough, on that very same day, the moon high overhead in the night sky.

And as for the fight, it lasted the entire night. The beast itself had grown stronger, too, after feeding on not only human prey but its own brethren, as well.

Bete fought with everything he had, blood pouring from his wounds, his bones snapping, sacrificing countless weapons. He repelled the mighty claws that had once rent his mother and father limb from limb, he dodged the great galloping feet that had once crushed his sister underfoot, and he smashed the sharpened jaws that had once fed on the flesh of the girl he'd loved. The dying cry of his enemy echoing out against the moonlit sky, Bete became a beast even greater than the Master of the Plains, brandishing the fang that had led him to this point.

Then.

The colossal beast came crashing to the ground, shaking the very earth and leaving Bete standing alone, his body bathed in red. He'd won. He had consumed the strong. His fang was victorious.

Body battered and bruised and broken, he cried out, the same as he had on that day that started it all so, so long ago.

Joy, anger, sadness, futility, pain—everything welled up inside him, forming one giant ball of emotion that burst out in a howl that crackled in his throat. Toward the moon, he howled, toward the dark night slowly fading into the light of the dawn.

*I won!*

*I devoured it!*

*I'm the strongest of them all!*

*I'll never let anyone take anything from me ever again! Never!!*

A trickle of blood wove its way down the fang on his face.

No matter how strong he became, that pain would always follow him.

Night's shadow curled itself around the half-ruined buildings and strewn rubble of the Pleasure Quarter's third district—the territory of the former *Ishtar Familia*. Down among the ruins, voices quiet, *Loki Familia* conducted their investigation. Their ranks were small: Finn and Gareth in the lead, followed by a few lower-level members and a very disobliged Loki. They conducted their search without light to help guide them, not even the glow of their magic-stone lanterns.

The Guild had stationed guards around the perimeter to keep anyone from entering the Pleasure Quarter, but they clearly hadn't assigned enough, as their group didn't run into a single soul on their way inside, and from the looks of the untouched rubble, none of the reconstruction efforts seemed to be making any headway.

"Any thoughts on all this, Finn?" Gareth asked slowly from his spot in the shadow of a nearby brothel, most of the others already dispersed to the four corners of the wreckage.

"Hmm…The way I see it, the enemy has to have left behind at least one key somewhere in the city."

"And what makes ya think that, huh?" Loki this time, giving a little snort from atop a dilapidated barrel she was using as a chair.

"Because Ishtar's been sent home," he answered, glancing over at his goddess. "We already have reason to believe Ishtar was colluding with the Evils after what happened back in Meren. Perhaps the Evils enlisted Ishtar as a source of funds, what with her grip on the Pleasure Quarter. And what would they give her in return for all that?"

"…The downfall of *Freya Familia*?"

"Indeed. Ishtar's antipathy toward Freya and her familia is practically common knowledge. So I can't imagine it would be anything but." Finn turned his eyes back to Loki.

"Mm, guess that's true. I bet she was plannin' on enlistin' Kali's help in luring Freya and her goons down into Knossos. Spoiled brat of a goddess, really. There's no way she wouldn't've asked for a key of her own so she could go slitherin' through the halls whenever she pleased."

"Hmm…" Gareth mumbled at this, stroking his beard in thought. "But wouldn't ye think the enemy'd wanna keep knowledge of a place like that well under wraps? Ye wouldn't think they'd be handin' out keys like candy, now, do ye?"

"Well, if what Lefiya learned from Thanatos is anything to go by, both the Evils and the creatures want nothing more than the destruction of Orario, meaning they'd come head-to-head with *Freya Familia* sooner rather than later anyway. Another obstacle to their goal, so to speak, much like us."

"I see what yer sayin'. They figured they'd use Ishtar as their front man to take Freya and her bunch down now—or weaken 'em, at the very least. Which is why they agreed to help, yeah?"

Finn nodded.

Hell, that demi-spirit they fought down in Knossos may have even been Ishtar's trump card.

"For Freya and her men to take out *Ishtar Familia* now…I would imagine this has the Evils reeling, too."

"Hmm, here I was thinkin' we'd lost everything with *Ishtar Familia*'s destruction, but…lookin' at it a different way, this might be the chance we've been waiting for."

"That it might. If Ishtar really was in possession of a key, then the Evils will do everything possible to try and retrieve it." Finn nodded, finishing Loki's thought. Though it was possible the Evils had already recovered the key, the way he was licking his thumb was evidence enough that the prum thought they still had a chance. "The Evils or us…Who'll be the first to find it, I wonder?…The fight for the key has begun."

"Lady Valletta! *Loki Familia* has been seen prowling about the palace in the Pleasure Quarter…!"

"Goddammit! So they're on the move, are they?" Deep beneath the earth in the man-made labyrinth Knossos, Valletta cursed under her breath at the news from one of her subordinates. The accessories dangling from her ears jangling, she furrowed her brow in indignation.

"What will you do, then, Valletta dear? If I may be of any help at all, do let me know," Thanatos said from his spot atop the altar, his black garments fluttering with the slight movement.

Valletta didn't respond for a moment. The cogs in her head were turning within the ethereal gloom created by the blue phosphorescence of the magic-stone lanterns.

"…There's no way they got a tip or somethin', is there?"

"I—I wouldn't think so, ma'am! There doesn't seem to be any rhyme or reason to their search. Word on the street is they're also approaching the former Amazons and prostitutes of *Ishtar Familia*…"

Valletta stilled, bringing a hand to her lips in thought.

Finally, she raised her head, as though she had reached some sort of conclusion.

"I want you to assemble all our assassins."

"Yes, ma'am!"

"And you, Thanatos! Go get that jackass Barca up here…Tell him to start making those cursed weapons of his. As many as he possibly can."

"Oh? You aim to take them on, then? Outside of Knossos?" Thanatos watched Valletta issue orders, his eyes widening as a smile rose on his face.

Valletta simply brushed her hair back. "Didn't wanna cause a ruckus up there, but…Well, what can ya do?" she retorted. "I'm not about to let Finn get his grubby little hands on even one of our keys."

Her lips curled into a vicious smile.

"—We're going to war."

# Unshed Tears

Гэта казка іншага сям'і.

Слёзы, якія не выконваюцца

The slight chill brushing across his skin was his morning wake-up call.

"..."

Bete slowly opened his eyes to find himself next to the window. As he went to move his limbs, stiff from staying in the same position all night, he noticed the blanket that had been draped across him. Glancing farther down toward the carpet below, he saw Lena fast asleep, her breaths soft, deep, and even. On top of the velvet chair nearby was a bowl of soup with a few vegetables breaking the surface, along with a meat sandwich—the dinner she must have made last night.

Gazing for a moment at the now ice-cold meal, he brought a spoonful of the soup to his mouth.

"Blech..." he half whispered before giving the rock-solid bread a nibble as well.

Still munching on the stale bread, he gave the girl at his feet, currently curled up like a cat in her blanket, a kick.

"Gwuaaah!" she yelped in surprise.


"It's time for that info you promised," Bete demanded, now out in the back garden (sorry as it was) and dousing himself over the head with a bucket of water. The werewolf had stripped to the waist, and more than a bit of drool had pooled in the mouth of the young Amazon watching nearby.

"Huh? Ah! I, uh...S-sure! Right!" Lena sputtered out, red-faced, before bringing herself back to the present. "It's, well, you see...Phryne and the other girls were always pushing me around, right? Sending me running all over the temple on this errand or that. Well, one day, that old frog tasked me with something really crazy! 'Find me Lady Ishtar's weak point!' she said." Her impression of the toad-like woman in question left something to be desired as she watched Bete give his skin and ears a rough rubdown with his towel. "'Course I knew I'd be skinned alive if I was caught, so I waited until Lady Ishtar was out one day and snuck into her room…where I just so happened to catch sight of a hidden door that'd been left ajar."

"Hidden door?"

"Yeah! And behind it was all sorts of crazy stuff—gorgeous veils, golden crowns! It musta been Lady Ishtar's secret vault. But anyway…That's where I saw it. On top of the desk in there was a small box, and inside the box was this little ball thing made of ingot. Definitely some sort of magic item."

Bete's ears perked up at this, and he threw a glance in Lena's direction.

"I didn't see if it had any kinda symbol or whatnot on it, but…Was the ball you're looking for made of a silvery type of metal? 'Cause this one was made of mythril, and it sure sounds like the same one from your drawing."

"What'd you do after you saw it?"

"Erm…I got caught by Tammuz. He was our vice captain. And you should have *seen* the look he gave me! Chased me right out of the room demanding that I 'forget everything I saw.' He's normally pretty quiet unless he's dealing directly with Ishtar, so I guess he decided to let me go, but…" She gave a little shiver from where she was seated cross-legged atop a nearby box, no doubt reliving the memory in her head.

"So this Tammuz fella. Where's he now?"

"Haven't seen him since *Freya Familia* attacked us…Considering he was Lady Ishtar's right-hand man, I wouldn't be surprised if he followed her up to Heaven, so to speak…"

"Which means…that thing's probably still there."

"Yeah, either in Lady Ishtar's secret room or in Tammuz's room."

This news got Bete thinking.

While there was no guarantee Ishtar or Tammuz hadn't taken it with them (or at the very least removed it from that room), there would certainly be value in checking it out.

Now that his head was considerably clearer after the cold water and crisp morning air, Bete made up his mind with a soft *"Let's do this!"* He would head toward the palace towering in the distance—Belit Babili.

"Hey, hey, hey! It's all right if I come, too, isn't it, Bete Loga? I mean, it'd probably be pretty difficult to find that secret room without me there, huh?"

"...Whatever."

*"Yippee!"*

Bete shot the now happily spinning girl a sidelong glance as he shook off the remaining water on his skin and slipped his battle jacket on again. And then he was off, leaving behind the high-class brothel with chipper Amazon in tow.

"You never went back there after your familia went under, huh?"

"Well, everything in the familia vault got evenly distributed out to all its members, you know? 'Cause *Ishtar Familia* had a lot of girls who weren't fighters. And everything got pretty crazy what with Aisha trying to take care of it all and, well, I guess I forgot to even go check...Ah-ha-ha."

The sky above them was cloudy as they walked, the ash-colored clouds completely obstructing the light of the sun. Bete couldn't help but imagine the rain that was likely on its way as he glanced up at the thick veil settling down over Orario's rooftops.

It was a ways away from the center of the attack, but even this small backstreet had suffered its own fair share of damage. The stone underfoot was cracked, and the magic-stone lampposts stood at awkward, bent angles—even part of the roof of a nearby brothel had been blown clean away, likely by some sort of magic, and others still had errant scimitars protruding from their walls. All manner of broken debris now littered the path in front of them. The fact that *Freya Familia*'s swath of destruction extended even to these outer buildings was evidence enough as to the power behind Freya's divine will—there was no way she'd planned on letting Ishtar escape.

And the carnage only increased as they made their way farther down the path.

Truly, the sight of the wreckage surrounding them might well have belonged to an impoverished slum.

"Careful, Bete Loga! The guards the Guild left here might be few and far between, but they're still adventurers, and we're in broad daylight. They won't need to be close to see us."

"Yeah, especially when someone's climbing around on all the rubble like a crazy monkey."

"Eh-he-he-he! I'm a monkey! Eek! Eek! Eek!" Lena stuck her tongue out at the werewolf, atop a pile of rubble as he'd described. "Meh, I'm not too worried about the guards. Just don't wanna get into any legal trouble or whatever if they figure out who we are. Plus, some of them might be Ganesha's guys, since they'll do work for the Guild every now and then," she added, jumping down from the dilapidated building.

As the path opened up in front of them, Lena beckoned Bete over to the side, and the two of them slipped between a gap in the buildings. Now that they were on the actual territory itself, it made sense to avoid the gardens, but as a bit of added protection, she guided the two of them through small back alleys and byways that were away from human eyes, as well.

Bete was suddenly quite glad he'd allowed her to come along.

*Wonder if Finn and the others are searching here, too…Prolly not in the middle of the day, though. That'd certainly draw attention*, Bete mused, the faces of his comrades floating to the back of his mind. Certainly, as one of the leading familias in the city, their presence anywhere was sure to turn heads, so the chance of Bete running into them here was slim at best. Even if they'd determined Belit Babili to be the main target of their investigation (as they likely had), it would take them days to scour the entirety of *Ishtar Familia*'s former home. There was no way they'd have reached the hidden room in Ishtar's chambers that Lena had mentioned yet—nor the room of a certain Tammuz, if it came to that.

*That reminds me—when should I go back? I know Finn told me to give it a little while, but…Ah, shit! Now I'm thinkin' about yesterday again! Not goin' back! No way…!*

Given that Aiz had already witnessed him, it was likely his status in the familia had already taken another nosedive. Meanwhile, the undying rage of those Amazonian sisters was probably growing like an inferno. Just imagining Aiz attempting to tell the story in her awkward fumbling way, how it would get exaggerated and over-embellished, made his heart drop. Nope, he definitely didn't wanna see them.

He cursed under his breath, hiding his thoughts behind his usual mask of hostility.

*Here I was just supposed to lone-wolf it up a bit...And now 'cause of this chick, I'm up to my neck in crazy,* he grumbled silently, throwing the girl in question a half-lidded glance as she walked along beside him.

"How come you went and fell asleep last night, huh, Bete Loga? After I went to all the trouble of making dinner for you!"

"I'll go to sleep whenever I goddamn well please, thank you very much."

"Yoooou! Werewolves never think about anybody but themselves! What about when I put that blanket on you, though, huh? Did you feel your heart skip a beat? It was almost like we were newlyweds!"

"Oh, shut yer mouth already, would ya?" Bete snarled, attempting to quash the overly familiar attitude the girl was taking with him. This game of "let's pretend" Lena kept pushing on him would end today. Once they'd finished their investigation, Lena would be out of his life for good. He refused to let her manipulate him anymore. Sure, the lovelorn Amazon would probably try to follow him back to his familia, but, well, he'd just ignore her. Yes, that's what he'd do.

He didn't like that being with her made him think back to things he'd rather not.

Everything that had led to the fang on his face.

*...Finish this up. Get rid of her. Get rid of her for good...*

And then—never again. That's what his heart decided. Only then.

His ears suddenly perked up on his head.

"..."

"Bete Loga?"

The two of them had emerged from a narrow passageway and were currently walking along one of the district's backstreets. Bete came to a stop in the middle of the wide road, rows of brothels on either side.

*Someone's watching us...*

He narrowed his eyes, directing a sharpened gaze at his surroundings as Lena turned around curiously.

*One of the Guild's guards? No. There's no way. They'd be all over us already. That and they certainly wouldn't be shootin' us a death glare or whatever this is.*

Certainly, the feeling of malice emanating from whatever was looking at them didn't belong to an ordinary adventurer. Whoever this was was different, much different. Filth that had crawled its way out of the darkness.

And what's more, their numbers seemed to be—growing.

"Wh-what's wrong?" Lena asked, herself more than a little flustered at the intensity of the first-tier adventurer behind her.

"Hey! You two! What do you think you're doing?!"

The voice came from in front of them.

Turning toward the sound, they found themselves face-to-face with two men, a human–animal person pair of adventurers, donning the all-too-familiar armbands and yellow scarves indicative of Guild affiliation—the guards Lena had claimed were few and far between.

Grabbing ahold of the whistles dangling around their necks, the two adventurers who'd been placed in charge of patrolling the restoration zone began making their way toward them.

"—Ngh! Hey, morons! I'd stay away if I were you!" Bete shouted, his fur bristling. The two guards, however, merely looked at him in puzzlement. Then, as one would expect, they brought their whistles to their lips, fully prepared to sound the alarm on these trespassing reprobates—

"—Nngah?!"

That one move was all it took.

All of a sudden, the necks of the two guards split open in twin waterfalls of blood.

The man behind them, shrouded in black and moving without a sound, had severed both their carotid arteries with one sweep of his dagger.

"Wh-what's...*What's going on?!*" Lena screamed as another dark figure leaped from the nearby roof to land next to the animal person, their own rapier drawn. Meanwhile, the two adventurer guards, not even knowing what hit them, sank to the crumbling cobblestones with a gurgling *slop*.

"Y-you *killed* them...!"

"Ngh...!"

As Lena struggled to find words, Bete growled next to her, jaw tight and teeth grinding against one another. His eyes were focused on one and only one thing: the hooded assassin, swathed in black, who was leisurely turning to face them as they pointed the bloodied black dagger at the pair.

It was then that the shadows appeared, a multitude swarming across the rooftops to either side of them.

"Wh-what's happening? What's going on...?"

"Get yourself a weapon!"

"Wh-what?"

"I said *get yourself a goddamn weapon*, you ignoramus! Or are you gonna just stand there and let them kill you?!" Bete snapped, causing Lena's shoulders to jump. But she did as she was told, snatching up a spare scimitar that had been left behind after *Freya Familia*'s attack.

The swarm of enemies around them had appeared in a flash, almost as though their every move had been coordinated, and Bete's face twisted into a snarl as he watched them form a ring.

*More of those Evils bastards? The assassins who attacked Tione?!*

He remembered the other Amazon talking about them after they'd escaped Knossos.

But why were they here? Why now? What did they have to gain by attacking him like this?

Even Finn and the others had always assumed the Evils would never launch an attack like this on the surface. His suspicions about the group that had appeared before him now, completely undercutting all their previous assumptions, simmered in the back of his mind like a rufescent flame.

When all of a sudden…

"Oh, of all the—! And here we were just hopin' to do a bit of lookin' around!"

"That voice…!" Bete growled, his tone low as he turned toward the new, decidedly feminine shadow that had just jumped down from off the roof.

That same fur-lined overcoat, that same undershirt that covered nothing but her chest, that same pair of leather pants. Yes, Bete remembered the woman standing in front of him now, waving her sinister-looking oversize sword.

Valletta Grede.

The Evils commander who'd set all those traps for them down in Knossos.

"What? You alone, Vanargand? And what's that Amazon brat for? Don't tell me a mutt like you is actually trying to *breed*?"

"Oh, go to hell, you pink-haired worm! What are you even doing here anyway?"

"I could be asking you the same thing. Running into a first-tier adventurer like you wasn't exactly in our plans!" The anti-aging effects of Valleta's Status made her look more like a woman in her late twenties than her actual age—somewhere in her late thirties. Her face was beautiful but severe, and at the moment, it was scowling as she gave her lips a rather disconcerting lick. "…But no bother. No, in fact, this might be just what the doctor ordered," she added, eyes narrowing like a snake on the prowl as she eyed the two adventurers. "The city's always so noisy this time of day anyway…"

Bete understood all too well what the roseate-haired woman was implying, a murderous aura already radiating from the giant sword in her hand. There would be no running away from this fight—that much was for sure.

*Damn! And now the brat's gonna get caught up in it, too…!* he lamented silently, throwing a glance at Lena next to him. It was too late for her to run away now.

Almost as if emphasizing his reproachful thoughts, the clouds overhead seemed to tremble, first one, then two, then drop after drop of rain spilling from the haze of gray. All it took was a second more, and then the sky opened up.

Rain pelting his body, he cursed himself and his own ineptitude. "You need to get away from here, you hear?!" he shouted at Lena.

"O-okay!"

But Valletta's voice was right behind hers, screaming at the top of her lungs.

*"Sic 'em, boys!"*

The response was immediate; every one of the black-robed assassins readied their weapons—jet-black cursed blades—and launched themselves at the duo.

"It's raining…" Finn murmured as he glanced out the window of his office in Twilight Manor. The storm had come on fast, and rain was now bombarding the surface of the glass while thick, heavy clouds turned the city sky an ashy gray.

*…What's this feeling? It's as though something dreadful is about to happen.*

Standing at the window and watching the rain patter the streets, he felt the most peculiar sense of foreboding wrap itself around his heart. With a start, the thumb of his right hand began to throb.

Then…

"Captain!"

Raul burst into the room. Drenched from head to toe and breathing heavily, he looked as though he'd just seen a ghost.

"What happened?"

"I-it's terrible…" he started, lips trembling. "Down in the city, it's…!"

*"GYYAAAAAAAAAAAAAAAAAAAAAAAAAAAAAAAAAAAAH!!"*

The party that formed outside in the streets appeared as though summoned by the rain itself.

"Wh-what is it?!"

*"Dead! They're d-dead!!"*

"Someone was killed?!"

Almost instantaneously, the previously empty side street was overtaken by screams and chaos. The blood painting the stone cobbles swirled together with the rainwater, forming red rivers that flowed down through the cracks.

"Move, please! Let me through!" Lefiya pushed her way through the crowd, having heard the shouts while out and about with one of her friends. When her eyes landed on the carnage, she could hardly find the words to respond.

"I-it can't be…!"

Riveria encountered similar pandemonium upon arriving at *Dian Cecht Familia*'s hospital.

"Miss Amid! Over here, quickly! I need your help!"

"W-we can't stop the bleeding!"

The panicked cries of the healers seemed to harmonize with the thundering echo of the rain. Blood coated their clothes, hands, and skin as they rushed to carry in the wounded one after another. Hearing the screams of her own familia members, Riveria bolted to Amid's side, the healer herself stunned by the developments.

"A wound that can't be healed…Don't tell me!" Riveria took one look before nearly flying back out of the hospital, long silver staff in hand.

"G-guuuuuuaaaaaaaaaaaaaaaaaaaaaaagh!!"

"Th-the adventurers, they're…they're killing each other!"

A crazed battle was taking place to the tune of the rain in the city's back alleys.

The sound of metal on metal, blade on blade, echoed ceaselessly off the stone along with wild, bestial cries. Metallic sparks interspersed with flying spatters of blood as they fell to the ground below.

It was a merciless, violent attack right in the middle of the day, shrouded beneath a curtain of tempestuous rain.

"Somebody get the Guild! No, get an adventurer!" came the piercing shrieks as flustered civilians scrambled away from what seemed to be a familia dispute. Even the free people of Orario were all too familiar with the overwhelming power of their adventurers. Meanwhile, the maddened shouts of *Loki Familia*'s members continued behind them, echoing throughout the streets.

"Ngh!"

Aiz wove her way through the crowd and splashing puddles, unsheathing the sword at her waist as she flung herself into the dance of shadows beyond.

The screams and shouts continued all throughout the city, muffled by the pouring rain. Blackened blades descended like reapers' scythes, claiming their new blood.

Bete's metal boots, Frosvirt, smashed through the faces of his enemies, taking them out one by one together with their cursed weapons.

"Grrraaaugh!"

The assassin who'd just come flying at him went to the ground hard, tumbling back across the cobbles. But like clockwork, another appeared in his place to launch another attack at Bete.

"Shit!"

They came at him in waves, a veritable sea of robed assailants.

Cursing under his breath, Bete launched kick after kick at the incoming tide of enemies.

"*Bwa-ha-ha!* Get him, you miserable pieces of scum! *Get hiiiiim!*" Valletta shouted from the nearby rooftop, looking more and more like a tourist ogling the city's most popular attraction.

Down below, her laughter enveloped Bete's every blow.

And around him, stifling the entirety of the restoration zone, the rain continued to pour in a perpetual deluge. The soggy haze acted like a film, separating them from the outside world, nothing but the gray sky watching over their isolated fight.

"Hiii-*yah*!"

"G-guuuwwwah?!"

"—*GET DOWN!*" Bete shouted as Lena lashed out with the broken scimitar she'd picked up off the street. Lena did as she was told, stooping down just in time to avoid Bete's spinning kick. The incoming assassin was launched away just before his blade could reach Lena.

"Gwghhh?!"

"Th-thanks…"

"Don't just stand there! There's more of 'em coming!"

This was no time for words of thanks.

Even now, another swarm of black shadows was lunging toward them through the blurry haze of the rain.

"Those weapons of theirs are cursed! Do *not* let them hit you!" Bete growled as he stared down the approaching enemies.

"C-cursed?! O-okay! I'll try!"

The assassins were uniform in their attire: jet-black robes topped by equally dark hoods. And they didn't carry themselves like normal adventurers at all; their movements were surprisingly deft. In less than a second, they'd simply be gone. There was something inhuman about the perfectly emotionless eyes staring out from underneath their masks.

No matter how many of their comrades Bete and Lena took down, they seemed completely unaffected, coming at them again and again without an inkling of hesitation.

*These guys aren't Evils! They're hired assassins!*

He'd heard of them before—a familia more like a criminal association, talked about only in hushed whispers. They carried out the dirty dealings of their Goddess of Slaughter, but nobody knew where they came from or how many they numbered—an organization of cold-blooded assassins. Bringers of blood and death in the underworld, who killed in exchange for coins.

Almost as though confirming Bete's suspicions, he caught sight of the insignia on one of the assassins' fluttering cloaks: Sekhmet, veiled in a hood and mask of her own. The assassins themselves didn't seem to boast high Statuses compared to a typical Orarian adventurer—Level 3s at the very most—but Bete wasn't fighting them one-on-one, now, was he?

"Ggggh—grraaaaagh!"

Every single one of their attacks was a finishing blow, attempting to reap the very life from their opponents.

There was no uncertainty in their movements as the fresh waves of assassins attacked everything in sight with their long-bladed cursed weapons, even the bodies of their wounded comrades. Bete responded with a rush of his own, eyes flashing as his right leg lashed out, taking them down in one giant sweep. The sheer amount of friendly fire happening—and the assassins' lack of concern toward it—grated on Bete's first-tier-adventurer nerves.

These were an entirely different type of enemy from the Evils they'd faced in Knossos, who had at least still feared death when they were blowing themselves to smithereens. No, these men must have been brainwashed through years of sadistic training and upbringing, to the point where they didn't even flinch at using their own lives as a weapon—a band of true cold-blooded killers.

Then...

*"Waltz of blood!"*

The chants came at him one after another, morphing into waves of black energy and reddened mist.

*Curses and...anti-Status Magic...?! These guys are starting to get really annoying!*

One after another, they layered the curses and spells meant to lower the Statuses of their opponents. And they didn't care if these hit their comrades, either, which made them seem particularly low. In their attempt to weigh down Bete and Lena, they sent wave after wave of curses even if it meant sacrificing their own companions to do so. *Annoying* was an understatement.

*And I've got my own baggage to deal with, too...!*

He threw a glance behind him to where Lena was still struggling to deal with the assassins' erratic fighting style. While the girl's Status may very well have been higher than that of her opponents, their constant underhanded approach had her consistently coming up short.

Bete couldn't go on the offensive so long as Lena was there. He had to be constantly on guard, ready to grab her arm and pull her out of harm's way at a moment's notice, especially when the assassins began shooting off those spells.

On and on the battle raged under the watch of the crumbling brothels on either side.

Between the cursed weapons coming at him from every side and the throwing knives now flying toward him, he didn't notice the darkened shadow fluttering overhead until it was too late.

"Ugh!"

"*Shit!*"

One of the throwing knives grazed past Lena, drawing a small spatter of blood. The assassins didn't miss a beat, quickly moving in on the stumbling girl, but Bete beat them to the punch and kicked the whole lot of them away.

*Just how many of these guys are there? It's like they're never-ending!*

Bete cursed, realizing that they weren't making any progress.

"Gnngah…!"

Lena yelped.

"Unnnguugh…?!"

And again.

"Gah…!!"

And a third time.

"_____"

Suddenly, Bete realized what was happening.

The attackers were leaving him—and, instead, focusing on Lena.

*What the hell?!*

Why weren't they attacking him, one of the upper echelons of their most-hated *Loki Familia*? Why else would they go to all this trouble to drag these assassins out of Knossos? Weren't they trying to keep him from finding that key?

Then again, what was it Valletta had said earlier? That they hadn't planned on running into any first-tier adventurers—?

Bete began focusing all his movements around Lena.

Using his body as a shield to protect the girl from any more wounds from cursed weapons, he met the incoming assassins head-on and sent them soaring one after another.

*What the hell what the hell what the hell.*

Why were they coming at her en masse, almost as though that had been the plan the whole time—

*—Wait, don't tell me!*

Bete's heart gave a jump as a strange possibility crossed his mind.

What if he'd been wrong about this all along?

He hadn't gotten Lena mixed up in anything. In fact…

*—Oh, for cryin' out loud!*

No, Lena hadn't gotten mixed up in anything at all.

The only one getting pulled into things that didn't involve him—

And the true target of those assassins was—

"He-he-he."

Valletta's lips curled into a grin as she watched the battle play out from her vantage point on the roof.

"He-he-he-he-he-he."

Laughing, she watched Bete grow more and more anxious.

"He-he-he-he-he-he-he-he-he-he!!"

But when she looked at the girl, pained and suffering, she licked her lips with a wicked grin.

Jumping back for a moment.

"Thanatos…Just what do you plan on doing with so many cursed weapons?"

Down in Knossos, and back in the long hallway with mosaics covering the walls, a man appeared. Only one eye was visible through the swath of his bangs. His hair and skin deathly pale, as though never having seen the light of the sun, he was a ghost of a man with large, dark bags underneath his sunken eyes. It was none other than Barca, a man driven by the desire to fulfill the legacy of his ancestor, Daedalus.

"You plan to challenge *Loki Familia*...?" he asked the god now standing unaccompanied in the hall, his tone incredulous. "On the surface? Are you mad? To do so would be nothing short of suicide."

Thanatos was silent for a moment, then simply shrugged. "Those were my thoughts at first, but...it seems we may have been mistaken."

"Mistaken...?"

"Indeed. Dear Valletta seems to have really lost her head this time—not that I wouldn't generally say the same thing about you. Yes, she's in quite a tizzy."

"..."

"Even I, the God of Death, was taken aback."

He wasn't exaggerating, either. He'd truly been impressed. With a shake of his silky, deep-purple hair, he narrowed his similarly colored eyes, turning toward the still-silent Barca.

"You see, our dear Valletta is going hunting"—he paused with a smile, almost as though sanctioning her actions—"for Amazons."

"Amazons are being attacked all over the city?!" Finn shouted.

"Y-yes! Even now, they're...There are already so many bodies...!"

"...Their affiliation. Is there any connection?!"

"At least right now, they've all been from different familias, but...it seems like all the victims so far were originally from *Ishtar Familia*...! The ones closest to Lady Ishtar—the Berbera!"

At this, Finn furrowed his brow. "They must be trying to silence them to keep us from finding the key...!" he realized in a flash, as even then, the sound of clashing weapons began making its way in through the window. This had to be the work of the Evils.

Then their enemy must have given up on finding the key themselves. With no clues to go on, *Loki Familia*'s own investigation efforts must have had them on pins and needles, to the point where they'd decided to use brute force. Not even Finn would have thought they'd stoop to this level.

If they couldn't get their hands on it, they were going to make goddamn sure no one else would. And that meant eliminating the one source of info that might lead anyone to it.

It was a bold, immoral, in*human*, and altogether merciless plan.

"Who would do such a thing...?"

But already in the back of Finn's mind, the sadistic smile of a certain woman had sharpened into focus.

"Valletta...!"

"Lord Dionysus!"

"An attack out of nowhere, shrouded in shadow...A mass assassination?"

Back on one of the backstreets, still reverberating with the sound of rain and screams. Dionysus and Filvis were kneeling beside the slain corpse of an Amazon, a group of white-faced onlookers behind them.

The dead Berbera's eyes were staring blankly at the sky, evidence enough as to the warning-less strike that had taken her life. Blood was still dripping from the laceration that refused to heal; from what they could tell, the attack had taken place sometime last night.

"They're trying to wipe Ishtar's followers off the map...Thanatos and his lot have certainly chosen a disturbing route," he murmured, hia graceful features twisting in apparent distaste. Behind them, Lefiya pushed her way through the crowd.

"Miss Filvis! Lord Dionysus..."

"Lefiya..."

"Thousand Elf...You'd best look away."

But Lefiya's gaze had already fallen to the sprawled-out corpse on the ground, and her words left her. The demi-human lying there, being battered by the rain same as everyone else, was someone she had seen alive and well only last night.

"She's…one of the Amazons we asked for information…"

"Come back here!"

Tione shrieked, her Kukri knives flashing as she furiously wiped her sopping-wet bangs out of her eyes.

"Grruuaaaaagh?!"

"You *bastaaaaaaaard*!"

The black-robed figure fell to the ground as, nearby, Tiona slammed one of his peers and his jet-black weapon against the wall with her Urga.

"You…monsters…"

"Tione! Are you okay?!"

"Just what the hell is going on here, huh?! Amazons are getting attacked all over the city!" Tione howled, hands pressed to the torn skin of her arms as her sister, Tiona, ran over to her. Having heard the screams and rushed out to help, they were just starting to realize the gravity of their situation.

"Hey! Shit-for-brains! You know something, huh? You better spit everything out *right now*…!" She turned toward the assassin still lying on the ground, yanking him up by his collar. But it was too late—he'd already cracked something with his teeth, and in an instant, his eyes rolled back in his head. A bubble of blood popped between his lips as a scalding smoke hissed its way out of his mouth.

A strong acid, no doubt, to kill them quickly in just such a situation. They clearly didn't want any information on their plans getting out.

Tione ground her teeth together in maddened futility at her assailant's abrupt end.

"Goddammit…!!"

"Get the wounded to *Dian Cecht*'s hospital! Quickly now!!" Gareth thundered, his voice practically shaking the cobbles underfoot as he slammed his great ax into a swarm of incoming assassins.

Amazons with blood leaking down their faces. Amazons with stab wounds in their guts. Amazons whose wounds simply would not heal, the blood flowing, flowing, flowing. *Loki Familia* worked together, shouting back and forth as they hurried to carry every wounded Amazon they could find off to the hospital.

"Every one of their attacks is a suicide attack…!"

Neither the Amazons, covered in blood, nor the adventurers helping them were simply standing there. In fact, there were quite a few hero figures who had stepped up to the plate, facing off against the onslaught of assassins. However, their enemies had no regard for their own lives, and all they had to do was land one strike on one of their Amazonian targets to succeed in their mission.

After all, they fought with cursed weapons.

A single hit was all it took to inflict what might as well have been a deadly poison, spelling doom for the victim.

"Our numbers are dwindlin'. We don't have enough to protect 'em all…!"

It was a single, coordinated assassination attempt on the Berbera. And considering those Berbera were currently scattered about the city in their new respective familias, Gareth and his crew couldn't even begin to imagine the full scale of the attack. The rain was surely swallowing up more screams all across Orario.

Gareth narrowed his eyes beneath the low-hanging rim of his helmet.

"Gngh!!"

Aiz's sword went whistling through the throng of leaping assassins, sending countless bodies tumbling across the stone and the shattered remains of weapons spiraling through the air.

"Aiz! Don't let their weapons touch you!" Riveria called out from her position a short distance away. The high elf's long silver staff was mowing down a multitude of enemies of her own. Her jade-colored hair clinging to her forehead in clumps and the last thread of her composure all but vanished, she finished off her remaining opponents before dashing to the side of the Amazon they'd been defending.

"Are you unharmed?"

"I'm *fine*! And I never asked for your help, either! Just leave me alone!" the prostitute Aisha Belka shouted back as she thrust her large podao sword into the ground for support. Indeed, the ground was already littered with the bodies of the assassins she'd taken care of herself. Having narrowly avoided being wounded, the lone female warrior was breathing hard as she tossed a glare in Aiz and Riveria's direction.

"Aisha!"

"Samira?"

Another Berbera, this one with ashy-gray hair, ran over to the trio.

It was the same Amazon Tiona had been interrogating only the day before. Her skin scored with shallow wounds, like Aisha, she quickly filled in her fellow Berbera on the situation: what was happening all over the city, the scope of the wounded, and everything they knew at the present time. Once Riveria added in her own short explanation, Aisha brought a hand to her forehead and tightened her fingers.

"An assassination attempt...on the Berbera? Goddammit! Even with that Goddess of Beauty out of the picture, she still finds ways to make our lives a living hell...!"

"What do we do, Aisha? Even some of the high-class courtesans who were employed at the palace were killed...Ah! That's right! You haven't seen Haruhime, have you?!"

"Calm down! She's not on any familia list. Not even the Guild knows where Lady Ishtar hid her, so there's no way they'll find her!"

"Right. Then...erm...Phryne! What about Phryne...?"

"You really think that frog would let herself be killed by the likes of this lot? Don't make me laugh!" Aisha barked loudly at the frazzled girl, her responses a harried mixture of irritation and comfort. As the chaotic questioning continued, Riveria stepped forward with a request of her own.

"Our efforts to stop the attack are falling behind. By the time we heard the commotion and rallied our forces together to help, we were already too late. If you know of anyone who might still be targeted, you must let us know."

"Gimme a second! Let me think! Anyone else who might be attacked...?" Aisha snapped, her hand still on her forehead as her face twisted in frantic thought.

But her answer came in less than a second.

Her head snapped up, and a name left her mouth.

"Lena..."

"Huh?"

"*Lena...!*" she said again, her face a picture of horror as she dashed in the direction of the Pleasure Quarter to the city's southwest—and the location of Lena's secret place.

"Lena's in trouble!"

It was a knife to the shoulder that finally sent the girl to the ground.

"Unnggahhh!"

"*Dammit!!*" Bete howled as he sent the rapidly approaching black shadow sailing into the air with a high-speed kick. Repelling the white blades flying in his direction with his armguard, he focused everything he had on protecting the girl behind him from the bevy of cursed swords. His cheeks already bore a jagged pattern of wounds.

The rain-swept battle in the corner of the ruins had yet to show any signs of stopping as Bete and Lena put up a desperate, isolated struggle.

"B-Bete Loga..."

"It barely scratched you, ya idiot! Stop actin' like he cut off yer arm!"

Lena's eyes filled with tears as she watched Bete fight.

Using his sopping-wet body as a shield, he was doing his best to keep the girl on the ground safe from the incoming attacks. And attacks there were by the dozen—members of the Evils, of *Thanatos Familia*, had joined the fight, adding more fuel to an already chaotic brawl.

"It's me they're after…isn't it…?"

"Took you that long to figure out?!"

"Then…it's my fault you're caught up in this mess…?"

"…As if that matters! These are my enemies, too!"

Indeed, Bete hadn't gotten Lena tangled up in anything at all.

Quite the opposite, actually—Lena had dragged *Bete* into this mess.

The true target of the assassins was none other than the Amazonian girl behind him, the bearer of Ishtar's final secret. It had simply been fortuitous (or not so fortuitous) that Bete had been with Lena that day.

But even with the sparks flying down around him, he refuted the ignorant girl's trembling question.

No, this was his fight, too.

How dare she think this involved only her. No, she was gravely mistaken.

"…*Hyyyyyyyyaaaaaaaaaaaaaaaaaa!*"

The true target of the assassins' attacks was as plain as day.

Not Bete but, rather, Lena. And as Bete fought to ward off the attacks coming at them from every direction, he found himself unable to so much as retaliate. There were simply too many of them, too many cursed weapons, and Bete was falling prey to them together with their target.

This would never have happened had Bete been alone.

No, he could have used his ultimate weapons, his lightning-fast feet, to their full potential, mowing down the mob of assassins like they were nothing more than toys. Staying true to his namesake, Vanargand, he could have taken out every single one of them with his patented high-speed battle style.

But he had Lena.

A tiny little girl who couldn't fight off the multitude of attacks, who'd be crushed beneath their sheer numbers. A fragile doll who'd be killed in an instant if he didn't do everything in his power to protect her.

That thought alone was enough to make Bete see red.

The tattoo on his cheek, the fang chiseled into his skin, was throbbing.

No matter where he went or what he did, these weaklings, these helpless pieces of fish bait, were there to torment him.

And yet, in spite of all the grief he'd given her, he just couldn't abandon her now.

"Grrrrrrruuuu*uuuuuuuaaaaaaaaaaaaaaa*AAAAAAARRRGGGH!"

In the split second between his relentless flurries of defensive maneuvers, he slapped a lightning knife to his Frosvirt, wrapping his boots in a web of electric sparks. The resulting arc of lightning zigzagged its way through the throng of surprised assassins, culminating in a deafening white blast of thunder and electricity that plunged the world around them into a blind and soundless void.

For just a moment, the ceaseless wave of attacks, that perfect offensive they'd formed around him, came to a halt. It was now or never.

"*RUN!!*" he hollered, yanking Lena's arm and urging her along.

"O-okay!"

They slipped between the stunned assassins, bursting free of the tight circle ensnaring them—

"*And just where do you think you're going?!*"

"_____?!"

Only to see a whirling blade flying straight in their direction.

Bete threw his leg up in an attempt to protect Lena, the force of his lightning boots shattering the blade; but that same force also turned those broken pieces into flying shrapnel that cut his skin and battle jacket to shreds.

"*He-he-he-he-he!!* Did you really think I'd let you get away that easily? I'm having far too much *fun* for that!!" Valletta, the one who'd launched the cursed blade in their direction, squealed at them from atop her perch. The sheer destructive power and speed behind her throw, coming from the only Level 5 in their group of assailants, had increased all the more after the retaliatory strike from Bete.

What was more important now, however, was the huge gap this left in the duo's defenses.

"*Waltz of blood!*"

"_____?!*"

It was a direct hit, and the curses and anti-Status Magic finally took their hold on Bete.

"You're mine now, Vanargand!"

The assassins were on him in a flash, their eyes glinting as they leaped toward the now sluggish werewolf. Valletta watched in glee from on high as he reattempted his lightning attacks, but no matter how many of the black-robed assassins Bete took out, there were always new ones to take their place, ready with another blast of curses to further dull his movements. To make matters worse, they still refused to attack Bete directly; the whole lot of them were doggedly focusing their strikes on Lena.

The dull gloom weighing down his every move made him feel as though he were stuck in the middle of a giant spiderweb or, perhaps more accurately, a wolf in chains.

"You're a monster, you know that? Just how many people have you taken down to get to where you are, huh?" Valletta hissed as she watched Bete fight off not only the assassins but the *Thanatos Familia* reinforcements, as well, even in his labored state. Ten, twenty, thirty went flying, skulls crushed, ribs smashed, and blood spraying from their mouths in an almost constant deluge.

"But it ends now," she finished, her lips curling up into a smile. "And here I thought I was just gonna do a bit of Amazon hunting today...But look at what just fell into my lap! I'm finally gonna have your head tonight, Vanargand!"

Almost as though in tune with Valletta's euphoria, the jet-black shadows increased the fervor of their attacks. Deep wounds were beginning to form along Bete's shoulders, and the spark of electricity in his Frosvirt was all but dissipated.

"Gnnngh...!"

The Unhealable Curse had morphed into a fierce heat that was now searing across both his shoulders. Aside from the deep gouge in his right shoulder, the other cursed injuries he'd sustained were nothing but light scratches. He could still fight. But against how many more? And for how much longer? He let out an almost desperate roar, his insides burning as the assassins' relentless attacks continued.

And all the while, she watched him.

Having fought her own fight as well as she could, she dropped her arms uselessly to her sides. Her lips trembled.

"I'm sorry...Bete Loga..."

Even through the rain, her voice was just loud enough to make Bete's lupine ears twitch.

"You were right. About everything. I'm sorry for being so weak... for always getting in your way..."

*Oh my god, shut up!*

*This is not the time to be talking!*

*You're gonna make me sick whinin' like that!*

*This ain't the place for cold feet! For moanin' and wailin' and I'm sorrys! Pull yourself together!*

*Howl! Just howl already! If that's the only goddamn thing you can do, then you do it—*

Bete's head whirled with insults, all of them aimed at the sopping-wet girl behind him. Time was running out, and he fought against that ticking clock with everything he had, frenzied limbs flying, blood spraying, blades ricocheting, and kicks meeting the soft bodies of those assassins again and again. Seconds seemed to stretch into minutes; everything was slowing down, and the rain was now a dull roar as Lena's voice echoed in his ears.

He hated how annoying she was.

Hated the way his fang throbbed at that whimpering murmur.

"But."

Then...

"If it weren't for me...you'd be strong...wouldn't you, Bete Loga?"

Just like that, Lena's whispered words brought time to a halt.

"_____"

He threw a glance behind him, only to see Lena standing there, pools of what could have been tears or rain quivering just beneath her eyes and a blubbering smile on her face.

It was the face of a girl who was less than a moment's breath from turning tail and running.

*—Hey.*

*Wait.*

*You've gotta be kiddin' me.*

*Just what the hell you doin' there? What's gotten into that head of yers?*

*You think you can just start makin' decisions on your own? Huh?*

*You're a lousy piece of fish bait! You don't have the right to go rogue!*

*So don't move. Don't you dare move!*

*You're not goin' anywhere. You're just gonna stay right there.*

*Stay right there, you damn brat!*

Bete didn't even notice the rampant inconsistency in his thought processes.

How the words echoing in his heart right now directly contradicted the verbal abuse he'd been flinging in her direction only a moment earlier.

*—Weaklings should just stay in the back.*

*—Anyone who gets in our way needs to scram.*

No, Bete didn't notice the disparity at all.

And the girl behind him, water dancing in the corners of her eyes, smiled.

"Win for me, okay, Bete Loga? —And don't die."

Then…

She turned on her heels—and ran.

"—Lena!!"

How ironic that the first time he'd use her name would be at a time like this.

His voice cracking, he faced her retreating form—and screamed.

"Gnfph! He-he-he... *Bwa-ha-ha-ha-ha-ha-ha-ha-ha-ha-ha-ha-ha-ha-ha!!* After the woman, assassins!" Valletta howled from atop the roof, sending the remaining manpower after the fleeing girl. Bete felt a searing heat shoot through his body as he watched the bat-like swarm descend on Lena.

"————————————*Ngh!*"

As everything bubbled up into a wordless grunt, he took off after them.

"Did you forget about me, you overgrown mutt?!"

"Hngh?!"

But his pursuit was cut short when Valletta jumped down from the roof to land neatly in front of him.

"I'm the only girl you need to be concerned about here! I've got more to offer than that brat anyway!"

"I'LL KILL YOUUUUUUU!!" Bete practically exploded as the alluring Evils chieftain gave him a twisted, lascivious grin. He shot forward in a maddened rush at the woman standing in his way as she pulled a new cursed weapon from her fur-lined overcoat.

"A bit desperate, aren't we, Vanargand?"

"Shut the hell up!"

"Is that little vixen soooo important to you?"

"*I said shut up!!*"

Valletta flourished her jet-black dagger as she deftly blocked Bete's every attempt to move past her, enjoying herself thoroughly. It didn't help that the layer upon layer of anti-Status spells were turning into chains around Bete's arms and legs.

He was strong enough that even in his weakened state, Valletta couldn't land a hit.

But she didn't need to. She only had to stop him.

With every second that ticked by, his face twisted into an even more distorted grimace, which had his sadistic opponent giggling in glee. There was nothing that gave her greater pleasure than snuffing out the twinkle of life in her opponents' eyes.

"Have you found my little present yet, hmm?"

"?!"

"Those precious friends of yours! Gift-wrapped for ya in their own blood down in Knossos!"

Bete's hackles snapped to attention.

Her words were like the knife grinding further into the wolf's already tumultuous heart.

"It was me! All of it! I slaughtered those sniveling shit-for-brains where they stood!"

"...You..."

"I did! Woulda liked to take more time with 'em, though. Make it really grisly. But you little ass-biters were hot on my heels, so I had to be quick and dirty!"

"...I don't wanna hear it..."

"Killing that little healer was the best, though. So weak! Yet she kept trying to protect the others until the very end!"

"*Shut your mouth!!*"

Bete met Valletta's rapturous cry with an enraged howl of his own.

She'd killed Leene and the others. And that thought alone was enough to make Bete's entire world erupt into flames.

"How did Finn take it, huh? —Probably looked as pathetic as you do right now, huh? Like your precious little kitty just died or somethin'?!"

And then Bete's anger imploded.

Right into that smiling face.

"————————RRUUUUUUUUAAAAAAAARRRRGGGGHH!!"

His foot moved so fast it seemed to melt into the falling rain, shattering Valletta's dagger right in her hand.

"Shit! ...Well, guess that ends things here," Valletta cursed as she jumped up and away from the werewolf, throwing a quick glance down at her shattered blade before tossing it behind her. "Though if you keep it up, you're gonna get yourself killed!" she added with a stiff laugh at the werewolf's now bloodshot eyes. Despite the cautionary nature of her words, her voice itself was full of amusement. "Go on, then, Vanargand! Though it might already be too late! Ha-ha-ha...*ha-ha-ha-ha-ha-ha-ha-ha-ha-ha-ha-ha-ha-ha-ha-ha-ha-ha-ha!!*"

And with that, the woman disappeared into the rain.

Bete didn't even wait until she was fully gone—he was off in an instant.

The rain flooding his vision only further propelled his fury. *Outta my way! Beat it! Get lost!* he screamed to himself as his legs thundered against the ground below so sluggishly it nearly drove him mad. And the rain seemed to respond, losing ever so little of its fervor as though scared into silence by the wolf's advance.

He caught sight of an all-too-familiar scimitar lying abandoned on the cobbles.

All of a sudden, the curses that had been binding his body came loose, and he felt infinitely lighter even as his heart squeezed in his chest.

*Faster, faster, faster.*

Following the strewn bodies of the assassins Lena must have fended off earlier, he propelled himself even faster through the rain-swept ruins.

Down, down that ruined city street, he ran.

And then.

"..."

The road opened up in front of him, and there she was.

The rain was pelting her body, sprawled across the crumbling stone.

She must have fought it out until the very end. Her copper skin was painted red with blood, and her arms and legs were a tangled meshwork of cuts and gashes. Protruding from her stomach, almost like a gravestone, was a black dagger.

Blood dribbled from the wound slowly, steadily, and silently into the puddles below.

Bete stood there frozen for a moment, then dashed to the girl's side, kneeling next to her. The splash of water he sent up painted her cheek, causing her eyelids to flutter open, ever so slowly.

"Is that...you...Bete Loga...?" she murmured through red-stained lips, one hand rising unsteadily into the air. "I can't...see very well... Everything is a...blur..."

Without even realizing it, Bete reached his own hand out to meet hers, gingerly, carefully. Lena's hand responded with a soft squeeze, almost as though her slender fingers themselves were smiling.

"…Hey."

Bete urged.

"…Hey."

Bete began to tremble.

"…Hey!"

He couldn't seem to say anything else, almost as if his lips were broken.

Lena's blurred dark eyes began to droop as the softest, slightest smile crossed her face.

"Bete Loga…I'm sorry for being so…weak…"

"_____"

"I couldn't keep my…promise…"

As the words faded, so, too, did the last bit of warmth from her body.

Time stopped there.

With the last ounce of her strength, Lena gave him one more silent smile.

"I really wanted to…stand alongside you…"

Those were her final words.

As the last of her strength ebbed away, her thin fingers slipped from Bete's grasp. Almost as if on cue, another gurgle of blood trickled from her body, the last spark of life inside her fizzling into nothing.

"…"

The rain sounded so loud around him. Was Heaven weeping?

Bete didn't make a sound.

He didn't laugh.

He didn't cry.

He simply stared down at the girl on the ground, her wet hair clinging to her face. Time seemed stuck in an endless loop.

"Lena!"

When the girl's name was finally called, it didn't come from him.

It was Aisha, out of breath as she dashed over and followed by a startled Aiz and Riveria.

Bete acknowledged the girls' arrival by turning his head to the side and slowly rising to his feet. The three rushed forward in an instant. Aisha took the lead and pushed past him without a word, but she stopped before she could kneel beside the girl on the ground.

She'd directed a trembling hand only halfway toward the girl's body before her fingers curled into a fist.

Aiz and Riveria both took a knee beside her, their faces grim as they removed the dagger and began preparing vials of medicine and healing spells, as useless as they both knew they would be.

And Bete watched all of it, eyes dark.

"It's cursed...!" Riveria murmured as she observed the jet-black dagger.

Aisha's gaze snapped up at this, her voice terse as she directed her anger at Bete. "What did I tell you, Vanargand?! If you let anything, anything at all, happen to her, I'd...!!" she hissed, her eyes boring into him.

But Bete didn't have a response.

He simply stood there, the rain soaking his skin as he returned Aisha's incensed gaze.

Then, finally, his lips moved—forming a smirk.

"Heh. And just what was I supposed to do, huh? Damn brat ran away on her own."

Aisha's eyes tightened.

"She was just gettin' in the way anyway. Annoying as hell."

"Bete..."

"It's like I've always said. Can't do nothin' for a piece of fish bait."

"Bete..."

But now that he'd started, he couldn't stop, the words coming back to him like a rushing waterfall. Ignoring the looks from Aiz and Riveria, he simply kept talking, kept sneering.

He continued laughing.

"They'll all end up like this. Dead on the sidewalk and helpless to do a thing about it...And don't say I didn't warn 'em!"

Aisha erupted, sparks alight in her eyes.

*"NGH!!"*

Overcome with rage, she grabbed Bete by the collar, fury building up like an inferno as she launched her fist straight toward his stupidly smirking face.

Only, in that split second before her fist connected...

"_____"

It came screeching to a halt.

The only thing that ended up hitting Bete's face was the pouring rain, forming rivulets that cascaded down his cheeks.

Aisha simply stood there, frozen, her eyes wide.

And for the life of him, Bete couldn't figure out why.

Why?

Why did her fist stop?

What was that look she was giving him?

What was that shock coloring her eyes?

*The hell you lookin' at?*

*I'm smilin', ain't I?*

*Just like I always am!*

"You..."

*Hey! Just whaddaya think yer lookin' at, huh? I got somethin' on my face?*

*Can't ya see I'm laughin' at 'er?*

*So why stare at me like that?*

*Why aren't ya layin' in to me?*

"..."

Aisha wordlessly lowered her fist, releasing her grip on Bete's collar. With one final pitying glance, she turned away.

Meanwhile, Riveria took the motionless girl on the ground into her arms and carried her away.

Leaving Bete behind.

"......Bete."

Only Aiz remained, looking unsure how to approach the werewolf or of the right thing to say.

So she simply watched him, standing there with his back to her.

The rain never stopped.

"…What the hell was that?"

Why hadn't she hit him?

*Why?*

Why had she looked at him like that?

*You think you can just look at me however you want, huh—?*

It was humiliating, was what it was.

Letting what should have been his scornful grin slide from his face, he ground his teeth together so hard they were liable to break.

Rage—and other emotions—were churning through his veins like fire.

And yet, he was powerless to do a single thing.

Unable to so much as scream, he turned his gaze toward the sky above.

And toward the unfeeling rain, beating against his skin.

It had been raining that day, too.

The Master of the Plains vanquished, Bete started his triumphant return to the Labyrinth City.

However, all that awaited him upon his arrival were the weeping faces of his familia—and the corpse of his beloved.

"＿＿＿＿"

Bete suddenly found himself overwhelmed, the dry rattle of the ground trampled beneath his feet crashing down around him.

It wasn't supposed to have been anything special. They were just going into the Dungeon, same as normal. Just the typical Dungeon raid, same as normal. Then suddenly she'd wound up dead.

It had happened so fast. The Dungeon had bared its fangs and taken her before she'd even had a chance to resist.

The woman who'd been trying to get strong for Bete's sake; who'd done everything she could to shed the skin of her former, weaker self; who'd disregarded her own strength and paid the ultimate price. And Bete hadn't been there to protect her.

"B-Bete..."

The rest of his familia was an equally sorry sight, whimpering and wounded. Some had lost limbs, some whose bodies hadn't even recovered from the excursion into the Dungeon, and others with tears running down their faces as they apologized to Bete over and over again. No one blamed him. No, they blamed no one but themselves and their own lack of strength, cursing the world in hopeless melancholy.

Her corpse had been so pale, as though free of regret or pain, as though nothing had happened at all.

*Why?*

*Why?*

*Why couldn't she have been stronger?*

*Why did she have to be so weak?*

*Too weak to fight off the world, to fight off fate, to fight off truth.*

*These weaklings.*

*They can't do anything without me.*

*Without one of the strong there to protect them.*

*Didn't I grow stronger to escape all this?*

*So why is it still happening? Why are the things I love being taken away from me?*

A ridiculous number of questions tumbled around in his heart before fading into nothing. A whirlpool of thoughts he couldn't turn into words, despair cutting deep into his very being.

Glancing at his comrades, still weeping helplessly on the ground, he absentmindedly rose to his feet.

"Bete...I'm sorry."

The voice came from Víðarr this time, the god turning his gaze toward Bete.

Something inside Bete snapped.

Before he even knew it, his hands were gripping Víðarr's collar and holding him aloft.

"Don't you say that to me! A god ain't supposed to apologize!"

"Bete, stop!!"

"A god—a god ain't supposed to admit it!!"

Bete continued to scream, tears running down his face even as his fellow familia members raced forward to pull him away. He wouldn't let Víðarr apologize, not when those words were an acceptance of the sacrifices made by the weak.

It felt like the entire world was affirming Bete's despair. The tears—the anguish—refused to let him go.

What was Víðarr even apologizing for?

Why was he apologizing to Bete?

Bete didn't understand. All he could do was howl, the raw emotion coursing through him like a raging river.

It was decided that Víðarr and his broken familia would leave Orario.

Bete didn't go with them.

He'd washed his hands of them. As though hoping to make them hate him, his daggerlike words practically drove them out of the city, like he wanted to keep them far from the Dungeon. And the Guild had no choice but to allow their departure if they wanted Bete, now a second-tier adventurer, to stay in Orario. Bete didn't even see his former friends off on the day they left.

With Víðarr's half-withdrawn blessing still on his back, making it possible for him to convert, Bete kept on fighting, throwing himself into battle after battle. He dove solo into the Dungeon, injuring himself, losing blood by the bucketful but still cutting down monsters left and right. He'd become a wolf starved for even more power, even greater strength.

But still, the phantom pain radiating from the tattoo on his cheek, his fang, refused to let up.

In fact, if anything, it got worse. He'd destroyed his enemy, so why did the pain continue to follow him wherever he went?

The slow burn that plagued his entire body could not be cooled.

It was around this time that Bete began to lash out, his tongue as sharp as a knife.

*—Beat it, fish bait!*

*—Know your place!*

*—I'd say yer all bark and no bite, but you don't even got the bark!*

He berated everyone and everything, and those around him grew to despise the lone wolf without a familia. And they'd attack him, again and again, trying to take him down, only to ultimately be bested. His despair simply couldn't be stopped.

Not a day went by that he didn't pick a fight. Like clockwork, almost, he was wreaking havoc at the pub beneath the red-wasp sign. Not even the disgruntled dwarf who ran the place could be mad at him, almost as though taking pity on Bete's plight.

Bete wasn't going to be taken down by the strong.

No matter how much they hurt him, how much they stole from him, how much the despair hounded him, he would keep fighting, keep moving forward. Because he'd promised himself that he would feast on their flesh and grow strong himself.

Yes.

What had finally dethroned Bete was not the strong—but the weak.

The powerless beings unable to fight back against a world where only the strongest survived.

And no matter how strong he became, his strength could do nothing to change that.

No matter how strong he became, he couldn't save those fragile beings.

Before he'd even realized it, he'd come to despise the weak, powerless to change their fate, with every fiber of his being.

Hating them, loathing them, berating them with words of ridicule and scorn.

Thus, the lone werewolf, broken and friendless, continued his ravenous quest for strength, spurning all those around him. Alone, he fought his way forward along his own path.

Until, despite not having a familia, he took on a new name—Vanargand. Yes, that's what they called him.

Night's curtain had descended over the city.

Pitch-black shadow enveloped the empty streets, the broken magic-stone lanterns flickering softly and the stains of blood still peppering the back-alley cobblestones. The rain had yet to let up, still pounding the city streets as though attempting to bore into the stone itself.

It was this never-ending rain that Bete listened to now, sitting in silence atop a rather plain sofa.

"Bete…"

Aiz murmured from where she stood next to him. She'd yet to find the right words to say, simply gazing down at the werewolf. He hadn't even bothered to wipe the rain off himself or tend to his own wounds, still bleeding from the curse.

Darkness yet reigned outside the window of their room in the *Dian Cecht Familia* hospital. Aiz had led Bete there after the attack. The werewolf hadn't said a word as the rain continued to pelt his skin. Even now, she could tell his weather-beaten and bleeding back needed to be looked at as soon as possible.

"…You should…really dry yourself off…" she started. If there was nothing she could do about the wounds, she could at least dry him, but before she could approach him with a towel, the door opened with a rattle.

"I apologize for the delay."

It was Amid.

Her normally immaculate uniform was now covered in blood, and deep bags sagged beneath her eyes as sweat ran down her skin.

Aiz could tell immediately.

She was dangerously close to a Mind Down.

"Amid, have you…been using your magic…all this time?" Aiz asked anxiously.

"Mine is the only magic currently capable of lifting the curse…I sincerely apologize for making you wait, Mister Bete," Amid replied, voice calm and face showing no signs of strain.

Amid had been working nonstop, attending to the endless stream of Amazons who had been brought to the hospital after the attacks. Her pride as a healer, however, didn't allow her even a moment to herself, and she immediately took to tending Bete's wounds. Holding her right hand over the multitude of scratches on Bete's back, as well as the deep gash in his shoulder, she began her spell, the white glow of magic enveloping his skin.

"…The Amazons…How are they doing?"

"We've saved who we can. But there were still some who were simply brought in too late. We did everything we could…" Amid explained. Though she'd done her best to save them all, some had simply been too far gone. The attacks had likely started the night before, and by the time the victims had been found and brought to the hospital, even Orario's highest-level healer, Dea Saint, could no longer save them.

Though her delicate, doll-like features betrayed nothing, by the looks of her tightly clenched fist, knuckles white from the strain, her head must have been a whirlwind of self-reproach and regret.

"Did the…body of a kid get brought here?"

"…Those who did not make it were taken to the First Graveyard," she explained, not quite answering Bete's question. There would be no room for extra bodies, after all, in the hospital.

Bete's expression didn't change. Instead, his amber eyes simply stared down at the hardened face of the girl on one knee in front of him. Water dripped from his damp gray hair.

Aiz was the only one to look away.

"The assailants have been identified as *Sekhmet Familia*, the shadow of the mainland," Amid continued, trying to change the subject to something more neutral. As beads of sweat formed on her temples from the fatigue, she kept her thin lips moving. "Considering the targets were former members of *Ishtar Familia*, I would gather this is the work of a god with a deep resentment toward

Ishtar...A goddess, perhaps, plagued with jealousy, who hired the assassins to take out the last of her familia. At least, that is what the Guild has surmised."

"..."

"The assassins, too, in line with the laws of their familia, refuse to say a word as to who hired them, even going so far as to kill themselves...The Guild has apparently given up on trying to extract details out of their ringleader," she continued, almost businesslike in her tone.

It made sense that the Guild would leap into action after what had happened. They must have used Status Thieves on the assassins' bodies in an attempt to extract the name of their god, resulting in nothing but a myriad of unanswered questions.

While the Berbera had been able to kill many of their attackers (they *were* adventurers of Orario, after all), the cursed weapons of the assassins had finished the deed for them in many cases. What's more, the assassins didn't fear death, throwing themselves at the Berbera in near-suicidal attacks in order to wound (and curse) their victims. The combination of these two factors was what had led to a frighteningly high victim count. When the assassins found themselves at a draw with their target, they'd simply killed themselves. And it was no different with the assassins *Loki Familia* apprehended in their rush to help, either.

Aiz watched as Amid tended to each of Bete's wounds. The werewolf himself was uncomfortably quiet until she'd completed her task.

"I've finished with my ministrations...However, your wounds will still need a while to fully heal after being afflicted by such a strong curse. Please take some time to fully rest and recover," Amid asserted as she rose to her feet and made to leave Bete's side.

Only, the moment she tried to move, she appeared to grow faint, and Aiz rushed to help her before she could collapse.

"Amid...!"

"I...apologize...I appear to have...used a bit too much...Mind..."

Aiz bit down on her lip as she held the other girl close. Amid's breath was ragged. Aiz needed to get her somewhere she could rest, but as she made to leave, she suddenly stopped. Could she leave Bete alone at a time like this?

"Get her outta here, would ya? She's an eyesore," said the wolf from behind her, arrogant as always.

That much was the same, but still, that static expression of emptiness on his face worried her.

She stood there, not entirely sure what to do, before finally opening the door with Amid still in her arms. "Stay here...okay? I'll be... right back."

And then, with one look behind her, the golden-haired, golden-eyed swordswoman walked out the door.

Silence returned to the room.

The only sound was the rain, now vexingly loud against his ears.

Having sat as still as a statue for so long, Bete finally slowly rose to his feet.

"..."

His amber eyes turned toward the window and the view of a rain-swept Orario beyond.

The fang on his face twisted, and his reflection in the window glared back at him like his own worst enemy. And so his arm rose to punch it wide open, smashing glass and reflection both.

"I apologize for getting you mixed up in this, Antianeira."

Finn was standing in front of the group of injured Amazons on the first floor of the soaring Babel Tower at the center of the city. Even now, in the middle of the night, the entryway to the Dungeon was bustling with activity. All those affected by the "Amazon hunt" had gathered among the crowd.

Most were former *Ishtar Familia* members, now having suffered two attacks in only a matter of weeks, but there were also noncombatant courtesans, as well. Joining them were members of *Loki Familia*, hired as bodyguards by the Guild, along with a few from *Ganesha Familia*. All those in danger of being targeted had been ordered here together, with only those in critical condition still in *Dian Cecht Familia*'s hospital—a swiftly made administrative decision to keep from losing any more Berbera, given how the upper-class adventurers were so important to the city's influence.

In front of the Amazons and courtesans, their features taut with anxiety, stood Aisha. She was facing Finn, Tione, Tiona, and the rest of *Loki Familia*, her long black hair flowing down her back.

"It appears that our investigative actions were what prompted the ringleaders of this attack to take action. While I can say I never imagined they would go to such lengths…that is no excuse for what happened. Please accept my sincerest apologies."

"There's no reason to apologize, Braver. This wasn't your fault. Even a child could tell you as much. No, the only ones at fault here are those bastards who did this," Aisha responded, refusing the spear-equipped prum's apology. As clear as the enmity on the bereaved Amazon's face was, the fury wasn't directed at the despondent crew in front of her. "Besides, it would have happened sooner or later, yes? Even if you and your people hadn't gone snooping around."

"…"

"Goddammit! Will that goddess never leave us alone? Even after she flies the coop, she still haunts us." Aisha sighed, taking Finn's prolonged silence as an affirmative. She already knew about the key that *Loki Familia* had been asking her girls about, and she'd surmised most of what had happened in Meren, from the violas to the "secret organization"—namely, the Evils—that Ishtar had been dealing with. The gorgeous Amazon didn't even need to pry into Finn's and the others' dealings to be utterly and entirely fed up with the apparent root of all evil her former goddess had left behind. Turning her long, narrow eyes toward the sky, she scowled at the heavens where Ishtar now resided.

"You weren't able to protect us. To save us. But we don't blame you for this. It is a shame that we, as warriors, will have to bear…Tell that Vanargand of yours as much, too."

"Bete? Why bring him up now?"

"…You didn't hear?"

At this, Aisha was silent for a moment before finally explaining. She told him everything, about Bete and about Lena.

Finn's green eyes widened in surprise, as did Tiona's and Tione's and everyone else's standing behind them. All of them were shocked at this unexpected news.

"The look on that werewolf's face…No, it's nothing. Anyway, you can keep your concerns to yourself. We're grateful for those of us you've saved, but your help won't be necessary any longer."

And with that, Aisha walked away. The rest of the Amazons, too, seemed to shake off their anxiety, turning their focus instead toward the rallying voice of their leader.

Finn remained silent, lost in thought.

"The Amazon killed in front of Bete…You don't think it's that same girl Lefiya told us about earlier, do you? The one on a date with him?"

"…Can't imagine it'd be anyone else. Maybe he was looking for info on the key, too? Only they got attacked along the way…"

Tiona and Tione mused to themselves, prompting the rest of the familia to start wondering out loud, as well. At the front of the group, Finn gave his thumb a lick.

He stood there in silence.

Before finally raising his head.

"We'll use Bete as bait."

"?!"

The sudden announcement was enough for Tione and the others to question their ears.

"The Bete Loga I know isn't one to stand by quietly after an event like this. No, my gut says he's already out there *raising hell*."

"…!"

"In fact, he's probably on his way to the Evils as we speak…to Valletta and her crew, thirsty for revenge. And not quietly, I may add. We'll use him as a diversion. While the enemy has their sights set on Bete, we'll cut off their escape route."

Their path back to Knossos, in other words. Without it, they would be trapped and isolated aboveground, the prum explained.

"And then, we'll take that opportunity to relieve them of their key."

The series of announcements was met with shock after shock from the rest of his familia.

Tiona, Tione, Raul, Anakity—everyone. Without a moment's indecision, they were just going to use Bete's emotions to their own advantage and gain the upper hand; seeing their captain, Braver, discuss it so coolly was enough to make the younger familia members gulp uneasily.

"We'll station someone to keep watch on Daedalus Street. I'll set up camp outside the entrance to Knossos in the Old Sewerway. We'll also keep a few people here, as well, just in case they decide to use the second entrance to the Dungeon to return to their hideout. Raul, tell Gareth that I'm putting him in charge of Babel—"

"F-Finn?!"

"Sh-shouldn't we stop and think about this for a moment, Captain?!"

A rather flustered Tiona and Tione cut off his orders.

He turned his green eyes toward the two twins, who were now leaning forward anxiously.

"No? And here I thought both of you detested Bete, hmm? So much so that you wouldn't even look him in the eye?"

"That's…well…This is just too awful, if you ask me!"

"Isn't the whole point of a familia to look after your friends? Like back in Meren, when you and everyone else came running to our aid…! Th-that stupid werewolf, too!!"

The two insisted, even as Finn retained his mask of emotionless leader-hood.

And it was true—not even the two Amazons understood exactly why they were so against Finn's plan, considering the hatred they'd been harboring for the wolf only a short while earlier. It was the same for the rest of the familia behind them, too, all eyes practically glued to Finn.

"You don't agree? How about I change up the wording, then?"

Finn mused, turning his gaze from Tiona to Tione and then to the rest of the familia behind them. "We're going to stake everything we have on Bete."

"‼"

A second ripple of shock ran through the group.

Tiona and the others stared at him wide-eyed and stunned as Finn doffed his mask of authority, anguish and heartache clear in his wry smile. After scanning the group once more, he let his eyes fall toward the open door to the tower and the rain-drenched shadow beyond.

"Because nothing we say can stop him any longer."

"Finn, that imbecile…He's really done it this time," Riveria murmured, her sullen voice melting into the pouring rain. She'd just been delivered Finn's orders.

She was in *Dian Cecht Familia*'s hospital. Lefiya was gulping for breath after relaying the command to the elves who'd been left in charge of guarding the few remaining Amazons yet to be healed.

Though Alicia and the others looked at the younger elf in disbelief, Lefiya reaffirmed her words with a nod of her head, streaked with rain thanks to her mad dash from Babel.

"I…I agree it's…unprecedented. Even for Mister Bete, this cruel plan is simply not like the captain at all…"

"No, it's because he understands Bete…and has faith in him. That's why he can issue such an order."

"Huh?"

"Then I shall play the part of the villain," Riveria cut in with a sigh, as if about to launch into a soliloquy.

Still confused, Lefiya looked toward the high elf for an answer, but then—

"Riveria!"

—Aiz appeared from the back hallway.

"Bete is gone…He left on his own…!"

"Is that so…? I suppose this was expected. Everything is going according to Finn's plan."

There would be no stopping it now.

Ignoring Lefiya and the other flustered elves behind her, she closed her eyes for a moment. And when she opened them again, she rushed quickly toward Aiz.

"Follow him, Aiz. Don't let him out of your sight. You'll be the only one he has now…"

"I…Okay. Understood."

Riveria didn't even bother filling Aiz in on the rest of Finn's plan. With a single nod, Aiz was off, dashing past Lefiya and the other elves and toward the hospital door beyond. Just before she disappeared, Riveria called to her one last time.

"Aiz. When you see Bete as he is now, do you think he's like how you…?"

"…?"

"…No, it's nothing. Go on." Riveria shook her head, almost as though apologizing for stopping her. Aiz looked back, her head tilted to the side in confusion, but did as she was told and put the hospital behind her.

Riveria narrowed her eyes as she watched Aiz disappear into the night.

The rain descended like a never-ending deluge of spears.

And through that rain, Bete made his way down the city streets.

He was alone, and the city practically deserted, though by no fault of the rain—rather, the attacks that had taken place earlier that day. In fact, to see the streets so desolate was nigh unprecedented in a city like Orario. With the sound of the rain masking everything and everyone in sight, too, Bete might as well have been the last person left on earth for all he knew.

His wounds were deep. He'd lost too much blood. He needed food, items.

But even despite the brilliant, fiery-red emotion coursing through his body, Bete's mind was surprisingly calm. He was the prime example of someone built for combat, both as an adventurer and as someone raised in a tribe of warriors.

They would come for him again. Valletta and her crew. He was sure of it.

If he let his hackles down, blatantly walked around like this by himself, he'd be an easy target. There was no way they wouldn't attack him—it was a chance to take down *Loki Familia*'s mad dog. Which was why he wouldn't call for help. No, he *couldn't* call for help. Bete would never allow himself to stoop that low.

The dim light of the magic-stone lanterns casting his shadow on the stone below, he walked, completely lost in thought—until a shadow flickered behind him.

He came to a stop, realizing quickly who was following him and wrinkling his face in annoyance.

"Bete."

She appeared from the darkness, vermilion hair soaked and her body dripping with water.

Bete's thoughts first wandered to the goddess's footwear. What had happened to what she'd said before, huh? About not wanting to get her shoes wet?

But as the faint light of the magic-stone lanterns brought her into view, Loki didn't seem too concerned about them now, bag slung over her right shoulder and ill-dressed for the rain, same as Bete.

"…What the hell are *you* doing?"

"Oh, you know, was just thinkin' I might be able to see you, so I took a little stroll outside the house, and whaddaya know? There you are! Bingo!"

"You really shouldn't go outside alone, you know…Did you even hear what happened today?"

"You worried about me?! D'awww, yer sweet, Bete!" Loki cooed, her buoyant, bubbly voice in sharp contrast to Bete's low growl.

She approached the werewolf, leaving a few steps between them so that goddess and follower stood face-to-face.

"Bete. Here."

"…"

"Potions and mruit. Eat 'em if you need," she said as she tossed the bag in his direction. He caught it in one hand only to see that, indeed, a few vials of medicine and some pieces of the dungeon fruit were peeking out from the top.

It was almost as though she'd seen through everything. Bete felt his irritation rising at the goddess's too-perfect sense of timing.

"You're not gonna try 'n' stop me?"

"And what would happen if I did, huh? You'd end up blamin' yerself for the rest of your goddamn life, yeah? That's what I figured, at least."

She was really grating on his nerves now. She and those eyes that could read him like a book. In fact, she was quite possibly the last person on earth he would have wanted to see right now.

As she looked at him with those slit-like scarlet eyes, he felt something stir in his memories. They were the same—her eyes and Víðarr's.

"…Looks like you went and got yerself hurt again."

Something snapped inside Bete at those words.

With an almost audible *crack*, he felt his blood rush straight to his head.

And before he knew it, he was shouting.

"Stop actin' like you understand anything about me at all!!"

" … "

"Hurt? Who's hurt, huh? The only person I'm pissed at is *me*!"

" … "

"Those Evils bastards did me over real good, yeah? Me, the one who's normally kickin' around the other weaklings, laughin' it up. But I'm nothin' but a piece of fish bait myself! I'm a disgrace!!" His words came pouring out, all the pent-up emotion inside him released like a bomb with his silent goddess in the blast zone. His hand tightened around the bag, knuckles white from fury. "I'm not strong enough! Not powerful enough! I need to get stronger! Much, much stronger—than anyone else!!"

His words were true.

However, he'd left out one piece.

The motivation behind his quest for power. The true form of his unquenchable thirst.

Even he himself pretended not to realize the true target of his emotions, instead baring to the world nothing but his fang—the fang of a raging, starving wolf.

"...Kinda sad, innit?"

But none of that mattered in the face of his goddess.

The howl of a wolf that sent shivers down the spines of those weaker than him meant nothing to her, who could see straight through his Status, the symbol carved into his back.

Loki stepped forward silently, bringing her hands to Bete's face even as he stared at her, breath ragged.

"That this is what it takes for you to get stronger," she murmured, tracing the distorted tattoo, the fang, on his cheek.

Between them, the cold rain continued to fall. Light from the magic-stone lanterns illuminated their faces, their shadows stretching out across the stone below. For just a moment, the two shadows formed a single silhouette: that of a happy trickster comforting her world-condemning wolf.

"Gngh...!"

But it was not to last, and Bete batted her away with what little strength he had remaining.

He stepped past her, fully prepared to keep on walking.

Almost as though running away.

"You know, Bete. Víðarr told me a little bit about you," Loki said simply, not even turning around as Bete walked away.

Bete's feet came to a halt.

"Even bein' from the same place up in Heaven 'n' all, he and I never really saw eye to eye. Completely unapproachable, that one. Everything went over his head."

"..."

"Which is why I never really took to heart what he told me when I ran into him in the pub that one night, drunk as he was and gettin' all mushy..."

*—There's a certain rambunctious wolf under my care.*

—*But I worry that staying with me, staying with my familia, will end up killing him.*

—*If ever he were to escape from my grasp, would you look out for him, Loki?*

Víðarr's words in Loki's voice echoed in the rain.

Bete clenched his teeth, then simply kept on walking, leaving the words of his god—all but his father—behind him.

Loki watched his back disappear into the rain before accosting him one last time.

"Have you figured out what that fang of yours means, Bete?"

—But he'd already figured that out long, long ago.

Meeting them was probably fate.

Making enemies left and right, drinking and fighting through the night, the familia-less Bete happened upon a number of unfamiliar faces one night in his usual pub.

*Loki Familia.*

The city's greatest familia, it, along with *Freya Familia*, had been on a race toward the top ever since Bete had stepped foot in Orario all those years ago. And they were here now, seemingly celebrating a successful expedition in the Dungeon, all of them laughing, having fun, and extolling one another's valor in their endeavors. Bete watched them for a while in silence before, in typical fashion, he began his tirade.

"Heh, what kinda adventure can a bunch of wusses have, huh? Don't make me laugh! You guys'd be nothin' but a bunch of big ol' roadblocks for the real adventurers!"

*Loki Familia* had been quick to respond. With their god present, they'd tried to stick it out for a while, but the more of Bete's abuse they took, the more irate they became, until finally, they'd had enough, the whole lot of them moving in on the werewolf. Bete responded with a kick that sent all of them to the floor.

*"Bwa-ha-ha!* What a crazy wolf! All by yer little lonesome, yet ya fight like you've got a whole army behind ya. What a kook!" came the voice of their vermilion-haired goddess, now ogling Bete in amusement. Her narrowed eyes opened just slightly as she gulped down the rest of her drink.

Bete could feel the others staring at him—a boy clearly unfit for battle, a dark-haired catgirl eyeing him in awe, and a golden-haired, golden-eyed girl who didn't seem to care one single bit. He couldn't help but be disappointed that *Loki Familia* would turn out to be nothing more than this. Only, before he could even finish his thought.

He was blown away.

The fist that hit him full-force sent him flying all the way across the room.

"Yer spoilin' our drink, boy. So why don't ye just keep yer yap shut?"

Bete looked up from the table he'd slammed into to see a dwarven soldier staring down at him.

"Indeed. Quite the smart words for someone who is, themselves, nothing but a craven pup."

The voice came from a high elf mage this time.

"While your words don't seem of genuine arrogance...I must admit, the desperation is more than a little amusing."

And the next, from a smiling prum warrior.

They made up *Loki Familia*'s elites, its strongest team of fighters. And a set of first-tier adventurers whose fame he'd been hearing of nonstop since arriving in Orario.

Sitting in the face of the truly strong, Bete first balked. Then smiled. Then raged.

He leaped to his feet with a furious shout, abandoning himself to the furor racing through his body like wildfire. Only to be brought down single-handedly by the dwarf.

Again and again, he was slammed into the floor before rising to his feet, stubbornly refusing to learn his lesson, and getting sent straight back on his hindquarters. The rest of *Loki Familia* watched the violence in white-faced shock. The dwarf he'd first exchanged punches with—Gareth Landrock—went above and beyond even their wildest imaginations, now a veritable monster in the way he was attacking Bete, seemingly intent on smashing the werewolf's unwarranted conceit into a thousand pieces.

Finally, unable to take it any longer, Bete collapsed to the floor.

He didn't move. His hand was clenched so tightly into a fist, it was trembling, its gray fur standing on end. It was a sight that reminded Bete of the many weaklings he himself had sent to the floor, reveling in their humiliation. But now he was the one tasting the cold, hard ground, a flavor he'd not experienced in quite some time.

—*I found 'em. I finally found 'em.*

—*The crazy-strong punks I've been lookin' for.*

Even as he lay there on the ground, a smile began to form on his face while Finn, Riveria, and Gareth watched him from above.

And then he howled. But it was no longer the howl of the strong. No, he'd become the weak.

Finn and the others looking on in bewilderment, he rose to his feet, charging toward the *Loki Familia* adventurers only to be sent flying one last time, his strength finally depleted.

Still, Bete smiled.

Even as the anger continued to course through him with such force it sent shivers down his body, he whispered a silent word of thanks for this fated meeting: He'd finally found someone stronger than him.

Having witnessed the entire affair, Loki promptly scouted Bete.

The astute leader, the eccentric mage, and the ridiculously powerful dwarven warrior who had beaten Bete to a pulp—all three of them knew their strengths and weaknesses, using them to their advantage as they faced off against adventure. What's more, not a one of them was accepting of those who didn't get stronger, and the rest of *Loki Familia*'s members did everything they could to meet those expectations.

*This is where I need to be*, Bete thought, finally having found a place where he felt comfortable settling down.

Though even after he was officially inducted, he remained a loner. Making no attempt to mingle with the rest of the familia, he continued his crude tirades of insults, pushing away his new colleagues and instigating almost daily fights with Riveria. About the only contact he had with anyone besides Finn and the other elites was Raul, and even that was only because the poor boy had gotten the short end of the stick as the familia liaison, barely able to talk to Bete without sweating despite the fact that they were almost the same age.

As for Bete, well, he challenged Gareth every chance he got:

*"Tenacious little bastard, ain't ya?"*

Bete would always hear this before getting his ass solidly handed to him. It didn't take long for Bete to become recognized as the token "belligerent werewolf" of the familia.

It wasn't until the grueling expeditions in the Dungeon that Bete's relationship with the rest of the familia improved. While the harsh conditions didn't put an end to his altercations with Riveria—the wolf was constantly dashing out ahead of the group on his own—there was something assuring about the sight of him up ahead that calmed the nerves of the rest of the familia behind him. It was around this time that his colleagues began viewing him and his abusive diatribes with awe and aspiration rather than fear as Bete quickly forged his way to Level 4.

It was during these treks to the Dungeon, Bete in the lead as they fought tooth and nail against whatever surprises awaited, that he, too, began to reevaluate his colleagues—Raul, Anakity, and all the others. Seeing their faces stained with blood and dirt, hearing their determined cries of war, reminded him of the beloved tribe he'd lost long ago.

*—They may be chumps, but they ain't short on guts.*

They were ridiculously stubborn in the way they kept on fighting until the bitter end, the very picture of adventurers. And the reason they could? Because they had complete and utter faith in the voice that was guiding them. To think that a leader would have this much influence on those who followed—though Bete would never say it, even he had to acknowledge the greatness of Finn and the others.

Even still, casualties were unavoidable.

Though Bete and the other stronger adventurers were able to escape by the skin of their teeth most of the pinches they got themselves into, the weaker ones weren't so lucky. The Dungeon was constantly filled with the wails of the weak. Just one more thing that ground on Bete's nerves.

Which was perhaps why that girl became a sort of savior to him.

Aiz Wallenstein.

A golden-haired, golden-eyed beauty of only ten years. Bete had originally looked down on her as he did everyone else, only to have his words stolen from him after watching the ferocious way she fought.

Her practically emotionless features might as well have been those of a doll.

And though they were just about polar opposites when it came to temperament, Bete imagined his younger sister would have looked something like her if she were still alive.

That long golden hair.

Even more vibrant than that of the girl from his youth.

That relentless spirit, yearning to grow stronger.

So familiar to when *she* had loved him and strived to follow in his footsteps.

Aiz had been like a sister to him back then. And though he'd berated her for charging headlong into incoming swarms of monsters—"Pot calling the kettle black, are we?" Riveria had pointed out—he'd taken to her immediately. The stronger she grew, the less she needed saving and the more the crazy thought inside Bete's head grew: *If only she had been that girl back then.* It was a stupid, selfish wish, and Bete felt ashamed for even thinking it. Still, as Aiz grew, changing from a girl into a woman, he became even more lost, until, before he realized it, he was falling for her. That profile of hers, visible from his spot a few paces behind, just looked so much like *hers*, the girl he'd once loved so much.

But there was one difference between Aiz and that girl.

Aiz was *strong*.

Stronger than any woman he'd ever known. Any *person* he'd ever known. Once she invoked her magic, she surpassed even Bete, and if no one stopped her, she'd be rushing ahead, wiping out a whole throng of monsters single-handedly, her skills with a sword enough to make Bete swoon.

No amount of power was enough for her.

She craved it, even more wildly and recklessly than Bete.

And while that aspect of her did nothing but make Loki, Finn, Riveria, Gareth, and the others fret, Bete wasn't worried in the least. No, he approved of it.

*"Don't you change a bit. You hear me, Aiz?"*

*"…?"*

He still remembered their exchange that one night long ago. A night that Aiz had probably long since forgotten. Bete had approached her out in the manor's courtyard, where she'd been impassively swinging her sword.

*"You're strong. That's all that matters, so…don't you change."*

It almost sounded like an appeal.

A desperate, selfish request from the wolf who didn't want to lose the fourth person in his life who'd ever meant anything to him.

*"No."*

But Aiz wouldn't have it.

*"…I need to be even stronger."*

It was an answer that brought a smile to Bete's face.

He respected her more than anyone, this girl and her unparalleled strength.

She was definitely his ideal woman.

Someone strong. Who didn't know the meaning of compromise. Who continued pushing forward, unforgiving of her own frailties. This created a sort of kinship between them, and Aiz became the closest to Bete in all of *Loki Familia*.

*—I hate weak women most of all.*

Those words had become somewhat of a mantra for him at this point, the armor protecting him from the pain of his past.

But they didn't work on Aiz.

On the "Battle Princess," who abandoned herself to combat.

*A woman like her wouldn't…*

Almost subconsciously, Bete felt a kind of hope begin to build up inside him.

Bete had been beaten down by the shortcomings of the weak too many times in the past to put any effort into women. Which was why he refused to let himself grow attached to anyone who wasn't the ideal now.

At some point, watching that girl grow stronger, their fierce competition raging on, became the one joy in his life.

*Loki Familia*'s roster was constantly changing. One year after Bete joined saw the induction of Tiona and Tione and, a year after that, Lefiya. The rambunctious girls were always pestering Aiz, and as time passed, Aiz began to smile more often.

Bete, on the other hand, was not at all happy with this more "mellowed-out" version of Aiz the newcomers were drawing out of her. Even if the changes were good for Aiz herself, Bete could feel the "ideal woman" he'd created in his head start to blur.

He began lashing out, giving the girls grief, first as an extension of his selfish desire but later, simply out of jealousy. And Bete, too, even without realizing it, was starting to lose his edge.

*Accept it.*

*It's not a bad thing.*

*This isn't like before, where you prided yourself as a lone wolf.*

The fang on his cheek, the pain in his chest—they were disappearing. However.

"*—Probably looked as pathetic as you do right now, huh? Like your precious little kitty just died or somethin'?!*"

Valletta's shrill voice rung in his ears.

It wasn't only Leene's face that weighed on his heart. It was Lena's, too.

Bete brought a hand to his cheek, fingers digging into his skin.

"Haaah? Finn and his cronies have set up camp in the sewers, have they?"

Back in the restoration zone of the Pleasure Quarter, a number of figures continued to prowl about the now deserted ruins, melding into the shadows and rain—Valletta and her crew of assassins. They'd set up temporary camp in Belit Babili, the grandest of the quarter's structures. After hearing the news from one of the *Thanatos Familia* patrols, Valletta curled her lip in disgust.

"Yes, ma'am! It seems they also have sentries posted on Daedalus Street…and in Babel Tower."

"That obnoxious little mouse! Should have known he'd already be on top of things…So he plans on keeping us from returning to Knossos? Then…he's after our key?" she mused, pulling out the magic item in question, a small orb engraved with the letter *D*, from her fur-lined overcoat.

True to *Loki Familia*'s hypothesis, Valletta and the rest of her assassins had been using the sewerway beneath the city to move around. It was also how they'd arrived at the Pleasure Quarter, where they'd set up base now. By putting men there, on Daedalus Street and in Babel, they'd effectively cut off every one of their escape routes back to Knossos.

Valletta cursed in annoyance, then gave a voracious smile.

"Then they don't care about all the Amazons we're slicin' to pieces? He-he-he…This is just like during the Twenty-Seventh-Floor Nightmare. How many people you gonna sacrifice, huh, Finn? And all without batting an eye…!"

"Wh-what should we do, Lady Valletta?"

"Oh, don't get your panties in a twist! Thanatos and the rest of his guys are already at work as we speak, gettin' ahold of Levis or whoever. And once that monster shows up, well, Finn can say bye-bye to this little net of his," Valletta responded coolly despite her underlings' growing panic. They simply had to be patient and wait for Levis and the others to cut a hole through *Loki Familia*'s web.

She turned her attention from her fellow Evils to the hired assassins.

"Hey! You guys about done cleanin' things up yet?"

"Yes, ma'am! Our comrades in arms have successfully wounded almost all targets with the cursed weapons. Though some were able to escape due to *Loki Familia*'s intervention, most of their leaders, at least, have been silenced..." the chieftain of the group explained, to which Valletta responded with a wave of her hand.

"Good enough for me."

The number of people aware of the connection Ishtar had with *Thanatos Familia* was few, indeed. And those who knew of the key Ishtar possessed were even fewer—likely only those very close to the goddess. They shouldn't need to worry about any of the remaining Berbera now gathered in Babel.

The only thing Valletta hadn't planned on was *Dian Cecht Familia* or, more specifically, Dea Saint. But it was ridiculous to think that she alone would be able to heal every one of the Amazons wounded by one of Barca's cursed weapons. Which meant that today, almost all the Amazons had been killed—a thought that filled Valletta with sadistic joy.

The sight of her, smiling viciously, was enough to make the rest of the Evils associates tremble.

Valletta Grede.

On the Guild's blacklist now for six years, she bore the alias "Arachnia."

As a member of the Evils, she became intoxicated at the sight of blood, abandoning herself to the very cruelest of pleasures and reportedly responsible for the deaths of more adventurers than anyone else—a natural-born killer. Taking lives, for her, was the ultimate symbol of power, or at least that's what she had asserted to her sworn enemy, Finn, in years past.

The assassins in the room looked on in emotionless silence as she suddenly dropped her smile and lifted her head.

"All that's left is...Vanargand."

"What do you mean...?"

"When we ran into him this morning with that Amazonian brat, he was clearly on his way to the palace. At a time like this? No way that's a coincidence…" she hissed, the cogs clicking into place in her head. "He was definitely looking for the key. In fact, that little minx we killed might very well have given him some kinda clue—*We need to take him down.*"

This announcement set the entire camp abuzz.

"Vanargand probably wouldn't seek help, would he…?"

"As if! No way in hell that blockheaded mutt would go to his familia with his tail between his legs. If he's got his sights set on revenge, he's gonna carry it out himself…I know it. I *am* the one who massacred his cute little friends down in Knossos, after all, *he-he-he-he-he.*"

Adventurers like him were all too easy to read, she added, her smile deepening.

Even if the lone wolf, Vanargand, had any information on that key, he wasn't going to keep it to himself; instead, he'd come straight to Valletta to settle the score. She could practically see him now, veins popping in his eyes as he marched his way toward them.

"All right! I want y'all to do everything you can to find Vanargand—"

But then something interrupted.

The howl of a wolf off in the distance cut off Valletta's words before she could finish.

"…So he's calling *us* out to play, is he?" She laughed, sliding her tongue across her smiling lips.

The sound echoed throughout the entire city, masking even the steady sound of the rain.

Humans and demi-humans looked up in surprise from inside their homes, wondering if they weren't hearing thunder; the Guild members currently out managing the situation came to abrupt halts; and adventurers raced outside, gazes turned toward the sky. Every god in the city knew that *something* had started.

The whole of Orario heard the howl of a wolf.

"Is that…?"

"It couldn't be…!"

Anakity and Raul murmured in surprise, both of them tasked with watching over the Amazons currently housed in Babel Tower.

"He's mad now."

"Aye. I'd reckon there's no stoppin' 'im now."

Loki and Gareth exchanged words from in front of the great white spire, both their eyes turned in the direction of the rain-filled clouds as the werewolf's howl trembled against the sky.

"Lady Riveria! Is that…?!"

"Indeed. That would be Bete…It's started, then, has it?"

Riveria responded to Lefiya's question from within the *Dian Cecht Familia* hospital, one eye closed as she confirmed the sound of Bete's voice.

"Ngh…?!"

Aiz raced forward through the pouring rain in the direction of that lupine shriek, her feet speeding toward the Pleasure Quarter.

"————————————————————————————!!"

And Bete, standing atop the roof of a dilapidated brothel.

Looked toward the night sky, congested with clouds, and howled.

He wanted to make sure those assassins hidden in the darkness knew exactly where he was.

The battle was about to begin.

And this howl, this furious roar of a werewolf, amber eyes red with rage, was its harbinger.

# BATTERED
# WOLF

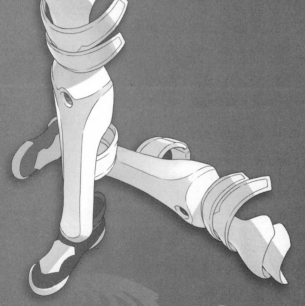

Гэта казка іншага сям'і.

Нядобра-сіняках воў

A scholar once said that there were three reasons why werewolves would howl.

The first was to assert their dominance over the enemy.

The second was to locate fellow companions who'd strayed from the pack.

The third was to strengthen their bond with their own kind, conveying the depths of their souls by calling at the sky.

According to Bete, however, these reasons were dead wrong, entirely missing the mark.

Howling was an oath.

When their throats trembled, they considered it a signal of their own readiness, carved into the heavens themselves.

A promise of absolute will, devouring the sun, devouring the moon, devouring everything as they looked to the sky and the gods gazing down at them and met them eye to eye.

Yes, all you had to do was howl.

No matter what kind of plight you may find yourself in, no matter how much the enemy may beat you down, no matter how much your body may cry out in pain.

Release the courage and the power built up inside you and make that pledge.

You'd grow stronger, faster than the you of a mere one second earlier.

Only then did you have the right to step onto the battlefield.

The oath Bete had made now—was a pledge to hunt.

To stain his claws and fangs a brilliant red.

And he hurled that conviction all the way to the heavens. The shadow-choked sky trembled, almost as though frightened, and even the rain seemed to weaken in response to his call. In the split second of clarity, he saw a golden outline shimmering faintly through the sea of clouds.

Bete's lupine ears shot up straight atop his head, his gray fur standing on end like sharpened needles.

It was time.

They were here. Assassins drawn to his howled oath that was neither a show of force, nor a beacon for lost comrades, nor a shared bond between friends.

They would be prey for his claws and fangs.

He gazed out over the ruined city, amber eyes flashing.

The assassins raced through the streets, melting into the surrounding darkness.

They made not a sound, not even the pittering pat of the rainwater bouncing off their speeding forms, almost like living shadows as they glided forward. Black robes fluttering, they made their way toward the high-rise building sharpening into view between the cracks of the dilapidated brothels, drawn toward the howl of a wolf, still reverberating from atop a roof.

As they approached, they drew cursed weapons from their robes—the sure-kill blades they'd been provided by the Evils. They been promised not only large sums of money for their work but these weapons, as well. More fatal than even the deadliest of poisons, such weapons would likely be beneficial to their familia of underground crime, allowing them to spill blood with even greater ease. Another step in changing the world for the better, or so the assassins believed. Such teachings were drilled into their brainwashed minds since the days of their youth.

The moment they arrived at the complex mesh of back roads, the thirty-something assassins dispersed. They would surround the building where their enemy stood. First-tier adventurer though he was, he could be taken down by only one hit from their cursed weapons, his death inevitable. A few sacrificial explosions of their own would do the trick. As would their synchronicity. And once he was injured, they would attack, as swift and sure as the early-summer rain, taking down the wolf in the process.

Yes, they were certain of their victory. Only...

*...? The howl, it...?*

The unique pitch of the lupine cry seemed to change—and, in an instant, a foreboding chill washed over the group. It was almost as if the wail of searing fury had morphed into a sort of inhuman melody, as cold and merciless as the moon overhead. Those amber eyes seemed to be staring down at each one of them, even though they were scattered among the streets.

All of a sudden, the wolf was gone.

"?!"

And in that moment came an agonized shriek from one of their kin.

Killed. In less than an instant. By a set of fangs plunging onto the ruined streets.

The silent flock of assassins didn't have so much as a chance to tremble in shock before there was another scream, followed by the earsplitting roar of a wolf. Like thunder, it shrieked through the shadow, almost as though the previously hidden wolf was reasserting his presence.

*H-how...?*

How were they supposed to stop him like this?

They needed to see through both sets of eyes: the hunter and the hunted.

The werewolf had the years of experience in his tribe to rely upon, making him a natural-born hunter.

What's more, he had chosen the path of the adventurer in his quest for strength.

But today, just today, Bete had forgone all that, reverting back to his roots and the wild wolf who lived inside him.

*—Their enemy was a true-blooded alpha wolf.*

For the first time, these supposedly emotionless magic bullets, these assassins who were trained to remain calm in even the direst of circumstances, found their breath coming with shudders of horror. The pinpricks on their skin were enough of a warning that this was a hunter more skilled than even them, and that thought gripped them with fear.

"*GrrruuuaaaaaaAAAAARRRRGGGHHH————!!*"

With each kill came another roar.

A show of power. That he, the wolf, was here. And they were next. All of them. It was the howl of a starving wolf who couldn't be stopped.

Their reaction was immediate, all of them moving off on their own either in attempts to apprehend the wolf or to hide themselves from his attacks. But that just made them better targets; the gray-furred wolf was following their every move as though anticipating their actions, and one anguished shriek after another rent the air around them.

The wolf's nose was as keen as ever, seeking them out even through the rain and the residual smells of their fallen companions.

It almost felt like their cursed weapons were an ill omen, the stench of blood simply too strong.

*The others…?!*

As the last scream ripped through the air, the leader of the group realized all too clearly that he was the only one who remained.

He was the one who'd laid the final blow on that Amazonian girl.

As the strongest of the hired assassins at Level 3, he'd thrust his blade in the brat's soft abdomen even after most of his comrades had already fallen at the hand of her resistance. Though he hadn't been able to stay and watch the light fade from her eyes thanks to the wolf running at full speed toward him, he'd been satisfied that they'd finished the job. Another necessary sacrifice to lead them into the new world. What had she said, he'd wondered, in those final moments before her death? Imagining it had left him with a darkened sense of accomplishment.

But now that same cutthroat had gotten himself driven up against a cliff, surrounded on all sides by a sea of blood.

It defied everything he knew. Using the darkness of night to take them out, that was *their* livelihood, what *they* were supposed to excel at, so how had their enemy flipped everything on its head? Just what *was* this wolf? Not an adventurer, not a hunter, no, something else, something much more fiendish, more repulsive.

He didn't even notice the way his hand was shaking, fingers curled around his cursed dagger in a grip of death.

Sometimes, the unknown that so enchanted adventurers brought with it a feeling of excitement.

Other times, it brought nothing but a deeply rooted sense of terror.

The convoluted byroads circling like a labyrinth around him, the assassin chieftain made to escape. But then…

"_____"

His exit was cut short by a hand reaching out from one of the nearby alleyways, gripping him by the neck and pulling him into the darkness.

"_____*Guwaaaagh?!*"

His throat was crushed in an instant, the fingers curling around his windpipe like a jaw snapping shut, and his body was slammed to the ground. He hadn't even had a chance to use his cursed weapon. His shoulder dislocated from the force, he dropped his dagger to the stones below.

Groaning in pain, he tumbled across the street, picking up trash and dirt along the way. Then, his neck trembling in effort, he slowly raised his gaze.

He saw, backdropped by the night sky and cutting a sharpened profile against the landscape of the back alley—the horrifying visage of a wolf.

"Ah…gnnaah…khaaah…?!"

One step, then another, the werewolf approached in complete silence, and the assassin chieftain quickly readied himself to take his own life.

But suddenly, he found that he couldn't. With his crushed throat, he wasn't able to bite open the lethal chemical embedded in his teeth. And with his dislocated shoulder, he wasn't able to so much as grip a weapon.

The wolf's metal boots came down on his cursed dagger, shattering it against the stone.

Then, looking down into the revealed face of the assassin—the werewolf, Bete, spoke.

"Howl for me."

Yes.

That's what he needed to do. Howl.

Howl for the new world to come.

But he couldn't.

And with those amber eyes as vivid and brilliant as the moon, an expression dripping with pure, unbridled bloodlust, Bete plunged the supposedly fearless assassin into the uttermost depths of despair.

All that came from his fractured windpipe was a crackling whisper of dry air, almost like a broken flute.

"If you can't even do that—"

The werewolf raised his arms, fangs gleaming a brilliant crimson red.

And as the assassin experienced true guttural fear for the first time in his life, those claws came flying down at him.

"*—you don't belong on the battlefield!*"

It was at that moment that he blacked out.

"Hey, Finn, did…something happen? To Bete, I mean?" Tiona asked, Urga at her side.

They were down in the Old Sewerway that sprawled out beneath the city. Finn had led a small party there to set up a sort of blockade to keep Valletta and the rest of her group from escaping back into Knossos.

"Like, why he's always going on…callin' people fish bait… chumps…weaklings…Makin' fun of people and stuff?"

"Tiona…" her sister, Tione, murmured as she, the captain, and the rest of the group turned toward the younger Amazon at her question.

Tiona had long been intrigued by why Bete acted the way he did, ever since she'd first met him, actually. But it was only now that she was finally trying to get an answer about her constant debate partner.

As she and the rest of the group turned toward Finn, the prum captain stood in silence before finally throwing them a glance.

"...Bete doesn't talk about himself much. Not even I know if something happened in his past," he started, eyes turning in the direction of the flowing water underfoot, almost as though looking far, far beyond the sewer itself. "So what I can offer is only conjecture..."

"He's unbelievably socially inept."

Back in *Dian Cecht Familia*'s hospital.

Riveria stared out the window at the slowly receding rain as she responded to the question posed by Lefiya and the other elves.

"Socially...inept?"

"Indeed. Disastrously so," Riveria confirmed with a soft sigh. "Everything that boy says, the scorn, the ridicule, the extreme threads of logic he follows—he's only trying to motivate people. To spur them on in the only way he knows how."

"Oh..."

The words brought a memory to Lefiya's mind.

When she, Filvis, and Bete had been about to storm the twenty-fourth floor's pantry, Bete had criticized her again and again and again, saying the young elf constantly required protection from the wolf.

*You satisfied like this? Havin' to count on others 'cause you can't protect yourself?*

*As long as your magic's the only useful thing you got, you'll never be anything more than baggage.*

*You are soft.*

She remembered how crestfallen she'd felt, biting her lip and pushing on in spite of his words. But then, he'd yelled *that*:

*Don't admire the old hag, surpass her!*

"Surpass Riveria Ljos Alf." That's what he'd told her.

That hadn't been mere encouragement. That had been the true spirit of a wolf starved for power. Constantly irritated by the weaklings surrounding him, he tried to push them to stand up for themselves.

"Bete's words go far beyond what's necessary. Harsh to the point of antipathy. Or perhaps…he believes that the only way to push others past their limits *is* to hurt them," Riveria continued, eliciting surprise from the other elves, including Lefiya, just returning from the sea of her memories. "It got to the point once where Finn, Gareth, and I were forced to call him in for a talk. Though, thanks to Loki's 'help,' there was a bit too much alcohol involved…" the high elf recalled, amusement dancing in her jade-colored eyes as though watching the scene play out in her mind.

"—*When yer strong, you've gotta pick yerself back up no matter what happens. Someone spat in your face? Someone humiliated you? Someone stole somethin' from you? You get right back up!*"

They'd refused to let Bete leave the room until he explained the reasoning behind his constant berating of others, and after a few of his usual exchanges of blows with Gareth, he'd finally opened up, ignoring the wounds he'd incurred and gulping down his drink.

"*Because that's what it takes. You've gotta lose someone. You've gotta lose a part of yourself. You've gotta make a mistake…You've gotta get to the point where you can't forgive yourself. Only then do the strong change,*" he'd continued, slamming his glass down on the table to the surprised shock of Riveria and the others. "*But the weak will always be weak! No matter what happens, those failures just sit there and yuk it up! They'll always be weak—always!! Living trash until the day they get torn to pieces!!*"

The eyes of Lefiya and the other elves widened as Riveria relayed the wolf's words. At the same time, they realized the mistake they'd made.

Bete's unruly conduct, his heavy-handed principles of meritocracy, had been nothing more than the ultimate shakedown. A ritual for digging up and forcing adventurers to face the wounds of their past. An awakening that would send them upward.

They were words of abusive encouragement that would kick the truly weak to the side.

An inhuman, arrogant, and cruel divider of the strong from the weak.

A special privilege that, according to him, could be bequeathed only by the strong.

"...But there...there must have been a better way of doing that! What he does goes far beyond 'socially inept'! Not everyone is... going to have that...strong of a spirit..." Alicia asserted.

A Level 4 in *Loki Familia*'s reserve crew, she'd likely hit a wall in her abilities herself; she was forced to swallow her tears and keep pushing forward no matter how her heart threatened to break. Lefiya, too, found it hard to condone Bete's harsh criticism. Riveria, however, simply nodded.

"Indeed. You're right about that, Alicia...But there is more than that behind his actions. He also greatly dislikes...when those whom he refers to as 'weaklings' take the field, so to speak."

He wanted to ensure only those with the proper qualifications joined the fight, she explained.

And at least to Bete, he'd already come up with the solution.

The high elf's thin voice, laden with pity, faded into the rain outside the window.

"Would you like to know what he said...? When I criticized him for pushing his own values on others?" she asked with a sad smile, the Bete in her memories playing out across her eyes.

*"You gonna say the same thing once they're dead, huh?*

*"You'd rather they end up dead than get their 'feelings' hurt, huh?*

*"It'll be too late once they're ripped to pieces!!"*

Even Bete knew just how tactless he was.

*"RuuuuuuuaaaaaaaAAAARRRRRGGGGHHH!!"*

Letting out a mighty roar, he went from assassin to assassin, his attacks a ceaseless rampage. Kicking, clawing, mauling, he allowed his rage to carry him, not stopping until every shadowy figure in the restoration zone was nullified.

And at the forefront of his mind throughout every swipe of his limbs were the images of his past. The faces of every adventurer he'd seen die before his eyes, Leene and Lena included.

He couldn't stop screaming.

Why?

Why did they have to be so weak?

Why did they have to *stay* so weak?

Why didn't they try to get stronger?

How could they sit there, laughing, in a world where only the strongest survived?

Why, when such a cruel fate awaited them, didn't they—?

The despair and anguish were taking control of him now. Bete had been beaten down by the weak for too long, and there was only one solution in his mind.

He had to train, become even stronger, and protect them.

He wouldn't lose anyone. Never again.

But even that was just something he told himself.

Because no matter how strong he became, no matter how hard he tried to protect them, the weak still slipped through his fingers, as impossible to hold on to as a fistful of sand.

That left him with only one choice—he had to push them away.

He ridiculed them, laughed at them, hurt them.

The only ones allowed on the battlefield were those who could howl back at scorn of the strong.

The weak had to be able to howl.

If not, if they couldn't change—their corpses would only keep piling up.

Like his father. Like his mother. Like his sister. Like his childhood friend. Like *her*.

Like the kindhearted nurse who'd healed his wounds.

Like that Amazonian girl.

And so Bete would keep screaming.

He would keep scoffing, taunting, deriding any weaklings who tried to set foot on the battlefield.

"He...just didn't want anyone to die?" Tiona asked, half in shock, after hearing Finn's response.

"What an idiot! As if he can just keep that from happening!" Tione cut in almost instantly, her voice ringing off the walls of the sewer.

If that was the case, then it was Tiona and Tione who were the disillusioned ones when it came to death. The two who had taken more lives than they could count within the prison located in their home country of Telskyura, and who had since then been protecting this two-person world they shared.

As the rest of the party stared on in bewildered astonishment, Tione couldn't hide her anger. "I mean, really! How the hell does he think he's gonna be able to protect everyone, huh? Even people he doesn't even know!"

"No…I don't believe that's what he's trying to do," came Finn's soft response. And as Tiona, Tione, and the rest of the group looked toward him curiously, a wry smile formed on his face. "Quite the opposite. The reason he can't stop his abusive tirades is more…"

"…selfish, I would say. And not just a little bit, either."

Loki mused with a smile identical to Finn's.

She was on the first floor of Babel Tower, the large, circular hall bordered by countless doors. Around her, the members of *Loki Familia* who had been tasked with guarding the Amazons through the night—Raul, Anakity, and the others—attempted to deduce the true meaning behind her words.

"What do you mean by…selfish?" Raul asked.

"Whenever the lad sees someone weak by his standards, he catches a glimpse of his own past…and his former self. It ticks him off, ye might say," Gareth, who had been put in charge of the Babel task force, responded with a stroke of his beard. He'd traded blows with Bete more often than anyone else in all of *Loki Familia*, which was what gave him the authority to surmise what even Bete couldn't bring himself to say.

"Ticks…him off…?" Aki repeated dejectedly.

"What? Ye didn't take him as the charitable sort, did ye? As if! It's as Loki just said. The boy's own lack of social skills makes him all the more contentious," Gareth continued, tossing the catgirl a smile. But the smile quickly disappeared as he looked toward the door.

The far-off howl of a werewolf came trickling in once again from far away.

"Nay...that lad hasn't changed a wee bit since the moment I met him..." he murmured.

*Even in a group, weaklings are still weaklings.*
*Living as a weakling means having everything stolen from you, leaving you to blubber and snivel your life away.*
*I'm not gonna be like that. And I'm not gonna let anyone around me be like that, either.*
*So shut up with your whimpering and your moaning and your crying.*

They were words that had been echoing in Bete's heart for as long as he could remember. Even now, as he raced throughout those dark alleyways, they continued. Whether they were simply random memories or regret at the women in his life he'd let die, he didn't know.

"...Even that rabbit brat stood his ground."

The words left his mouth before he even realized it.

A murmur melting into the pouring rain.

He remembered that night and the adventurer he'd ridiculed while drunk as a skunk.

And how that boy hadn't liked to be called weak.

It was that tiny thought that had brought the boy to tears, made him rise to his feet and throw off the shackles of his weakness.

That fight against the minotaur had shaken Bete to his core. Ashamed of himself, incensed that he could be losing to a chump like him—and yet, though he hated to admit it, a little excited, as well.

That was the first time in his life Bete had found himself in awe of someone weaker than him. It was almost like he'd been waiting for him, for that gallant figure to come into his life.

Because even Bete understood.

Not everyone could become a warrior. Not everyone could become an adventurer.

They couldn't be Aiz and the others. They couldn't be that boy.

And yet, in spite of all that, Bete couldn't bring himself to abide weakness.

To stay weak was a sin. Evil, almost. To sit around laughing and smiling, then to weep, collapse, bawl, and scream every time they lost something. Bete hated those screams most of all. And he refused to accept them, the same as he refused to accept the young wolf from his past.

He'd heard so many screams by this point. Too many.

They needed to go away.

And if they weren't prepared to do that, he'd make them.

Shameful powerless chumps like them didn't deserve to live.

The battlefield recognized none but the strong—.

"It seems to me…that Bete just can't give 'em up. That's why he keeps on scoffin' and ridiculin' 'em," Loki mused as the rest of the group looked on in silence. Though she might have been over-thinking things, there was something about her voice that made it hard to doubt her theory. "Then, when they don't change, he gets pissed. Starts fights. Even though it'd be much easier on him to just let it be."

This claim shocked Raul and the other onlookers.

Certainly, Bete's tirades never stopped. Picking on them, tossing insults—never once did he take a break from giving them a hard time. So if what Loki was saying was true…

Then his actions were really just a completely maladroit form of encouragement.

Acrimonious cheerleading that even Bete himself hadn't realized he'd been doing.

"Why didn't you tell us this sooner?" Raul asked, tears welling up in his eyes thanks to this glimpse into Bete's soul. "Then, he was doing the same for Leene and the others? Telling them…Telling them that even after they're reborn, whoever, whatever they are, that he doesn't want to lose them again…?!"

Hearing this was enough to make the animal person Cruz and the human Narfi hang their heads in shame. Even Aki had her gaze pointed at the ground, lip between her teeth.

Bete had always pushed the weak away. Even when looking after his own companions, he was nothing but himself, to the point of violence. Almost as if that was the only thing he knew.

As Raul and the others pressed Loki for an answer, she merely shook her head softly.

"Because you wouldn't have understood," she murmured, lips pursed almost morosely. "No matter how much we may say we get 'im, none of us ever will. Hell, Bete himself prolly doesn't understand."

"What's more, that lad's philosophy'd be naught but a nuisance to most others, aye?…The whole negative-over-positive-reinforcement schtick," Gareth continued.

Loki raised her head. "Havin' said that, there is one thing for certain…" she started, almost to herself, as she made her way over to the door to look up at the night sky laden with tears.

"That fang of his isn't a fang at all. It's——…"

—The fang on his cheek was throbbing.

Burning, scorching, almost as though it were crying tears of blood.

*"Goddammit…!!"*

Hand against his cheek, he ran, abandoning all other thoughts as he pushed himself faster and faster.

Reinforcements had arrived, and as they came screaming at him, he launched them into the wall, one by one. The blood burst like geysers from their mouths and painted him and his fang a sanguine red.

*"Have you figured out what that fang of yours means, Bete?"*

Loki had asked him earlier.

But Bete had already figured that out long, long ago.

Its true form was so obvious.

Bete's fang wasn't a fang at all.

It was a scar.

Beneath that lightning bolt–shaped tattoo on his cheek was the scar that had started all this. The very first wound he'd ever received, when he'd first learned about this dog-eat-dog world of cruelty and had been beaten down by it, that he'd carved into this form on his face.

The fang that his father had long taught him to polish had cracked long ago.

And now that wound was proof of his weakness.

His fang, his strength, was nothing but a disguise.

Strength and weakness combined to form that un-healing scar. The proof of his origins, carved right within his own starving body. A blood oath he'd made to himself, that he would devour the strong and press ever forward.

Every time Bete felt his own weakness, he grew stronger.

When he lost his family, his sister, his childhood friend, *her*, his companions.

Each one of those times, Bete had cried—howled.

And then he'd rid himself of that weak flesh and devoured new strength.

His wounds tormented him, chiseled him, carved away at the weaknesses in his body. And with every person he lost, they grew. The blood spilled became his strength, and the Bete of the past hadn't even noticed.

He was a wolf sewn from wounds.

A powerful being built from the lives of the weak he'd abandoned.

"Grrruuuaaagh!"

"Ghngh…! *Urrraaaagh!!*"

He repelled an incoming strike with his armguard. Sparks flying, he sent the soft body of his attacker flying with a single punch. Again and again, his hands, claws, and fangs were painted with blood only to be washed clean by the pouring rain.

Bete's fang couldn't protect anyone.

Bete's fang knew nothing but pain and suffering.

Bete was capable of nothing but inflicting pain. His strength was nothing but a sham.

But still he would continue to bare his fang of lies, the wounds beneath it piling ever higher.

Hurting himself, hurting others, all because he refused to accept their weakness.

Howling at the weak, devouring the strong.

Until that gaping jaw of his was finally ripped from his face.

*"Protect that jaw of yours—and that fang—at all costs, yes?"*

Víðarr had been right.

Bete could do nothing but inflict pain. He could do nothing but howl.

Nothing but push people away. Nothing but gripe, complain, and demand.

*Weaklings should all just disappear!*

*Doesn't it annoy you, too?!*

*Howl, why don't you?!*

All he could do was wait for the howl of the weak.

"RUUUUUUUAAAAARRRRRRRRRRRGGGGGHHHHHHH!!"

Heart and throat trembling, Bete roared.


"Bete…"

Aiz's feet came to a stop at the sound of that lonely howl.

*"You're strong. That's all that matters, so…don't you change."*

All of a sudden, the meaning behind those words Bete had told her so long ago became clear.

He'd been baring a part of his heart to her, the way he might to a sister, to a lover, desperate not to lose someone else. A bumbling, graceless plea from a bumbling, graceless wolf.

Aiz stood there in front of the restricted restoration zone of the Pleasure Quarter and simply listened to that echoing cry.

Even the heavy rain was starting to wane, almost as though it had no tears left to shed.

"All of them…gone? That damn Vanargand. And even with the effects of the curse keepin' him from healing all the way…He's somethin' else."

The Evils base in Belit Babili was in an uproar.

None of the assassins who had been dispatched to take care of Bete had returned. Even the continuous lupine howl had faded into the shadows, as though signaling the subjugation of his prey.

But Valletta was undaunted, still wearing her ever-present smile as she gazed out across the shadow-strewn ruins of the Pleasure Quarter from the top floor of the palace.

"That lone wolf is even more riled up than I expected. If I don't get my act together, Mister Big Bad Wolf's gonna have that revenge of his after all."

"L-Lady Valletta! We've completely run out of assassins! Wh-what should we do?!"

"Oh, stop being such a pussy! Clearly, runnin' straight into his territory was a bad idea. So what do we do? We simply invite him over here, yes?" she hissed at the obviously flustered *Thanatos Familia* flunky next to her. Turning toward the group of robe-clad men, she jerked her chin toward the restoration zone outside the window.

"I really ruffled his fur back there. That guy wants us dead, and he wants to be the one to do it. We lure him over here and he'll come whether he wants to or not…He's really gone off his rocker this time, which gives us the advantage," Valletta explained coolly, despite the fact that most of her playing pieces were gone.

The countless battles she'd already survived as an elite member of the Evils had given her a keen eye when it came to strategy like this. And what's more, the power she wielded as a Level 5 was enough to place her among even Orario's leading adventurers. There was no doubt about it—this villainous woman who'd gone up against Braver and the rest of his crew time and time again was one of the strong.

"We might not have a lot of curse casters left, but we've got cursed weapons and magic swords comin' out of our ears, don't we?"

"Y-yes, ma'am…" the man replied with a nod.

Valletta smiled. "Then I'm gonna send us out a little invite. Get the party ready, boys. Only instead of cake, I wanna see as many traps as those little heads of yours can devise."

*They've stopped coming...*

Bete thought as he downed one of Loki's high potions, currently hidden within the darkness of the backstreets. Wiping his chin once it was gone, he tossed the empty vial onto the stone. His amber eyes narrowed in thought.

*They run outta guys? There's no way. I haven't seen that woman make an appearance yet. But I still don't know where they're comin' from. Do I howl again? See if more come runnin'...?*

Perhaps out of some sort of pride at their shadow-born lineage, the assassins had refused to give away any information on their allies, terrified as they were. Despite the unceasing sensation of fiery red constantly pulsating through his body, Bete figured he might as well try, so he slipped out from the safety of the shadows and back onto the streets.

Crumbling buildings, abandoned weapons and strewn shards of the same, burned rubble.

Racing past debris that looked straight out of a city of ruins, he set his sights on the tallest building in the district...when all of a sudden, he noticed something underfoot.

"..."

It was a trail of blood.

A snakelike red path, almost as though someone had been dragging a body.

It was very clearly deliberately placed to lead him somewhere, continuing on down the street. Bete stared at it in silence for a moment, then took off.

Corner after corner he turned, the trail of blood leading him down the convoluted web of streets.

"This handwriting..." he murmured, looking at a piece of scrap building material that was resting beneath an overhanging archway. On the side of the stone block was a message written in red.

*Come to the palace, Vanargand! We're so looking forward to welcoming you!*

He pored over the blood-scrawled Koine, the "paint" likely coming from the corpse of the assassin slumped against the nearby wall.

Perhaps by shoving a cloth of some sort in his open wound and using it as a paintbrush? But the light was already gone from the battered corpse's eyes, and bloody rivulets streaked from its multitude of lacerations. Bete didn't throw more than a glance at it, instead simply staring at the personalized invitation.

He recognized this hastily drawn scrawl.

It was the same as the one written on the walls of Knossos when they'd found Leene and the others dead.

Bete clenched his fist so hard it shook, and then he was off, leaping atop the roof of a nearby brothel. His eyes went to *Ishtar Familia*'s home, the great palace towering tall and proud above the darkness of the crowded buildings.

Then, with a sudden jerk, he looked straight up.

The rain had come to a stop. And through the swath of dark clouds, the dim blue of the sky above was peeking out. The moon, however, was still hidden behind the sea of gray.

With one last silent look, Bete hopped down from the roof and set his sights on Belit Babili.

He arrived at his destination without a hitch, not even having bothered to stay on his guard during the trip. Now that he was standing so close to Belit Babili, it was hard for him to deny its majesty, even though it was crumbling after *Freya Familia*'s attack. It boasted all the grandeur and prestige of a royal desert palace, not a single celch of it lacking in luxurious extravagance, right down to the finely chiseled lions gracing its many columns. The cracked golden facade covering the entire building was a symbol of both opulence and decay. And across the circular garden guarding the palace's entryway stood a colossal door, the familia's emblem—a veiled courtesan, currently missing entire chunks of stone from her face—looking down from on high.

Paying none of this any heed, Bete charged straight past the damaged remnants and into the palace proper.

He was greeted by a grand elephantine hall of white marble, also in a state of disarray. Though the hallways visible all the way up to the ceiling many floors overhead seemed nigh uncountable, Bete didn't even have a chance to get lost. No, a red carpet had already been laid out in preparation for his arrival.

Not one of cloth—but one of blood.

"Well, isn't this artsy-fartsy..." Bete mumbled, his brows furrowing as he followed the trail of blood. It took him down a long hallway, then down the stairs past a hidden door that had already been opened for him. He sped along in silence, the air around him growing colder and colder.

Upon reaching the bottom of the stairs, he passed by the crumpled corpse of an assassin, then followed the path until he reached an enormous underground hall, not altogether dissimilar to the one he'd just left at the palace's entrance.

Tall, broad columns lined the open space on either side, supporting the ceiling more than ten meders overhead and almost reminiscent of the underground sewers he'd infiltrated with Loki a while back. Magic-stone lanterns, too, were fastened sporadically across the rows of columns, giving the space an ethereal glow.

An underground chamber of this size...Had Ishtar been planning to keep some sort of monstrous pet?

"——I knew you'd come, Vanargand," came the sudden voice, almost unimaginably loud as Bete scanned his environs. Then she appeared, fur-lined overcoat flapping as she stepped out from the shadow of a pillar about eighty meders in front of him and smack-dab in the center of the hall.

"You bitch..."

"And you came alone, too; how wonderful! Can't teach an old dog new tricks, I suppose. Your kind is as easy to read as ever!" Valletta jeered, belting out a laugh and ignoring the murderous look in the werewolf's eyes. Her fingers were curled around the grip of a one-handed sword—a cursed weapon, no doubt. She raised it now to the height of her chest, thrusting it in Bete's direction as she continued to push at his every button with endless joy.

"The two of us know each other *far* too well to need pleasantries at this point. Besides, I wouldn't want any of your little friends poking their dirty noses into our business. And the way I see it, you wouldn't, either."

"..."

"Come on, then!"

Now that the prologue was out of the way, Bete's eyes flashed with a sharpened glint.

He could already sense the presence of the ten-, twenty-some assailants hiding in the shadows of the surrounding pillars. This was a trap; that much was for sure. But none of that mattered to Bete. Not now. He was ready to kill, no matter how many enemies came at him.

Fury coursing through his veins, he took a step forward. But...

"?!"

That's when he noticed it.

*What's...?*

The stone floor was ever so faintly glowing, myriad geometric shapes shimmering faintly on the surface. They were a reddish-purple color, just about masked completely in the amaranthine phosphorescence of the magic-stone lanterns lighting the room. And they covered the entire length of the room, each one of them 120 or so meders across.

The round shapes seemed to center around Valletta in the middle of the room.

Bete narrowed his eyes.

"What's wrong, Level Six? Don't tell me you're scared! You wouldn't run away with your tail between your legs now of all times, would you?"

True enough, Bete didn't have much choice in the matter now.

Was it magic? A curse? Or something else entirely?

At this point, though, he didn't really care. This hungry wolf had only one thing on his mind: killing and eating his prey.

He stepped forward, metal boots landing in the range of the reddish-purple circles.

"——He-he-he!"

With one grin from Valletta, the battle began.

Bete shot forward, kicking up and off the stone.

Only for Valletta to leap to the side, dashing back into the shadows of the columns to escape.

*What, you don't wanna play?*

Bete hissed as he raced after Valletta, who was now making use of the entire width of the underground chamber to duck and dodge away from the wolf. She let out an even louder guffaw, and though Bete knew she was trying to goad him on, he couldn't stop the anger from bubbling up inside him. Column after column he smashed in his pursuit as the woman cackled in glee.

It was like he was stuck in an endless loop. Though clearly the faster of the two, he realized that no matter how many times he tried to attack, one of her *Thanatos Familia* goons was always there to block him.

The rosy glow of the magic-stone lanterns overhead. The reddish-purple haze of the patterns underfoot. Together, they made for an ethereal, otherworldly ambience, and in the midst of that world of color, Bete's face twisted in increasing irritation.

"Don't let him touch me, you worthless pieces of scum! Ha… *Bwa-ha-ha-ha-ha!!*"

Again and again, they leaped from the shadows, the obedient servants protecting their mad queen.

It was a deadly game of cat and mouse. Or hide-and-seek, perhaps, only this hider was having the time of her life shooting blades at the seeker.

Valletta's features seemed to glow red in the light emanating up from the floor.

"———*GruuuuuaaaaaAAAARRRRGGGHHHHHH!!*"

"Gngh?!"

Bete let out a roar as he suddenly charged forward, his fist just barely missing Valletta's throat. The force, however, was enough to carve clean through the stone floor, and the gust of wind it created was more than capable of launching her into the air.

She tumbled backward, forced to thrust her sword into the ground like a staff to slow her slide and pull herself back up to her feet.

"Shoulda known...gettin' too close to you was a bad idea..." she hissed, her ever-present provocative smile still on her lips as she brushed the dust from her cheeks. At the same time, another group of attackers rushed forward to meet him, and Bete grimaced.

*I missed?! Goddammit!*

Bete cursed himself and his own missed opportunity. She was only a Level 5. He should have been able to take her down easily. Was his own rage hindering his movements?

He scowled, throwing himself at the incoming enemies. Limbs flying, he aimed punch after kick at the clingy gnats, decorating the underground hall with their blood.

Then, he set his sights back on Valletta, who herself had already put some distance between them.

Next time. Next time he'd have her for sure. And with that oath, his amber eyes ran red with murderous resolve.

There weren't any traps, or at least none that he could sense immediately. *Just try and dodge me now*, he raged, the maddened fire inside him building into an inferno.

Only—there was one thing wrong with that thought.

Valletta's trump card was already in place—and had been for some time.

"___"

The first thing that clued him in was the sudden change in light.

Then, her followers, the *Thanatos Familia* disciples he'd already blown away, began gradually, ever so slowly, catching up with him. Tears and blood streaming down their cheeks, they pointed their cursed blades at the werewolf, faces half-crazed.

It was so strange.

They were somehow speeding up.

Or no.

Not even that——

"*He-he-he.*"

It was so faint at the beginning, Bete himself hadn't even noticed it.

"*He-he-he-he-he.*"

But it was becoming clearer and clearer as time went on.

"He-he-he-he-he-he-he-he."

As Valletta's smile grew in voracious amusement, Bete's movements began to slow, and he finally became aware of just what was happening.

*What's...going on?*

His limbs felt heavy.

Like his whole body was made of lead.

It wasn't that the enemies were moving faster. No, quite the opposite.

*Bete* was the one who was moving slower—laughably so. Hilariously so.

"Took damn well long enough——but now, the time has come!"

Just as Valletta's spit reached the ground...

The enemies' attacks began to hit.

"Gngh!"

It came from the back first, a light scratch that left him briefly in shock.

Though the gash itself wasn't deep, the searing pain of the curse made his fur stand on end, and with a quick half spin, he sent his elbow into the jaw of the offending assailant. They swept toward him in constant waves, sending up panicked wails as their swords came flying—a fierce retaliation, as though avenging their fallen comrades.

Bete repelled what incoming cursed blades he could, but his movements were so sluggish. *Too* sluggish. He couldn't respond fast enough. His body could no longer keep up with the rapid-fire perception of his first-tier-adventurer mind.

He was evading less and less, forced to defend more and more.

*This...!*

Bete could sense it now.

The strange change that had befallen his body.

His *movements themselves were being restrained* at an accelerating speed.

"How ya feelin' there, Vanargand?"

"?!"

As Bete barely managed to leap away from an enemy attack, he felt Valletta's sickly sweet breath directly on his cheek. How had he allowed her to get so close? Only a second ago, she'd been running away from *him*! He hurled his fist like a bolt of lightning at that vicious smile, only for Valletta to quickly duck out of the way.

Her eyes flashed as she activated the blades on her boots, sending out her leg in a high-speed horizontal kick.

"Hrraaauugh!!"

"Gngh?!"

The two strikes landed direct hits on his Frosvirt, shattering not only a section of their armor but the inlaid yellow jewels, as well. With their core gone, the mythril Superiors fell silent.

"You don't think I know about your nasty old magic-sucking boots, huh?!" Valletta laughed, moving like an acrobat as she directed a kick toward his upper body while standing on her head. When her leg struck his armguard, she used the recoil to jump back, reclaiming the distance between them.

Bete, meanwhile, now completely robbed of his weapon and power, stumbled backward.

Losing his Frosvirt was bad, for sure, but his biggest problem now was still the overwhelming weight slowing down his body. It seemed like every second that passed saw his reaction time worsening. No, his power, too.

He threw a glance first at the cracked jewels on his boots, then at his arms and legs, and finally, down at the still-glowing reddish-purple pattern decorating the floor.

*The more I move, the worse it gets. That thing must be lowering my Status...!*

"Took you long enough to realize, you great big galoot!" Valletta called out, her voice only adding to the already building panic in his gut. "Let me introduce you to my own special brand of magic!"

"!"

"I call it Shaldo! I suppose you could call it a type of...barrier magic," she explained, her voice reverberating through the underground hall as the attacks on Bete came to a momentary halt.

Almost as though responding to her call, the geometric patterns on the floor seemed to glow even brighter.

"But this magic isn't a barrier at all. What's more, it has an annoyingly long chant, and it dissipates the moment I step outside it. Not even that useful in real combat, either, given how much Mind it zaps. Damn thing!" she ranted, clearly irritated at the one magic spell she possessed. "However," she started again, lips curling upward. "It's perfect for a trap. Even more so for catching impudent little beasties who can't rein in their own rage!"

"Ngh…!"

"As you might have guessed already, Shaldo is a Status Down spell. It saps the power and speed of any uninvited guest who steps inside…And the more they move around, *the worse it gets.*"

Whether she simply had time to spare or was enjoying this opportunity to bestow his death sentence, Bete wasn't sure, but Valletta gave him all the details about the features of her spell. Listening to it, however, made the color drain from his face.

A type of anti-Status Magic, then, but one that didn't require repeated castings, able to continuously drop an opponent's Status all by itself—rare magic, for sure. And if the chant really was as long as she said, its power had to be massive, with no way to break it aside from Valletta's previously revealed conditions. It seemed that no matter how many of them there were inside it—one, ten, even a hundred—all of them would have their Statuses lowered by this super-wide-range spell.

"The more you scuttle around, the tighter the invisible strings of my magic!"

Everything inside the reddish-purple circle.

Was Valletta's castle. Her prison.

In other words…

"That's right, my little flea. I'm the spider…and you've walked straight into my web!"

Bete's eyes widened in shock.

"There's no running away now, Vanargand! You've been rampaging about so much already, the threads of my web are already alllllll over you!"

It was true.

Bete's Status had dropped so low by this point, he'd breached the level threshold. If he had to guess, he was down to a Level 4 already, which was perilously low. What's more, Valletta had slowly lured him straight into the center of the barrier. Even if he used every ounce of strength he had left to try and escape, who knew how many attacks he'd have to fend off before he made it to the edge? And with every block, every dodge, his Status would plunge even further.

The frenzied wolf had truly fallen straight into her trap.

"Now then…let's play! Ready yourselves, my inept minions!!"

As the strident command echoed off the walls, the rest of the Evils materialized from the shadowy expanse behind the columns. Every single one of them—wielded a magic sword.

"_____"

Time came to a halt.

Then Valletta's voice rang out again, and in one simultaneous sweep of their swords came an explosive wave of fire.

"_____—Gngh?!"

First flames, then lightning, then ice, they bombarded him with all variety of magic attacks. Like rain, the barrage fell upon him from all sides, and though Bete was able to dodge the raging hurricane thanks to his unparalleled dynamic vision and motor reflexes, the brilliance of those same abilities was already rapidly fading. And thanks to his broken Frosvirt, he couldn't absorb the magic, either.

The second shadow Valletta had painted across the floor—her Shaldo—had him in its icy grip.

It was even worse than a curse. A permanent set of chains that had been wrapped around his entire body. He truly felt like a flea caught in a spider's web. The more he struggled, the more those threads wrapped around him.

Just like the spider's prey, left to await its inevitable end at the hands of a ghastly predator.

"Ngh?!"

One of the magic blasts finally hit its mark as Bete attempted to flee the barrier.

It was a direct hit, dyeing Bete's vision a fiery red.

"Gnghaaah!!" he screamed, the pained cry torn from his throat.

"Just die already!" Valletta shouted, a sadistic smile on her face as another simultaneous blast came flying at him.

"*Nnggaauuugh——*"

The wolf's shadow flickered in the midst of the blinding flash.

"*Again!*"

Like heralds of death, the *Thanatos Familia* servants raised their voices, sending forth another murky stream of light in an attempt to bring the giant werewolf to his knees.

They went through magic sword after magic sword as they rushed, half-frenzied, to carry out Valletta's orders; as soon as one sword broke, they simply grabbed another one and chipped away piece by piece at Bete's frame.

Not even the spilled blood on the floor could withstand the attack, evaporating in the brilliant gleam as the entire chamber thrummed with the building waves of colossal magic power. It became a veritable concerto of light, with Valletta holding the conductor's baton.

"*He-he-he-he-he-he-he-he-he-he-he!* Kill him! *Kill him!!* Kill the little *Loki Familia* hotshot! And then? I'm coming after you, Finn!!" Valletta squealed, practically climaxing at the scene of absolute liquidation in front of her.

Beneath her feet, Shaldo gave its own flash of euphoric light, almost as though joining her in riotous laughter.

"This..."

Back aboveground in the Pleasure Quarter's restoration zone.

Aiz had just happened upon the very same message that had led Bete to Belit Babili.

"*Come to the palace...Vanargand...*" She slowly read aloud the bloodred Koine words on the piece of stone beneath the archway. She'd caught sight of the trail of blood almost immediately upon entering the war-torn district of brothels and had followed it to this spot posthaste.

She threw a concerned glance in the direction of the abandoned assassin corpse, then made to leave, prepared to follow the clue and find Bete. Except...

"Hn...?!"

A sudden vibration underfoot brought her to a halt.

It was faint, almost like an earthquake. And while it wasn't strong enough to throw her off-balance, the intermittent shock waves that followed were enough to clue her in to the fact that something wasn't right.

Kneeling down, she pressed her hand to the ground.

The rumbling against her palm made for a sort of haphazard melody, almost as though a great many bombs were going off underneath the earth's surface.

"It's coming from...underground...? No!" With a start, she realized what was going on. Her head popped upward, and she took off in a flash.

Kicking off first from the ground, then the walls, she leaped free of the streets and onto the roofs of the surrounding brothels. She raced ever forward, row after row of shingles beneath her feet and the shadowy visage of Belit Babili, standing tall and solemn, in her sights.

Making a beeline toward that towering palace, she ran, moving among the rain-swept slopes and dilapidated crags of the buildings below.

The cacophony of explosions continued in the underground chamber, so numerous that Bete had lost track of them.

"Grrugh...Gah...!"

Smoke fizzled from his skin; Bete himself was only just managing to keep from collapsing to the floor as globules of scorched, congealed blood dropped from the wounds now littering his body.

"Tenacious little bastard, aren't ya?" Valletta hissed, the depraved delight momentarily fading beneath her furrowed brows at the sight of Bete still standing.

It didn't last long, though—that unforgiving smile of hers returned within seconds.

*But this is the end, Vanargand. Once my Shaldo's got its grip on you, it never lets go.*

Even now, the wolf's entire body was being bound tighter and tighter by the invisible threads of her masterpiece glowing underfoot, not only sapping his Status but completely inhibiting his escape, as well.

*One quick stab from a cursed weapon'd end this right quick...But why take the risk? There's no need to get that close. Even as he is now, one misstep could see his teeth in my neck!*

Yes, there was no need to rush things. Not anymore. Better to just keep on doing what she was doing, chipping away at his life bit by bit from afar.

He was much too wounded to make any attempt at escaping now, after all.

*And it's a good thing I lured him down here, too. Don't wanna risk his going all beast mode on me...No, there's nothing Vanargand can do to turn the tables now.*

The biggest risk one took confronting a werewolf on the surface was their transforming under the light of the moon. And once that happened, they were said to possess power far greater than that of any other species.

The rain may have stopped up above, but they were safe below the surface, where not even the slightest trace of moonlight could filter through.

Valletta let out a loud peal of laughter, completely assured of her coming victory. Hearing this was enough to bring smiles to the faces of her minions, as well. For them to take down a first-tier adventurer, after all, would be a major step toward attaining their life's greatest desires.

Seduced by thoughts of joy, excitement, and an appetite for destruction, they released yet another salvo at the already crippled werewolf.

"...Tsk."

Bete grimaced through the bolts of lightning, shards of ice, and flaming embers as they formed a whirlwind around him. He clenched his hand into a fist, muscles practically shaking from the sheer fury rushing through him.

"Dammit...dammit...*dammit*...DAMMIT!" he groaned, teeth grinding against one another.

He was angry with himself. With Valletta and her men. With the world. The fang on his cheek felt like it was on fire, the pain buried inside begging to break free.

His world was red.

The anger had taken control.

He cursed the world. Cursed fate. Cursed reason.

A white heat overtook his vision. His thoughts were a raging, chaotic mess. He couldn't accept this. He couldn't accept *himself*. Just like he hadn't been able to accept much of anything for as long as he could remember. That scar, that wound from his past, was always there to prolong the anger inside him. Bete's heart was a constant storm of turmoil on the battlefield.

But there was one thing for certain, and that was if he kept going like this, his anger would have nowhere to go. It would completely destroy him.

The fiery rage from having his companions torn from him. The inferno of enmity at seeing that girl get killed.

They were unacceptable.

Not everyone could be protected. Not everyone could be saved. But Bete was the only one who couldn't seem to put out the flames.

The *strong* were the only ones who couldn't forget.

The cries of the weak as they fought back against the world.

The tears of the frail when they were forced to yield to fate.

"——*Goddammit!!*" he roared, cursing his own self.

And then, raising his head, he looked through the waves of flames to meet Valletta's smile head-on.

He decided, then and there, to break the one "commandment" he'd given himself.

The one selfish act he'd childishly told himself he'd never resort to, even in the face of certain death.

All of a sudden, the memories of the past few days flashed across his amber eyes.

Then.

He began weaving his song.

*"Chained Fros, king of the wolves——"*

And casting his spell.

"Wha…? Vanargand using…m-magic?!" Valletta stammered, completely taken aback.

This wasn't possible. How could she not have known about this? *Loki Familia*'s Vanargand was a meaty powerhouse who belonged on the front lines with the Amazons. That was why he had to rely on his metal-boot Superiors if he wanted to use any kind of magic.

A look of panic crossed her face. This kind of trump card might actually be able to turn the course of battle. There was no way she was going to let him get away with this.

"Don't just stand there! Hurry up and fry 'im!!" she screeched, her underlings releasing another wave of fireballs and lightning bolts. But Bete made no move to dodge or even block them, his eyes shut and arms dropped to his sides as he focused everything he had on the chant. Withstanding direct hit after direct hit, he simply stood there, continuing his spell as the world of shadow around him lit up in a brilliant phantasmagoria.

*"The first wound: Gelgja, the fetter. The second wound: Gjöll, the cry. The third wound: Þviti, the hammer. The ravenous slaver your only hope, may it form a river, mixing in the tide of blood, to wash away your tears."*

Bete wasn't capable of Concurrent Casting.

Nor was his magic power anything to write home about.

He'd never had any reason to spend time honing a skill he'd told himself he'd never use.

*"Never forget those irreparable wounds. This rage and hatred, thine infirmity and incandescence."*

Bete hated this spell.

It was a reflection of the caster's nature, as well as the contents of their soul.

*"Denounce the world. Acknowledge fate. And dry thy tears."*

And it revealed the weakness buried in his heart.

Brought his focus back to the scar he'd tried so hard to ignore these many years.

*"May the pain become your fangs, the lament your roar—and your lost companions your strength."*

He hated this spell more than anything else.

"What the hell are you guys doing? Are you even trying to hit him, you incompetents?! He's half-dead already—I couldn't have served 'im to you on a better platter!" Valletta screamed

"L-Lady Valletta, we're definitely hitting him...he's just—not going down!" one of her associates yelled back helplessly.

And it was true. Though the blasts from their magic swords were landing direct hit after direct hit, setting him ablaze, the werewolf's feet were still firmly planted on the ground. Even as his upper body rocked from each subsequent impact, his lips kept reciting the chant, almost as though some sort of caged beast was struggling to break free.

*"Free yourself of the chains that bind you, and release your mad howl. O lineage of enmity, pray use this vessel and devour the moon, drinking greedily from its overflowing cup."*

With that, the chant of the wounded wolf began to increase in speed.

Valletta, meanwhile, could only scowl in growing concern as more and more magic swords began to explode, having reached their maximum use.

"Gnngh...Fine! Then just attack him directly! Skewer 'im with your cursed weapons! Go, go, go!" she finally howled, completely giving up on the magic approach. Her followers were quick to respond, gulping as they took off toward the wolf.

Grabbing cursed spears, they leaped, four of them flying across the length of Valletta's magic barrier and quickly closing in on Bete with spearheads hurtling.

*"Bare your fangs—and devour all."*

Only…

Bete was a second faster.

His amber eyes popped open with a treacherous glint—then he released the chains of ego muzzling the colossal wolf of his magic.

*"Hati."*

The short name seemed to echo throughout the room.

Then…

A flaming pyre engulfed Valletta and her men.

"——*GGRRRRRRRRRRRRRUUUUUUUUUUUUUUUAAAA AAAAAAAAAAAGGGGGGGGGGGGGGGGGGGGGGHHHHHHHH HHHHHH!!*"

As Valletta hastily threw her hands up to shield her eyes, she heard four sets of screams. With a startled gulp, she made to strengthen her magic barrier, only to see the forms of her companions wriggling and squirming as they burned alive in the searing inferno—followed by the terrifying visage of the werewolf as he shredded them to pieces.

Through the multitude of embers he walked, four searing flames now sprouting from his body.

One on each of his hands and each of his feet.

Four flames, four parts, and at their center, a crimson inferno.

"Ha…ha-ha…*ha-ha-ha-ha-ha-ha-ha*! What the hell is this, huh? All that buildup for a stupid little enchantment? I ain't scared of that shit!" Valletta forced out a great guffaw, her earlier tension melting away.

While certainly it must have been a fairly strong enchantment to allow him to take down four of her guys even *after* the Status Down, it was still just an enchantment. So long as she didn't get close, that thing couldn't reach her. And considering Bete's abilities were still dropping by the second, he'd go down long before he got anywhere near her.

Bete, however, wasn't fazed by her laughter, not saying a word as he began walking toward her.

"Shoot him, you half-wits! And this time, make sure you blow him away!" she commanded, stirring the rest of her troops back into action. As they began their magic-sword barrage anew, the underground chamber was once more filled with a brilliant deluge of light, a whirling storm of flames forming around Bete.

"*Bwa-ha-ha-ha-ha-ha-ha-ha-ha-ha-ha*————————Huh?"

Only...

Her laughter among the explosions quickly came to a halt.

She watched.

As with every new wound opening on the wolf's body from the magic salvo, the flames encapsulating his limbs grew in strength.

The hellish conflagration pouring from his body grew more fierce, more crazed, the more he was attacked.

"L-Lady Valletta...?!" came the shaky voice of one of her fellow Evils.

Though the flaming wisps on his hands and feet had started out around the size of a shield, they were silently, and ever so certainly, growing. They were already taller than Bete himself. Even now, from where they stood a safe distance away, the malevolent waves of flame seemed liable to swallow them whole.

"It's like he's...eating the *magic*," one of the Evils associates muttered in awe.

And suddenly, they all came to the same realization.

The glinting hellfire in front of them was actually *absorbing* each one of the blasts from their magic swords. Just like Bete's broken Frosvirt—just like a *ravenous wolf*—the flames were devouring everything, magic and all.

As they watched the blaze grow larger and larger, they quickly halted their attacks in horror. Their zealous determination to take the wolf down first had been completely engulfed by the flames.

As it would turn out, though, their hypothesis was only half-correct.

Because Valletta noticed something else about Bete.

And that was the new burn that had appeared on his right shoulder.

It almost seemed to be in sync with the flame enveloping his hand, a hazy film of light hovering just on its surface as the wisp on his fist grew ever larger.

*Don't tell me—?*

Valletta swallowed hard, unable to believe what she was seeing.

Then, with a glint in his eye, the wounded wolf charged.

The speed was nothing compared to Bete's normal abilities.

However, it was just enough to close the distance between him and the stock-still enemies in front of him now. They barely even had a chance to react, their eyes widening as he leaped forward, flourishing the blaze on his right hand. It drew from the power of the three other mini infernos, swelling up to an unimaginable size as he sent his flaming fang flying.

Valletta immediately grabbed the shoulders of one of her nearby subordinates, using him as a shield.

Then…

"_____"

In one single swipe of his arm, the entire chamber erupted in a brilliant, incandescent hellfire.

It happened the moment Aiz reached the palace, bringing her wind-like rush to a halt.

The immense garden guarding the entrance exploded into flames.

"?!"

The mighty crimson roar burst straight out of the earth, splitting the ground with it.

Aiz barely had time to avoid it, forcefully diverting her forward momentum and activating her magic as the fiery hurricane swallowed everything.

*"Awaken, Tempest!"*

Protected by her armor of wind, she pushed back against the oppressive waves of heat.

"What the...?!"

The explosion was visible from even as far away as Babel Tower in the center of the city.

Like an incarnate of fire, the colossal pyre towered, a monstrous wolf howling at the sky.

"I-it's an inferno! And it's coming from the direction of the Pleasure Quarter...?!"

"Seems our boy has gone and used that magic of his."

"M-Mister Bete? Magic? Does he even *know* any?!" Raul sputtered in response to Gareth's awed murmur. The dwarf merely nodded as Raul and the rest of the stupefied *Loki Familia* members looked on.

"He does, indeed. Though he'd rarely deign to use it," he continued, throwing a glance at Loki, who confirmed his words with a nod of her own.

"True that. The only time we've seen it is when he first converted."

Gareth turned away from his bewildered companions and back toward the southeastern corner of the city, where even now the inferno had started to dissipate. "This magic of his...it feeds on magic power."

"Feeds on...magic power? Then, you don't mean...?"

"Aye...A type of magic drain, it is."

Bete's spell: Hati.

While the four enchantments on his arms and legs boasted firepower of their own, its true strength lay in its ability to drain other magic. Any magic-based attack it touched was absorbed, boosting its magic output and destructive power.

"Bete's Frosvirt is actually a downgraded version of the spell. Stubborn lad as he was, refusin' to use his own magic, he had Tsubaki make 'em for 'im to use in its stead," Gareth explained. Raul and

Anakity gulped at this new piece of information. Not even they, for as long as they'd known Bete, knew any of this.

"But…but why wouldn't Mister Bete use his magic if it's this crazy powerful…? Wouldn't that make him even stronger…?"

"His scars." Loki answered Raul's confused question.

"Huh?"

"Usin' that magic…forces Bete to face the scars of his past," she murmured almost sadly, looking down at her own palm as though picturing the Status on Bete's back. "You see, it's got one more attribute to it, as well. Its true feature, you might say."

"True feature…?"

"It's a damage drain…Meanin' that the more Bete gets hurt, the stronger it becomes."

"…!"

"It ain't like Tiona and Tione's Berserk magic. This thing basically has no limits on how strong it can get. It can even become the sort of column-like pyre we just saw earlier."

This news left Raul and the other's utterly speechless.

That was the true nature of Bete's magic, Hati.

As it absorbed more and more magic, the enchantment properties of the spell made it impossible for Bete to avoid burning himself in the flames. And as Bete took more and more damage, the spell would grow even stronger, the wounds on his body acting as kindling for the growing inferno.

His own pain and suffering would make the fang of that colossal wolf stronger, more powerful than ever.

"And *that* is the true form of Bete's fang…or its origins, I suppose," Loki finished sadly.

"He's only ever used it once in front of us," Gareth continued. "During an expedition. When the tail end of the party got 'emselves caught up with an Irregular. You remember, don'tcha? Raul? Aki?"

"You mean that one time five years ago?"

"I remember we were with the front line…but that a number of people on the back line got killed. Is that what you're talking about?"

"Aye…One after another, they were gettin' wiped out. So Bete cast his spell…and *incinerated all.* Aggro'd everything and wiped 'em all out. The lot of us were takin' care of our own enemies an' could do nothin' but watch…"

The only one who'd made it out alive from the group, and who'd seen firsthand the werewolf's rampage, had been Leene, Gareth further explained. The old soldier dwarf's voice was laced with regret.

The room grew silent, no one saying a word, as Gareth turned his gaze toward the door and the sky beyond. The earlier clouds were gone, almost as though frightened away by the flaming wolf, revealing the golden light of the moon.

"That lad…Once he shows 'is true colors, he's stronger than anyone I know," Gareth muttered as he narrowed his eyes. "Those blokes really stepped on the wrong wolf's tail this time."

"What the…hell…?!"

Everything was in flames.

Tossing aside the colleague she'd used as a shield, his body now slumped and charred to a crisp, Valletta rose to her feet, her eyes practically trembling as she took in the sight of the blazing red hall around her. From the collapsed columns to every nook and cranny of the grand chamber, everything was alight with crackling cinders as wave after wave of heat rose from the floor. It looked like the inside of a broiling-hot oven.

Valletta's cheek twitched. The sheer overwhelming power of the flames had scalded her skin. The rest of her troops, too, having quickly darted beneath the safety of the columns and barely hanging on to their lives, had lost all will to fight.

She turned her gaze skyward to where the blast had carved through the thick crust of the earth, leaving a gaping hole overhead. The dark sky was now connected to the hellish world below the ground.

——*Shit.*

She mentally cursed, sweat running down her face. And almost as if answering her fears, the visage of the fire starter himself, now standing in the middle of the chamber, had begun to change.

Clouds parting, the light of the moon spilled down into the underground chamber.

Almost instantly, Bete's gray fur stood on end, his muscles rippling.

Then, the pupils of his amber eyes turned to slits.

He was transforming.

Making him not only more aggressive but insanely more powerful, to boot.

The second Valletta realized what was happening, she screamed. "*Kill him! Kill hiiiiiiiiiiiiiiiiiiiim! It's not too late! Take him dooooooooooooooown!!*"

The maddened screech of her voice spurred what minions of hers remained into desperate action. The *Thanatos Familia* puppets didn't fear death—not with the promise of resurrection that their god had given them. Though fearful of the pain that would come, they would do anything to fulfill their life's greatest desire, and so they launched themselves at the wolf, shaky war cries tearing at their throats and blood, tears, and snot flying, almost like suicidal warriors dying for their cause.

But—

"——GNGGGH!"

Before they could even reach him, the wolf was gone, leaving behind a cracked floor in his wake and taking out two of them before they'd even realized what had happened. He seized them by the face, the flame on his right arm still increasing in fervor, and slammed them straight into the ground. Their bodies *shattered instantly* into flying, flaming chunks. At the same time, he lashed out with his legs, the scorching blades slicing through the upper halves of another set of assailants, turning them into nothing more than clouds of black dust. The Inferno Stones they'd equipped themselves with in case they needed to self-destruct began going off en masse, the resulting blasts acting as further fuel for Bete's Hati.

"Guh...wah...?!".

The supposedly death-accepting followers of the God of Death went white with terror.

Nothing they'd ever witnessed before could hold a candle to the brutality taking place before them now.

Bete had truly become one with his fang.

On his arms, on his legs, on his every limb.

Four fangs, forming the top and bottom of a fiery jaw, that would consume them whole.

His hands were the upper fangs, ripping apart the flesh of his enemies, and his feet were the lower fangs, crushing their limbs.

The merciless amber eyes of the werewolf shot straight through his terrified prey.

And then he opened his jaw, prepared to swallow the sun, the moon, the entire world.

*"G-GUAAAAAAAAAAAAAAAAAAAAAAAAAAAAAAGH!!"*

The few Evils who remained screamed, half-crazed, as they saw their final battle looming before them. Even as they quaked with fear, they rushed forward, a veritable army of the dead as they attacked the wolf. Bete sidestepped them easily, his instincts now as sharp and wild as a beast's, his fists turning his enemies' entrails to ash and his heels coming straight down on their heads in a vertical line of scorching fire that charred their bodies, cursed weapons, and everything. His flames swallowed what incoming magic attacks yet flew at him, growing ever larger as he annihilated every one of the God of Death's followers.

It was a dance of embers, a nigh uncountable amount, his punches and kicks leaving trails of fire in the air. It was a scene not of this world, truly reminiscent of the end of days, and as Valletta watched from a distance, her hands and feet shaking, she murmured in awe.

"It…can't be…"

Before she knew it, her companions were gone, and the giant wolf turned his sights on her.

Every single hair on her body stood on end, but in that split second…

A shadow suddenly descended from the hole overhead.

"S-Sword Princess…?!" Valletta's voice cracked at the progressively worsening state of affairs, while meanwhile, Aiz herself could only look around her in bewilderment.

"What's going on…?!"

*Shit, you've gotta be kiddin' me!*

As Valletta's thoughts became a whirl of obscenities, the golden-haired, golden-eyed swordswoman's gaze fell on the last remaining enemy left in the chamber.

She made to unsheathe her sword. Only...

"*Don't touch her!!*" came the sudden incensed order.

"Mister...Bete...?" Aiz stopped, stunned.

"You touch her and I swear...I'll kill you, too!!" Bete howled threateningly before turning his eyes back to the woman in question. Leaving Aiz to stand there in shocked silence, he took first one step, then two, then more and more as he slowly crossed the world of hellfire and approached Valletta.

"Th-this is insane...This is *insane...This is insane...!!*" Valletta began to see red as she watched the wolf chuck aside the bodies of her former comrades, leaving nothing between the two of them. Somehow that rage had washed away the fear and the dread, leaving her almost, just the tiniest bit calm.

*Gimme a break, Vanargand! You're really gonna come at me when your own body's about ready to fall apart...?!*

It didn't matter *how* much damage and magic his Hati had drained at this point—the wounds plaguing his body weren't about to heal anytime soon. He'd kick the bucket *far* before Valletta even got close.

*Plus, my Shaldo's still workin' its stuff! So what if he's transformed, huh? He keeps flailin' around like that and it'll suck 'im dry, back to the exact way he was before,* she calmly told herself, glancing down at the still-glowing reddish-purple patterns beneath her feet. She smiled despite the anxiety tugging at the back of her mind.

*Yeah, bring it on.*

*Let me cut you down to size.*

With a sadistic grin worthy of the name "Arachnia," she readied her cursed shortsword.

"Huh—?"

Until her wandering gaze froze in an instant.

The patterns underfoot, the ones spanning the entire length of the chamber, and Valletta's carefully woven barrier...

Were beginning to flicker, almost as though giving up a dying wail, their power being sucked into the ravenous wolf's fangs.

Magic drain.

With those two words, Valletta felt an overwhelming despair wash over her.

*This is insane... This is insane... THIS IS INSANE...!!*

Because Bete's Hati had one thing different about it from the weaker Frosvirt he normally employed.

It could eat *anything*. Attacks. Curses. *Even barriers*.

Anything that used magic power.

"B-but it's not even attack magiiiiiiiiiiiiiiiiiiiiiiiiiiiiiic!!"

Bete's fang, his scar, was one even Leene, as a healer, couldn't mend.

This time, the color really did leave Valletta's face.

If Bete sucked up her barrier and broke the Status Down binding him...

As Valletta grew more and more panicked, Bete lunged forward at lightning speed.

"RRRUUAAAAAGH!!"

"Gnnaagh?!"

He hurled his fist of flame upward, a sweeping uppercut right into her belly.

Valletta's body curled in on itself as spit went flying from her mouth. Before she could even recover, Bete was spinning on his heel, delivering a flying kick as powerful as a raging river that sent flames across the side of her face as she was launched across the room.

Still, the hungry wolf kept up the attack, the tremendous force of his fang pounding into her again and again and again for a multi-punch salvo that left her body a crippled mess.

"*GNGH...GRRAAAAAAAAAAAAAAAAAAAAAAAAAAAAAAAAAA AAAAAAAAAAAAAAUUUUUUUUUUUUUUUUUUUUUUUUUU UUGGGGGGGGGGGHHHHHHH!!*"

The scream of agony was enough to make even Aiz, with her years of experience on the battlefield, plug her ears.

Her bones snapping, her skin searing, even her tears themselves evaporating into mist, Valletta was beaten to a pulp. Bete's strikes carved through the very air itself, his left fist, his left *fang* delivering a resounding blow that sent her hurtling straight into one of the columns in the middle of the chamber.

"Bete!" Aiz suddenly cried, having come to herself, but not even her desperate plea could get through to him now. His fury had taken control.

He walked toward Valletta, now writhing on the ground, as his every step sent the stone below him up in flames.

"A-aggghhhhh...?!"

"On your feet," Bete ordered coldly.

He was doing everything in his power to keep from turning her into ash right then and there, his slit eyes simply staring at the woman on the floor.

Valletta did as she was told, pushing her trembling, half-charred body to its feet.

"E-enough already, Vanargand...I—I can't take it anymore...It hurts too much...Too hot...I-I'm begging you...! L-look what you did to me! I'm not even th-thinking straight!!" she pleaded shamefully. "I—I don't wanna die! I still haven't...That pompous bastard Braver...Finn and I...I still need to...have my way with him...So let me go...please!!" She forced a smile in desperate appeal.

"And what did you do, huh? When all those weaklings you killed looked up at you with those same words?!" Bete hissed back, the flames around him flaring up as her expression froze under his callous gaze.

They were so close. A mere five meders away. With only a single step, Bete could swallow her whole. Valletta could almost see the giant flaming wolf, his fangs bared as he stared at her from over Bete's shoulder.

"S-seriously?" she sputtered. "You're still mad about that Amazonian brat?! Or do you mean those friends of yours I killed down in Knossos? D-don't you think you're kinda barkin' up the wrong tree here?"

"..."

"You guys are adventurers, aren't you? Fully prepared to die at a moment's notice! That's just our way of life! Y-yours *and* mine!" Valletta stammered, already starting in on her high-handed excuses, while behind them both, Aiz's fingers unconsciously curled into a fist.

Bete remained silent until Valletta was finished, then answered softly.

"...It's true. You're not wrong."

At this, Aiz couldn't believe her ears.

"They died because they're weak. So perhaps my anger is misdirected...It's the duty of the strong to take from the weak, after all. That's just the way of this goddamn world," he acknowledged. It was the same thing he'd said to Aiz back in the pub.

That was right.

The strong could do anything. Could take anything.

While the weak were powerless. Constantly having the things important to them snatched away.

The weak shouldn't be allowed to live.

That was simply the way of the world, since the day life came into being.

"Th-then...?" Valletta started, a glimmer of hope in her eyes. But then...

"—*WHICH IS EXACTLY WHY!!*" Bete suddenly howled, his eyes flashing with rage.

"There's nothing wrong with me ripping you to shreds!!"

Valletta's face went stark white at the werewolf's outraged howl.

There was a loud *crunch* as Bete stepped forward, then Valletta turned tail and ran.

"G-gaaaaaaaagh?!"

That was enough for Bete. This piece of fish bait who couldn't even howl, who was running away with her tail between her legs, didn't deserve to live.

"*RuuuuuuaaaaaaAAAAAAAAARRRRRRGGGGGGGHHHHH!!*"

"G-G-G-YAAAAAAAAAAAAAAAAAAAAAAAAAAAAAAAAH!!"

He was on her, fists flying, legs sailing, and finally, claws curling around her face in an iron grip. He lifted her off the ground, slamming her into the nearby pillar and causing the very flames surrounding his body to tremble.

"*W-wait?!* I-if you kill me, you'll never...never find the key———!!"

"Oh, shut up."

Nothing could stand in the way of the hungry wolf now.

His fangs would systematically, impartially tear the flesh of his prey into thousands of tiny pieces.

Valletta's desperate appeal to the key was immediately quashed.

"*WAIT, BETE!!*"

Not even Aiz could stop him now. His fangs were bared.

"*BURN IN HEEEEEEEEEEEEEEEEEEEEEEEEEEEEEEEEEELL!!*"

The world around them erupted.

"———————————————————————————*AGH?!*"

The jaws of the inferno opened wide, and its tremendous roar completely masked Valletta's scream of agony. Her body was engulfed in flames, turning her into blackened ash in mere moments and frying her alive. She made for an even more wretched sight than that of the many monsters he'd previously incinerated.

And Aiz saw everything.

The spectacle seared into her eyes.

The world of death and destruction the werewolf had invoked.

The terrifying spectacle of fire and brimstone his fury had set into motion.

There, in that giant underground chamber of glowing red, Vanargand had writ the final page of the Evils' saga.

"*AWOOOOOOOOOOOOOOOOOOOOOOOOOOOOOOO———...*"

Enshrouded in flames and drenched in the light of the moon, the lone wolf howled into the night sky.

An indicator, perhaps, that he'd fulfilled his oath; to Aiz's ears, it

© Kiyotaka Haimura

sounded both ferocious and heartbreakingly sad. She watched him, embers singeing her face, sweat pouring from her temples, and her golden hair glinting.

While the wolf stood there, savage, gallant, and destitute in the flames.

The heinous "Amazon Hunt" that had rocked the city had finally come to a close.

As far as official announcements, the ringleaders who'd hired the assassins were still unknown. In order to avoid any unnecessary chaos, no one aside from *Loki Familia* was to know it was the remnants of the Evils who'd been in charge of the attack.

As for the battle that had taken place in the restoration zone of the Pleasure Quarter—and the giant pillar of fire that had been observed all across the city—the Guild had already begun their investigation. Both the Guild and its workers, as well as the whole of *Ganesha Familia*, were quite rightfully horrified upon discovering not only the corpses of the two dead guards but the scarcely recognizable charred bodies of the assassins around the scene of the attack. Though they fully understood that the perpetrator was a "certain elite member" of a "certain large familia," no word or even allusion to him was ever released. Instead, they were simply forced to concede that the threat to the city was gone and that there was no reason to "step on the beast's tail," as it were, by questioning the measures taken to do so. Even the Guild's upper echelons agreed that this was a matter best passed over. Indeed, aside from the fact that it was going to take a bit longer to rebuild the Pleasure Quarter, the goings-on from that night might very well never have happened, buried beneath the darkness from whence they came.

Upon observing the bodies of the assassins they'd recovered, it was clear there would be no more risk of attack; thus, the Guild released the protective sanctions they'd placed on the former members of *Ishtar Familia*. And with that, the usual peace returned to

Orario, almost as though the rain had simply washed away the night's tragedies.

Save one person, who now had to live with one more scar.

Back in the Pleasure Quarter in the city's third district, where the ravages of war still painted the restoration zone…

Bete sat alone among the debris in a corner of the ruins, the brilliant sunset staining his features. This was the exact spot where he'd last seen her face. He narrowed his eyes into the fiery sheen of the twilit sun along the western horizon.

"Bete…" Aiz murmured as she and Loki watched over him from a short distance away.

It had been two days since he'd taken down Valletta, and the wolf had yet to return to Twilight Manor. It was only by chance that Aiz and Loki had finally found him there. There was no telling how long he'd stay, either. Though at the very least, it didn't seem he'd be leaving anytime soon, as he'd yet to move during the few hours since they'd arrived, simply staring off into the ever-changing sky.

Bete looked so small sitting there—quite possibly the quietest Aiz had ever seen him.

"Let 'im have his sunset, yeah?…We go bustin' in there now without a care for his mood an' he'll just turn himself off."

"Yeah…He doesn't seem very…happy."

It was true.

The two short days he'd spent with that girl, his own self-reproach at being unable to protect those weaker than him, and plenty of other emotions that Aiz couldn't even begin to imagine—they should have washed through Bete by now.

Aiz let her gaze fall before turning toward Loki. "What do you think…we should do?"

"Heh, I may not've mentioned it to the others, but I've got myself a little plan up my sleeve," Loki replied with a sudden smile. "Aiz, I'm gonna tell ya somethin' and I want you to pass it along to Bete, all right? Should cheer him right up."

"…What is it?"

As Loki leaned in closely to whisper in Aiz's ear, the girl quickly nodded. It took less than a second. Then, Loki's words in her head and a look of determination on her face, she took off across the square. She could hear Loki's whispered "*You can do it!*" from behind her as she approached Bete.

But before she could get a word out, the werewolf beat her to the punch.

"You need something, Aiz?"

"Bete…"

"I don't feel much like talkin' to anyone right now, okay? So just beat it," he mumbled, not even turning around.

Aiz gave a little gulp but stood her ground as she eyed the wolf bathed in the light of the setting sun, the fang on his cheek glowing red.

Then, with a little *plop*, she placed her hand on his shoulder.

As he slowly turned to face her, she relayed the words Loki had imparted to her.

"I got you, bro."

She had spoken in a completely monotone voice.

"………………………………"

The sight of the emotionally challenged girl, her features absolutely deadpan as the ridiculous attempt at encouragement left her mouth, was enough to make Bete's cheek twitch.

"*BWWWPHHHH!!*" came the stifled laughter from the nearby shadows—and the provider of the phrase herself.

"………………?"

Aiz could only look on in confusion at the reaction she was receiving, tilting her head to the side with a silent *Huh?*

*Seriously…?* Bete, meanwhile, realizing things had gotten too unbelievable by this point, simply let out a sigh before rising to his feet. Saying nothing and bringing his hand down on the girl's head with a more-forceful-than-intended *donk*, he walked right past her.

Aiz brought her hands to her head as she watched him go, now even more despondent.

"Well, lookie who it is! What a coincidence runnin' into you here!" Loki popped out from the shadows like a bouncing clown to land in front of Bete's path before he could make it out of the square.

"You got some nerve sayin' that, you old hag..." Bete half glared at her, annoyed that the earlier ambience of his sunset had been spoiled.

"We've been lookin' all over for ya, you know? Whatcha been doin' these last two days, huh?"

"What do you care? 'Sides, not like everyone's gonna throw a party for me if I just waltz back home, now, is it?" Bete pointed out, referencing the two Amazons he'd left on less-than-stellar terms. Loki, however, just hummed through her nose, her smile never leaving her face.

"Hmm...I dunno about that..."

"...?"

But as dubious as Bete was in the face of his goddess's antics, he wasn't about to stick around any longer, and he made to leave the square for good.

"Hey, Bete. Time-out, 'kay? 'Cause Aiz really, reeeeally wants to ask ya somethin'."

"...Huuh?"

Bete turned around to see Loki's eyes widen ever so slightly in mirth—and Aiz running after him with a decisive air about her.

As his amber eyes met her golden ones, she took a deep, nervous breath, then gave her question voice.

"Bete...Please tell me...why are you always looking down on people? And...why is it that you want to get stronger?"

"Ngh—!"

"You didn't answer my question back...back in the pub that night..."

Bete's brows furrowed.

The girl's expression remained steady and strong even as she stuttered out an almost desperate question. There was no way he could blame things on alcohol this time. Nor was there any way for him to lie. Not in front of those eyes. That would simply be unacceptable.

Instead, Bete made to leave. Then—

"Answer her, Bete. That's an order from yer goddess, ya hear?"

"You..."

"C'mooooon! It's not like it's in front of everybody. Just this little chick here!...Even you understand it's a cryin' shame to up and leave without sortin' out these misunderstandings."

Loki's words felt like a knife to his heart.

And as his goddess's words pried away at the doors to his soul, he felt anger rise up inside him. Making a none-too-kind gesture, he turned back toward Aiz.

The swordswoman was standing just as he'd left her, waiting for his response.

Her features so reminiscent of those of his younger sister, her eyes invoking the same determination as the girl he'd loved back in *Víðarr Familia*, and her golden hair, fiery in the setting sun, just like the girl he'd lost on the plains.

Yes, this was the one person in the entire world he couldn't lie to.

Which was a realization Bete suddenly understood all too well.

His mouth seemed to open on its own, unable to fast-talk its way out of this one.

"...Because I hate weaklings. That's why."

"That's...all?"

"They're disgusting. I don't even wanna look at 'em."

"And?"

"Hearin' 'em cry gives me goose bumps..."

"And?"

"—*What else do you want from me?!*" Bete finally roared, unable to take the girl's unending deluge of questions. "That's our duty, isn't it? The strong are supposed to bad-mouth those weaker than 'em! If we don't do it, who will? And then what, huh? The chicken-livered wusses'll just keep on coming! Is that what you want?!" Bete howled.

It rushed out of him like a dam had been released, everything he'd been keeping stopped up inside, all the pain from his scar, flowing out of him and dashing itself against Aiz.

"They don't belong on the battlefield! They should all just stay in their little holes! Learn their place! Not run around boo-hooing at every single goddamn thing. Makes me sick! Pissin' and whinin' like a bunch of little babies!! What else did you think was gonna happen, huh? They were doomed to die from the start!!"

Their deaths flashed through his head as he carried on, his parents, his tribe, his sister, his childhood friend, *her*.

And finally, the final moments of the girl who'd tried to heal him—and the Amazonian brat.

All these thoughts plaguing his mind, plaguing his heart as he continued his tirade, he finally ended it with one last bellow.

"*I DON'T WANT ANYONE TO CRY ANYMORE!!*" he roared, his voice echoing in the scarlet sky.

And then it was silent. Only the sound of Bete's ragged breath cut through the tension.

Aiz stood there, shocked into silence, before finally, ever so slightly, beginning to fidget.

Apologetically, almost, making herself as small as possible.

"I'm…I'm sorry…"

"See?"

But the first person to reply to Bete's dubious grunt wasn't Aiz, in fact, but Loki. A smug grin on her face, she brought a hand to her mouth before yelling at what appeared to be no one in particular.

"You hear that? Pretty much what we thought!"

Bete found himself thrown for a loop, until, from atop the roofs of the nearby buildings, heads began popping up, one by one.

The entirety of *Loki Familia* was there.

"…………H-huh?" Bete sputtered, mouth frozen in a half-opened droop.

"We heard it loud and clear!"

"Sure yelled it loud enough."

"I'm not sure whether to be happy or…embarrassed…Aha… ah-ha-ha-ha!"

They were the voices of his peers—Tiona shouting happily, Tione shrugging, and Lefiya with her hands to her cheeks in red-faced chagrin. And the affirmations continued similarly among the rest of the bunch: Raul, Anakity, Alicia, Cruz, Narfi, and even a whole bunch of the lower-level familia members, as well. Rakuta and the rest of his party down in Knossos, in particular, had tears forming in the corners of their eyes.

Bete's confession had been successfully delivered.

"The things you've put us through…"

"Indeed. Perhaps if you could be a little less…aggressive about everything, it would make our jobs easier."

"Less aggressive? Bwa-ha-ha-ha-ha! We talkin' about the same Bete here?"

Now the voices came from the shadows of a nearby patch of rubble, Riveria, Finn, and Gareth emerging onto the square.

Bete had truly turned to stone now, nothing but his eyes shifting toward the trio with an almost audible *creak*.

"Aiz really, reeeeally wanted ya to return to the familia, yeah? So I may or may not've dropped a hint or two that we should pull an innocent little stunt, and, well…You can prolly gather the rest."

"And I'm, uh…sorry…about that…" Aiz apologized once more as Loki looked on triumphantly. Bete was still frozen to the spot.

So that's what had happened.

The other familia members had carefully, quietly hidden themselves away just out of Bete's range of perception while Finn and the other elites had absconded themselves completely, all of them waiting for the moment when Aiz would urge Bete to spill his true feelings.

"Wh…You…Dammi…G-gaaaah…?!" was all Bete could sputter as he attempted to find his words. And as he stood there, features strained and mouth bobbing up and down, Tiona and the rest of his familia came running over to meet him.

They all lined up in front of him with grins that could outrival even that of their goddess, and from within the boisterous bunch, Tiona's and Tione's voices could be heard loud and clear.

"Hey, Tione! You know what they call people like Bete, huh? I heard it from Loki!"

"Sure do. A jerk with a heart of gold."

"_____?!"

Bete's face went instantly red.

But they weren't done yet, with Raul and the other second-tiers quick to toss their own opinions into the pot.

"You made my heart stop, Mister Bete! *'I don't want anyone to cry anymore!'* So dreamy!"

"I always believed in you, Mister Bete!" "We're so sorry for misunderstanding you!" "So *this* is what the gods mean when they say someone is 'so cute it makes you want to eat them'!"

"Asshole on the outside! Teddy bear on the inside!"

"Nice ta meetcha, Teddy Bete!"

"This new Mister Bete is an absolute dreamboat!"

"——*You bastaaaaaaaaaaaaaaaaaaaaaaaaaaaaaaaaaaaaaaaards!!"

"P-p-p-p-please forgive uuuuuuus!"

The screams camse almost simultaneously as Bete unleashed his fist on the group of overzealous fans. Raul was only the first to go flying. Tiona and Tione didn't miss the opportunity to join in on the fun, either, loosing giant guffaws as they clamored along with the rest of the peanut gallery.

The sight of it brought a smile to Aiz's face and a set of amused looks from Finn and the other elites.

Once the two twins actually started *fighting* with Bete, though, Lefiya and her group quickly attempted to pull them apart, and loud laughter erupted from everyone in the square.

*Loki Familia* was back, just as Aiz had wanted.

"Well, then..." Riveria said suddenly.

She let out a heavy sigh, almost as though she'd been waiting for a signal. Throwing an almost criticizing glance at Finn, she waited for an appropriate opening in the hoopla before pushing her way into the circle.

"Bete, I must first apologize."

"Huh?"

"It's about Lena Tully."

Bete's previously reddened face turned stark white the moment Riveria mentioned the Amazon's name. The tattoo on his cheek twisted in irritation as he turned cold.

"There ain't nothin' to talk about."

"No, there is, Bete. Hear me out."

"I said there ain't! She's dead, ya hear? There's no point in holdin' on to people who ain't ever comin' back?!" Bete lashed out, not even listening to Riveria's appeal.

"Or is there?"

All of a sudden…

The girl in question popped out from behind a pile of nearby rubble, bringing Bete's world to a sudden halt.

"Yoo-hoo, Bete Loga!" Lena Tully called out, looking none the worse for wear as she cheerily waved in his direction.

"………………………………………"

"And before you ask, nope! This isn't a dream!"

But it might as well have been, the way Bete seemed completely stunned, so Riveria stepped in quickly to explain, her eyes closed.

"The day of the attack, Amid was able to complete her work on a magic item capable of healing the curse. Using her own curse-exposed blood, she was able to distill an elixir with anti-curse properties. Of course, the supply was limited, but…"

"………………………………………"

"As we moved among scenes of the attack, Alicia, the others, and I used what we had to heal all we could."

"………………………………………"

"By the time we found Lena, my supply was running short. I was just barely able to rid her body of the curse, and though she was still alive when I brought her to the hospital…I had no way of knowing whether or not she'd survive, so I told no one."

"………………………………………"

"That and at the time, there was still a threat of Amazons being

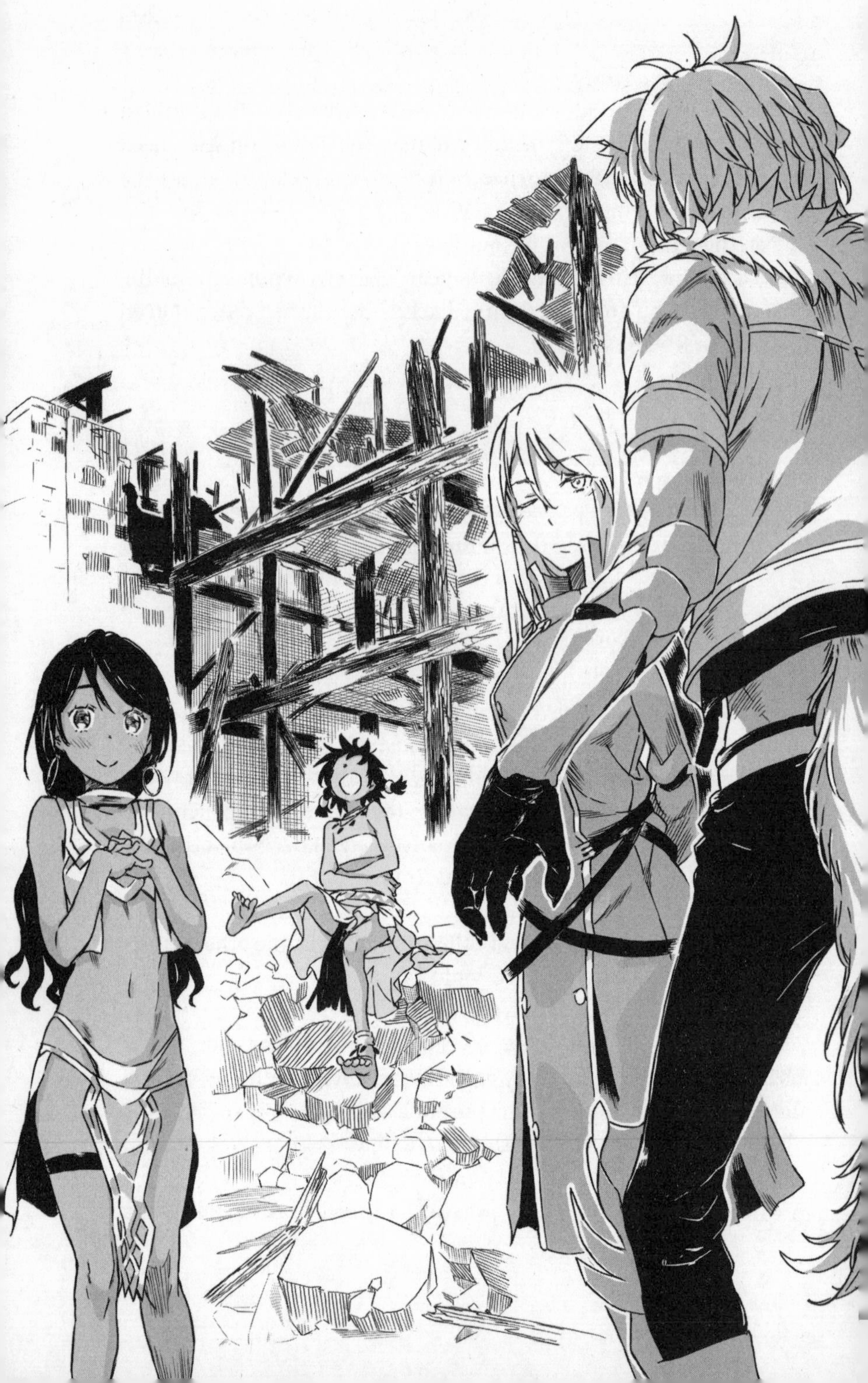

targeted, her included. Better to continue feigning her death for multiple reasons, then...So I decided to wait until things had cooled down," she finished. The detailed, long-winded explanation was evidence enough of the rare feeling of awkwardness she felt about the entire situation. "...So I ask you once again to please forgive me. You were hurting, yet I kept you from the truth."

Riveria threw an apologetic look at the girl in question—the very-much-alive Lena standing next to her—as Bete continued to flounder in silence.

"All of us, too. We only knew about it after we'd already taken care of everything," Tiona added.

"As did I. Riveria was operating on her own with this one. And trust me, she gave me quite the earful after hearing I'd left it up to you to...resolve things," Finn explained, his own voice remorseful.

Bete's gaze, meanwhile, had yet to leave the grinning girl in front of him.

"I'm so sorry for making you sad, Bete Loga! Though, you know? Hearing that you were all down in the dumps 'cause of little old me? Made my heart skip, you know! I musta made a pretty deep impression on you! You just didn't know how to express it, yeah?" she said with a smile, inching closer and closer to Bete, almost like a cat.

Bete lowered his gaze before shooting his hand out, letting it drop on Lena's head.

"Wh-wh-what are you doing? We're not gonna hug right now, are we? In front of everyone?! Bete Loga, you're so bold!" Lena tittered gleefully.

Suddenly, Bete's leg came flying upward.

*KER-PHWOMP!!*

"Guuwaaaagh?!"

His knee made direct contact with her abdomen.

The impact drew a curious squawking noise from Lena as her body curled in on itself.

And he didn't stop there, either. *KER-PHWOMP!! KER-PHWOMP!!*

His knee kept coming. A rapid-fire barrage of knees to the gut that made Lena's orange-pearl eyes practically bulge out of her head.

*"M-Mister Bete?!"*

"You're gonna kill her, you idiot!"

"You think I care?! *I'M GONNA MURDER HERRRRRRRRR RRRRRRRRRRRRRRRRRRRRRRRRRRRRRRRRRRRRRRRRRRRRR RRRR!!"* Bete roared, completely disregarding the surprised yelps from Lefiya and Tione.

His rage was unstoppable, entirely incomparable with his earlier anger, as he lit into the young Amazon. Not even Tione, frantically trying to pull them apart, could stop him. It finally took the entire familia, Raul and the others flying on him en masse, to bring the enraged werewolf, capable even of fighting off a first-tier adventurer, to a halt.

As the grand brawl ensued, Tiona darted in to pull the collapsed Lena out of the fray.

"H-hey! Are you okay?! You still with us—?"

"He-he-he…he-he-he-he-he-he-he…! My stomach…has been blessed again…I'll definitely get pregnant now…!" Lena laughed, an almost euphoric smile on her face as drool leaked down her chin.

*Th-the hell is wrong with this chick?!* Tiona drew back with a start.

Meanwhile, Aiz and Loki, now completely forgotten, could only stare in blank disbelief at the chaotic situation in front of them. It didn't take long for Loki to burst out in laughter, doubled over with her arms to her stomach. This was enough to draw in even Aiz, who brought her hand to her mouth with a giggle of her own.

Finn, Riveria, and Gareth looked on in shock at seeing the swordswoman laugh for what must have been the first time.

Was it because there was something funny about the way the red-faced wolf was howling in anger?

Or was it because there was something cute about the desperately apologizing girl darting in and out as she avoided the wolf's fist?

Or was it because there was something absolutely ridiculous about the way her companions were flailing in panic, trying to put a stop to the melee?

Or was it simply because she was so, so happy at the wild scene taking place before her eyes?

"D-don't be mad, Bete Loga! I'm *suuuuper* embarrassed at the whole thing, too, you know? But still, I can't deny that it makes me really happy!"

"*You think I care, damn cow?!*"

"I'm just ecstatic that I get to see you again!"

Bete's hand shot out in an attempt to grab her, his face completely red.

Lena, meanwhile, simply smiled, her eyes closed as tears dribbled down her cheeks.

On and on their voices continued, the wolf's howls of anger mingling with the delighted laughter of the Amazonian girl.

# Instead of
# Good-bye——

The morning sun glimmered in the sky to the east.

A group was on its way to the deserted First Graveyard, otherwise known as the Adventurers Graveyard, in the city's southeastern district—a group of Amazons, all of them donning attire reminiscent of dancers.

"Seriously! You really shoulda just come out and told us, you numbskull!"

*"Oooouch!"*

Aisha's fist came down on the crown of Lena's ponytailed head with a heavy *DONG!*

"B-but! Nine Hell told me I wasn't supposed to tell anyone! Besides! We weren't even supposed to leave the hospital, remember?" Lena insisted tearfully, reminding the other Amazon of the continued risk of attack from the assassins—and how Riveria had told them to lay low until things had cooled down. Whether they wanted to or not, they'd become part of the high elf's plan to "deceive the enemy by way of their allies."

The two Amazons were walking with the rest of the Berbera who'd been saved by Amid's secret curse-repelling potion—the same Amazons whose "corpses had been taken to the First Graveyard," according to the lie that had been spread.

"You were certainly a blubbering mess, Samira. Even went to all this work to prepare a grave already…"

"Wh-what did you expect? I just heard that all my friends had *died*! Why *wouldn't* I want to pay my respects…?!"

"I'm sorry for worrying you so much, Samira…But hey! You were on the ball with that grave! Guess I should have expected as much from our old ritual leader!"

"You don't look sorry at all!"

*"Yeeeoouch!"*

The red-faced, ashen-haired Amazon brought her own fist down on Lena's head, eliciting another yelp from the girl.

The group continued along with an air that was considerably inappropriate for a graveyard as they carted their shovels, pick-axes, and other various oversize tools. They'd need them to dig up the graves that had been made for them after they'd "died," as unexpected as that had been. Leaving them there would not only lead to more misunderstandings, it'd be ill-omened, to boot. Admonishing Samira as she continued to complain about all the money she'd wasted on their gravestones, they finally made it to their destination.

They stopped in the small corner of the graveyard their familia had purchased before being disseminated: the *Ishtar Familia* plots, where their former comrades who'd lost their lives in the Dungeon already slept.

"…Fallujah and the others…They're really dead, aren't they?"

"Yes, they've already been…buried."

While Amid's magic item had been able to save almost all the inflicted Amazons, there were still a few who had slipped through their fingers, most of them having been attacked in the middle of the night and their bodies discovered too late. There were also a few they simply hadn't had enough of the elixir left to save, making Lena and the others who had survived very lucky indeed.

Lena got down on her knees in front of the freshly made graves, a strangely reserved look on her face as she closed her eyes. She prayed for the happiness of her fallen friends in the next life—and that they might meet again one day under the same sun.

"…All right, let's clean these things up, then, shall we? Else these old girls who have to spend the rest of eternity here'll give us an earful!" Aisha exclaimed in jest, shattering the gloomy atmosphere that had settled over the group.

Smiles crossing their faces, they quickly got to work digging out the graves.

But then…

"Huh?"

"…? Aisha?"

Aisha had come to a halt in front of Lena, who'd been search-ing for her gravestone among the rows. Drawing the gazes of the rest of her peers, the older Amazon's shoulders gave a sudden jerk.

"Gngh…Ha-ha…*Ha-ha-ha-ha-ha-ha-ha!*"

She burst out in laughter.

"Wh-what's wrong? What's so funny?"

But Aisha was laughing so hard she couldn't even respond, her arms to her stomach and tears threatening the corners of her eyes.

"Oh, c'mon!" Lena puffed out her cheeks in indignation, then pushed past the other Amazon to see just what was so amusing.

"—Ah."

Lena froze instantly.

The grave Aisha had been standing in front of was none other than Lena's.

Completely white, it was clear the grave was fresh.

But what caught her attention the most was what was sitting on top of the carefully etched letters of her name.

Unable to believe her eyes, she reached out slowly, carefully, to take it in her hands.

"That wolf you've fallen for…he's really somethin' else." Aisha continued to giggle as she wiped at her eyes.

Lena simply clutched the item, her most beloved item in all the world, to her chest.

There was only one person who could have left this on her grave.

"Obnoxious doesn't even come close!"

Aisha's laughter continued from behind her as Lena's cheeks filled with a fiery heat.

This warmth in her chest.

This was happiness, a pure, unadulterated joy she'd never felt before in all her days fighting as an Amazon. Tears running down her cheeks, she turned her smile to the sky, shouting up at the sun.

"I love you, Bete Logaaaaaaaaa!!"

The bouquet of forget-me-nots clutched between her fingers trembled, as though smiling.

© Kiyotaka Haimura

## Status — Lv.6

| STRENGTH: | E 479 | ENDURANCE: | F 388 |
|---|---|---|---|
| DEXTERITY: | S 999 | AGILITY: | B 784 |
| MAGIC: | B 713 | HUNTER: | E |
| IMMUNITY: | E | MAGIC RESISTANCE: | H |
| INITIATIVE: | H | CHAIN ATTACK: | H |

### MAGIC

**Hell Finegas**
- Enhancement magic.
- Greatly enhances all abilities.
- Increase in bloodlust leads to a decrease in rational judgment.

**Tir na Nog**
- Spear-throwing magic.
- Adds the values from level and abilities to Magic, including latent values (extra points).
- Can be used only once every twenty-four hours.

### SKILLS

**Prum Spirit**
- Boosts the effects of magic and skills in times of adversity.

**Noble Brave**
- Provides high resistance to mind corruption.

**Dia Phiana**
- Temporarily allows Finn to use the development ability Lancer when equipped with a spear.
- Effects dependent on level.

**Command Howl**
- Expands reach of voice after speaking volume exceeds a certain threshold.
- During a free-for-all, expansion increases in proportion to the size of the battle.

**Ail mac Midna**
- Provides resistance to sleep. Increases ability to stay awake for long periods of time.
- Increases endurance against fire.

### EQUIPTMENT: Fortia Spear

- Golden-tipped spear.
- Crafted by *Goibniu Familia* for 130,000,000 valis.
- An exclusive prum weapon and custom order commissioned by Finn.
- Boasts a sturdy handle made of oathtree walnut and a golden spearhead made of amalgamated heroic alloy and dir adamantite. All components excluding the dir adamantite are rare materials from the Elanwood, the supposed birthplace of the fictitious goddess Phiana and her knighthood.

### EQUIPTMENT: Roland Spear

- Durandal.
- A piece from the Roland series of weapons crafted by Tsubaki of *Hephaistos Familia*.
- A long spear with a silver tip to contrast Finn's Fortia Spear.
- 100,000,000 valis.

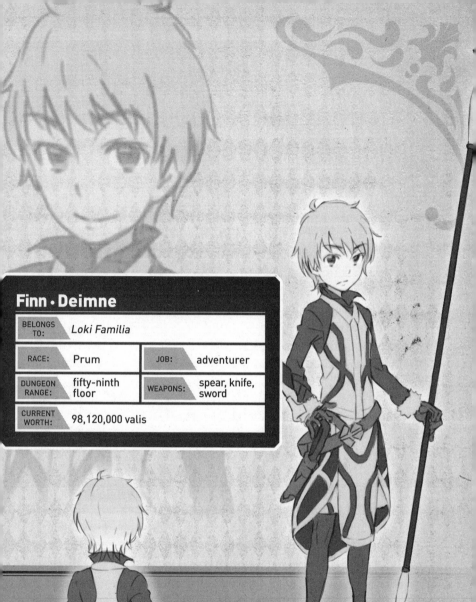

# Finn · Deimne

| BELONGS TO: | *Loki Familia* | | |
|---|---|---|---|
| RACE: | Prum | JOB: | adventurer |
| DUNGEON RANGE: | fifty-ninth floor | WEAPONS: | spear, knife, sword |
| CURRENT WORTH: | 98,120,000 valis | | |

FINN DEIMNE

# Afterword

With this book, Bete will finally be able to make it onto the cover.

Though I skipped a book since writing about the Amazonian sisters in book six of the side series, book eight will once again see my poor characters' rage take the front seat.

Back when I first started writing the main series, the only two characters in *Loki Familia* whose pasts I'd fully envisioned were Aiz's and Finn's. I hadn't put a thought into any of the other characters' backgrounds. Thus, when GA approached me about writing this side series, my first thought was, quite ineloquently, *Shit!* As you can imagine, the star of this book, Bete, was one of those in-the-dark characters.

Even among various stakeholders, Bete has always been vilified: "Bete's annoying," "Kill him off quickly," "Bete was so grating in the first book," "I'm actually amazed at just how annoying Mister Okamoto's Bete is in the anime." But for me as the author, I've never wanted to create easygoing, expendable characters. No, this character in particular was supposed to be the one to give Bell his original drive, a haughty, prideful kind of character. Which is why Bete turned out the way he did.

Getting kicked around can be a form of baptism, almost. And without that impetus, so to speak, neither they nor the things around them will ever change. Even if they try desperately to change them, they'll never change. That was kind of my basis for building up the character, bringing together a sense of frustration but also the feeling of looking up to someone into one entity.

The phrase "howl of the weak" comes up often when I'm trying to put this character into words, but more and more, he's starting to become the typical *tsundere*, much as I hate to admit it.

Anyway, it's about time I move on to my thank-yous for this volume (though, please be aware of some pretty major spoilers throughout). To Otaki, Takahashi, and all the rest of the staff at GA

Bunko, I thank you once again for all your help on this volume. To Chief Editor Kitamura, who wisely advised that "[I] can't kill Lena!" during our plot meetings, I'm even more grateful now that I've written out the epilogue. To Kiyotaka Haimura, who, once again, has supplied my work with the most wondrous of illustrations despite the grueling schedule, I want to get down on my knees and thank you. I'm also incredibly grateful to the staff, cast, and everyone else who made the limited-edition drama CD for this new volume possible. And, of course, you have my utmost thanks, as well, my readers, who have once again picked up my book.

Though this afterword is already getting rather long, there is one more thing I'd like to announce:

A new Sword Oratoria anime has been slated for an April 2017 broadcast. To have this little side story get the animation treatment the same as my main series is thanks to nothing but the overwhelming support of you, my readers. I can't thank you enough. I'm even more inspired now to keep working as hard as possible—after all, I can't let myself lose to the incredible work of the staff and cast on the new film version.

I hope to see all of you again in the next book.

All the best.

*Fujino Omori*

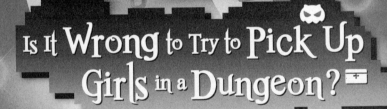